The Drunk'unn Boat

Darby Guise

Bear Skin Bob Press

The Drunk'unn Boat

One morning, when Gregor Samsa woke from troubled dreams, he found himself transformed in his bed into a horrible vermin.

—Franz Kafka, *The Metamorphosis*

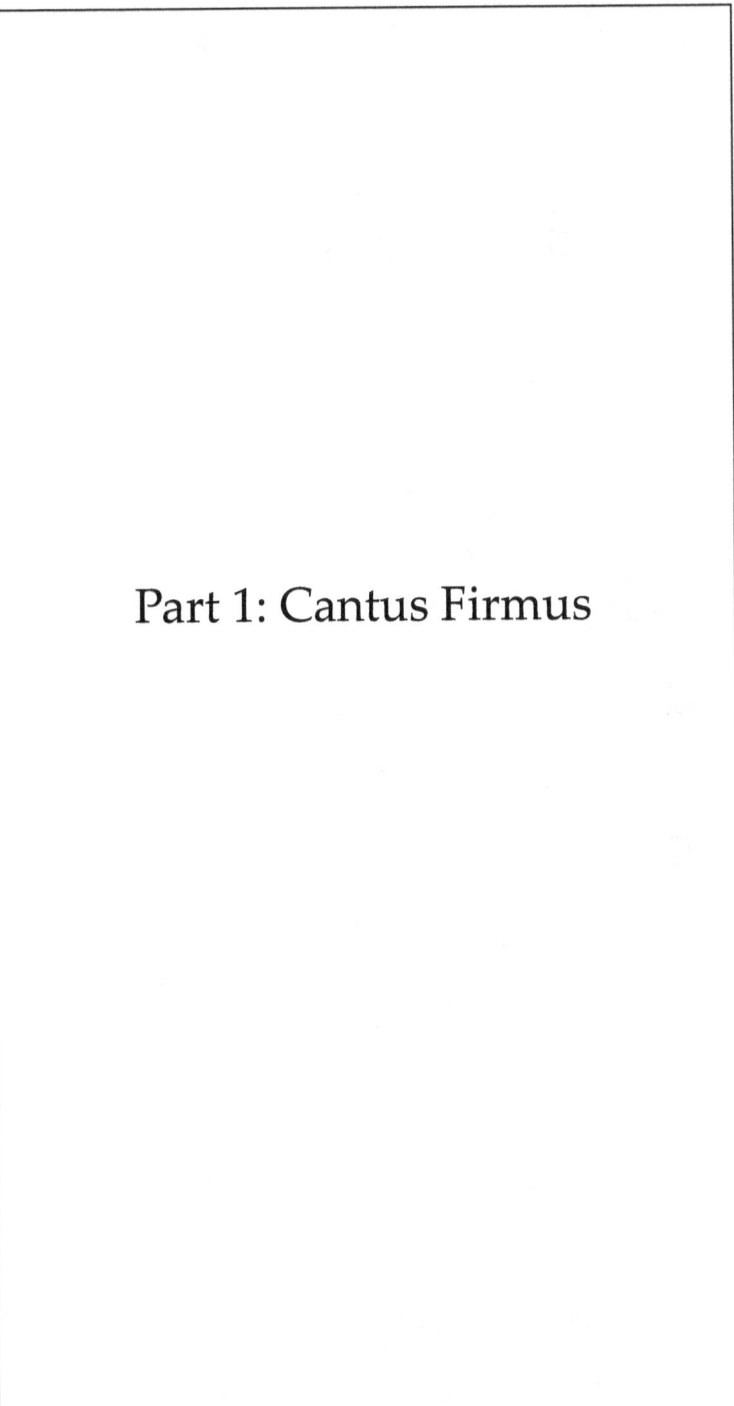

Part 1: Cantus Firmus

Chapter 1

Ricky Allen grew up in a split-level home on a lavish curving lane; the road led to his neighborly grocery store run by Dick Johnson. Ricky walked the length of the two-block journey at least three times a week. There, he'd buy whatever the coins in his pocket could afford, his preference aimed towards the sweets, and Dick would nod to Ricky each time he entered, asking him about his mother and voicing the same arsenal of happy-go-lucky platitudes.

"Till next time," said Dick, and Ricky walked out with his purchases: an assortment of candies and comic books tucked into a plastic bag—and a porno mag stuffed inconspicuously down the front of his trousers.

The stolen magazine didn't offer much to Ricky's eight-year-old mind from an enticing sexual perspective. It did little to stimulate his dormant hormones—but the anatomy and the form, the curvature and the poses, all left him reeling with curiosity and hopefulness; it seemed to open some doorway, which begot other doorways, deep in his imagination, parting the curtains to explore new horizons and never-before-seen vistas (at least for eight-year-old Ricky), even though these vistas were vague and still ill-formed and pretty gosh darn hazy; a minced oath whose central taboo, or gift, or key, was yet to be revealed or, quite possibly, would never be revealed but would work as the engine, an invisible and ghostly engine, turning and tuning young Ricky's urges and juices and desires and creativity. Who knew that such wonders and secrets could lie within a cheap porno mag, at least for Ricky, whose morally reprehensible decision to steal such lurid material had opened up something sacred and profound in his human soul.

His father was watching the news when he came down for supper. He paused in front of the television and heard the newsman talk of impending war, assassinations, and global catastrophes in the economic markets. The newsman said that the eventual tide of mayhem and destruction was knocking: the eve of battle was upon them. Best to prepare for the worst and hope for the best—something little Ricky assumed to be the founding principle for a man such as the newsman. His father extinguished the TV and smiled at his son; they entered the kitchen, and Ricky's mother heaped mashed potatoes and corn and a chargrilled pork chop onto his plate.

His pal George Dilgunk, a classmate he'd befriended on the first day of the first grade, knocked at the door and barged in unceremoniously the moment Mr. Allen had given his pudgy frame enough leeway to squeeze through. George was a habitual guest at the Allens'—and his fat, round bespectacled face made his somewhat uncouth disposition slightly more agreeable. Mr. Allen told him that Ricky was upstairs, and George mustered a "thanks" before disappearing down the upstairs hallway.

When Ricky pulled out the porno mag for George to see, he seemed less than interested... even a little bit nervous or ashamed. So Ricky thrust his treasure back wherefrom it came, to the shadows, beneath the bed, because George was disengaged, preoccupied, riled up somehow. But riled up by what?

An event—one that had transpired earlier that day, usurping the excitement of printed erotica: Judith, a friend of George's sister, an eighth grader, had called him into his sister's room. And he, curious George, went in expecting the group of girls to be there—his sister's pals—ready to call on him, their chubby mule, to descend to the kitchen and grab them their favorite afternoon snack. Instead, Judith, all alone, asked George if he'd ever seen *these* before, and she lifted up her shirt and showed the fat eight-year-old her breasts. George was knocked asunder and stood mute with surprise; he heard giggles from the far corner behind the bed, and Leanne's head popped out (another of his sister's friends), laughing at the scene. Judith turned towards her. "Okay, shut up. I've done it. My turn. Truth or..." And from that point on, George ceased to be a player within their perverse little game, and the stunned little man waddled back to his room in utter shock at having seen Judith's nipples.

Ricky called bullshit, not because he thought George was lying, but because he didn't know what else to say. Here he was excited over the simulacrum of boobs, whereas George had seen the real thing. And even still, the porno mag had unearthed something strange and uncanny within him (a turning point). Could he even imagine the riches George felt—or did he feel anything? Was it too much for his fat little friend? Was George now stunted and overwrought? Ricky didn't know. Perhaps this event would scar George or precipitate a new development in his depths as Ricky speculated the porno mag had done for him. When Ricky finally got around to asking George how he felt, all he could muster was an "I don't really know," followed by, "Want to play *Ratcatcher of Hamelin*?"

When Ricky arrived at school the next day, he was on the lookout for Judith. Her entire being had changed for him; she was somehow different now. Unique and wild and strange. She was special, but he couldn't necessarily articulate why. (A tangible being manifesting the inexpressible.) He saw her on the grass on the other side of the pitch where the older students hung out during their lunchtime recess. Even from afar, her newfound vibe sunk deep into his core, and he felt the flickering of what he surmised was a crush—a fluttering in his guts—and he watched her brunette locks sway as she darted around, goofing with the other boys and girls of her grade, and he articulated a plan, mumbled a ploy. He'd head over to George's (the sooner the better) when the girls were there: Judith, Leanne, and Trisha (George's sister). Then, he'd... oh, hell, he'd figure it out when he got there, or so he thought. In reality, he was just nervous—even with the idea, or the dream, or the imaginings. It all seemed so new, so beautiful, and so gosh darn painful, but why? Probably because it seemed within his reach, which brought about the fear, but the fear of what? The fear of failure? Or the fear of success? His feelings were still convoluted and mysterious to him; too fresh, too new, eight years was not enough to decrypt anything, and so he had no plan. He'd just show up when the girls were there and hope for the best—he didn't think it'd turn out well, but his mind was made up. "Might as well give it my all," thought little Ricky Allen.

It did not turn out well. George had invited him over, and the girls had been there, and Ricky had cornered Judith in the kitchen, and much to his surprise, he'd overcompensated for his nervousness and blurted out an order—jabbed it at her. "Show me *your* tits." She laughed, couldn't stop laughing, in fact; she pushed his head away in a joking and playful manner. He wasn't being taken seriously. He was a child in her eyes, as well as the rest of the world's (even in his own if he had to be honest). Why did he so badly want to see her boobs, anyway? To reconnect with that feeling, like a junky getting another hit, that strange discovery of new elixirs, like the porno mag, but better. Maybe if he explained this to Judith, the reasoning, but then he figured this wasn't such a good strategy; he lacked the vocabulary to articulate the argument in proper persuasive form. He went back up to George's room, greeted by a distorted parody of his goal. George stood half naked, displaying his pudgy little-boy boobs in a ridiculous and mocking manner.

So he went back to the magazine—the porno mag—it being the best he had. Not a bad consolation, really. It did not judge him, required no tactic to unearth its prize. There it stood, simply waiting to reveal itself. Ricky looked through it and began to trace over it. Placing a sheet of paper over its posed women and drawing their contours. He took these drawings to school, and their lack of explicit detail classified them as modest works of art, and one day, when he accidentally spilled the contents of his notebook on the floor, Ms. Laurent saw the drawings and (in reverential fashion) asked him if he'd drawn them; surprised by his answer and absolving his embarrassed look, she told him they were beautiful and to continue along this path; perhaps a poet or artist or madman lurked within his depths, a calling in wait. He went home, drew more, and decided to give one of his favorites to Judith—perhaps then she would flash him the *goods*.

He found her in the hallway, straggling behind, fussing with her backpack. He approached her and gave her the drawing without a word. She mumbled a "thanks" and rushed past, departing speedily without giving it the slightest glance. Later in the day, at the other end of school, taped to Ricky's locker, the one bearing his name (as was customary for all third graders), was the drawing he'd made—but with multiple additions. Penises and breasts and scribbling of all sorts accompanied the original work along with words like "fag" and "fuck" and "your mom" and "pussy," and he realized that perhaps giving Judith the drawing hadn't been such a wise move. He kept the vandalized art piece and placed it in his notebook. Upon later review, he saw it as his first collaborative effort and began to utilize it as a source of inspiration—less the foul language and more the mashing of tones and styles and colors. He introduced markers and pencils and collage techniques into his work; he cut from flyers and magazines; he created new pieces that displayed an artistic leap forward from the simple line tracings of before and heralded a new creative dawn for Ricky Allen, the gifted eight-year-old.

It would be a lie to say that Ricky was instantly noticed and propelled to notoriety by his peers and teachers as an artistic wunderkind—the sui generis boy of the elementary school— but he had enough momentum and childish enthusiasm propelling him onward that he quickly lost interest in Judith and found his calling elsewhere, fancying himself a godlike entity among the playground's riffraff, a sorcerer who could conjure the very things he yearned for most—particularly as his skills and tastes developed in equal measure over time; he was beginning to fill in and to see the fruition of his artistic ambitions and the development of a vocation in which he'd spend the majority of his brief life. But that's further ahead in our story, and for now, we are here, with Ricky Allen, age eight, uncertain, aloof, childish, and still four years away from the awkward and maturing phases of hormonal intoxication dubbed puberty. Good luck, young Ricky, unknown artist and prepubescent craftsman, we eagerly await your development and the fruits of your hard-earned labor.

Chapter 2

High school was different. Ricky had developed and created himself anew. He was confident, or he gave the impression of confidence. Girls swooned, and if they didn't, well... they were jealous and envious of the ones who did. How had Ricky established such a report with the student body? From eight-year-old artistic reject to wresting the power from the grasp of the school's handsome quarterback, emerging as the most popular and dominant male student: the alpha; how had he accomplished this rise to local adolescent superstardom in the teenage hierarchy? Easy—as a fit of luck, actually—his mother, a part-time lottery player, had won the jackpot. The Allens had won eight million dollars, and Mr. Allen had invested a portion of their winnings in profitable stocks, and purchased valuable properties, and grew their assets. (Accruing, growing, enriching.) And the Allens, once an ordinary middle-class family, had become one of the richest and most influential clans in the whole state. By high school, Ricky had acclimated, created a new identity for himself, cultivated a bad-boy persona—fellated frequently in the library, midday cocaine breaks in the handicap washroom—and the winning combination of money and amoral conduct had him courting many of the high school's most bold and audacious beauties while dismissing the authoritative staff with neglect and scorn.

But then Ricky died, true to form, when everything was great and prosperous for the young man; he drunkenly smashed his truck into a sturdy lamppost on Queens Boulevard. Julie Winters was with him, stunning beauty outfitted in a pink faux-fur chemise. The crash had ejected them both—neither wearing their seatbelt—and Julie had split her cranium, darting headfirst into a brick border; Ricky had skidded out onto the road and slid and worn out and broken the majority of his bones with lacerations and fractures and breaks irrefutably opting for his demise—although it took him a good five minutes to concede to this; and finally, the bloody pulp took its last breath, and the curtains were drawn, and young Ricky was dead.

The school made a big to-do about the whole affair and hosted a series of counseling seminars and grief stations for the student body; a vigil was organized for the pair of deceased teens that the whole school—along with the staff—was strongly encouraged to attend. Cellphones recorded tears, and grief-stricken videos were uploaded to online profiles, and well-wishers flooded the inboxes of both the Allens' and the Winterses' social media accounts. Some vile students uploaded anonymous comments praising the death of these two narcissistic youths. But their tirades were short-lived, and time marched on, and week by week, and month by month, the events normalized, and Ricky and Julie were barricaded in the minds of their peers and teachers and friends as an event, a tragedy demarking their seventeenth (or sixteenth, or fifteenth, or fifty-sixth, or whichever age they were) year on Earth, dating it; it being an introduction for many—their first real contact with death, in a proximal and unexpected sort of way. "It could happen to *anyone* at any time," thought some of them, and the saga of Ricky and Julie became a thing of the past, a sad and tragic memory, and the future adjusted to their absence.

But isn't Ricky our main player, the primary focus carrying this story, bearing the load of the narrative's weight? Shouldn't he be alive and engaged, changing and growing, in a constant state of conflict? Hadn't we even said that he'd become a gifted and gratifying artist—what the hell did he end up creating anyway, apart from a couple of tracings? Couldn't we switch to an alternate timeline, somewhere where Ricky was still alive, or perhaps one where he hadn't won the lottery or taken a fancy to young Julie Winters? We are, after all, in the driver's seat. Able to make sharp turns and ninety-degree cuts in whichever direction we choose. But perhaps our story should have some semblance of reality; keep a thin thread tied to the reader's world, united by death, a linear trajectory forward. Perhaps, thought the writer, perhaps.

He said he wanted to learn how to whisper a yell. And the world thought him a foolish and tasteless fuck. But to whom was he referring to? thought the writer, and the writer decided that narratives were made to be destroyed and to spit in the face of reality, and so he rewrote the lines and circumnavigated back, negating the linear rules. Ricky, age ten, is alive and well. His mother—who should have been out buying the winning lottery ticket—has succumbed to a stye infection (a narrative device to eschew the old timeline, diverge from its path), and she refuses to leave the house. The proverbial rewind button has been hit, and Ricky sits with his mother, harangued on the couch by an angry talk show host, yelling at them while spitting malice at the screen, and they enjoy the distance of watching someone self-destruct in their living room, brought to life by their fifty-two-inch television.

George knocks at the Allens' door, and Ricky jumps up from the couch and lets his friend in. They wander upstairs, the pair of rambunctious youths; four years as best friends and the ties of camaraderie are stronger than ever. George sits on Ricky's bed, and Ricky pulls out his notebook and shows George his new additions. Artwork designed to overstimulate the viewer; Ricky's talent for subtlety and shading lends his creations an unnerving efficiency. The viewer's eyes compete at multiple points, pulled in at various causeways, and a hypnotic allure permeates the work, tinges it with vertigo. George congratulates Ricky on another well-done piece, and Ricky shoves his notebook back underneath the bed as George relays to him a tale.

George's story:

Once upon a time, two grotesque dolls, created in a warehouse in northern Kentucky, escape the drudgery of their existence and leap out an unlocked factory window when no one is looking. Both dolls are seemingly identical except for the fact that one doll only has one eye. The one-eyed doll asks the other doll where they should go, and the two-eyed doll thinks for a bit, turning ideas around in its little doll head. They've only been in existence for three days and are, therefore, not overly educated on what lies outside the warehouse walls. They decide to wait for a sign and spend the night underneath a barren oak tree. In the morning, the one-eyed doll goes for a short walk and meets a cheerful 4-year-old girl. She smiles at the doll and asks where she's from and asks if she'd like to come home with her. The doll replies in the affirmative, and she leaves nestled in the young girl's arms towards a new and hopeful life. That night, in an unfamiliar bedroom, tucked into the young girl's bed, the one-eyed doll absconds and flees and goes back to the oak tree and finds her two-eyed companion there. She tells her what has happened and asks if she'd like to come along, back to the young girl's house. She agrees, and the two dolls head out. But before they enter the young girl's room, the one-eyed doll asks the other doll to remove one of her eyes. This putting them on equal footing because, she figures, if one doll is disfigured and the other is not, one will have an unfair advantage, or an upper hand, in procuring the girl's favor and ardor. The two-eyed doll agrees, and with the help of a rusty pair of pliers found outside near the garden hose, the two-eyed doll tears out and discards one of her eyes. The next morning, upon waking, the dolls explain to the young girl that they are a package deal, and the young girl is overjoyed at having not one but two new additions to take care of and love and drink tea with. A year later, tragedy strikes: one of the dolls (the original one-eyed doll) is attacked by the household dog and loses an arm and a leg in the scuffle. The young girl does her best to mend the battered doll, but her efforts are in vain. She promises to love the amputated doll regardless of her two missing limbs, but this doesn't cheer the doll up, who's delirious and depressed and sad. In an act of solidarity with her pal, the other doll (the original two-eyed doll) saws off one of her arms and one of her legs (what a saint (or psycho)) and the pair are practically identical once more. As time marches on, the young girl tries her best to love the disfigured dolls, just like before, but they are different now, and they can't stand up unaided, and they are a burden to her and the other toys, and they slow everything down, including teatime, and are constantly slouching with bad posture and are prone to sudden and unavoidable tumbles out of the blue. One night after waking from a strange dream, the girl has an idea; she grabs the two dolls and sets up a mock surgical table on her bedspread and sews and glues and tapes until dawn. In the end, the procedure is deemed a success: one is created from two. She's fused the dolls together—Siamese twins—and the pair are restored, with two eyes and two legs and two arms and two almost identical doll heads. A new being is born, and the young girl and her creature go back to bed and sleep a dreamless sleep until nightfall arrives and wakes them up.

Ricky didn't like George's story. He told him it was boring and could be cut down to "one is created from two," or something like that—really, he just couldn't figure out the point of it, or if it even had a point (But do stories need points? Are points surrogates for morals? Are overly straightforward and easily decrypted or one-sided tales the bastard offspring of the pamphleteer?). But this wasn't really true—the initial charge of oversimplification trumped up by Ricky—because there were lots of other "happenings" or "events" or "goings-on" occurring during the tale, or at least within it—between the lines, so to speak.

And wasn't a story just a bunch of tones and feelings when it was really broken down and looked at and analyzed? Shouldn't stories be measured based on how far they penetrate the reader's depths and dislodge and shake and entangle themselves around the audience's core? And don't some stories, perhaps the best ones, take time to really blossom and grow and be absorbed, like a seedling sprouting unannounced, and the host, never fully aware of it until much later, years perhaps, when it matures and grows, and its roots erode and extend and transform the terrain, and its influence cannot be ignored; aren't those the best stories? The real acts of genius? The tangible works descending to the deepest depths, expressing the inexpressible (a hypnotic Trojan horse), so mysterious and strange, revealing and unearthing the most baffling auras and tones within their viewer or reader or audience member?

Neither Ricky nor George extended their speech to articulate these arguments or ideas—them being only ten—still without the madness and intellectual rigor necessary to drill around their psyches and unearth those hidden prizes and contradictions. George was still hurt by Ricky's words though; he thought Ricky would be a supportive friend, kind towards his artistic ambitions, but this proved false. It took fifteen minutes for George's battered feelings to resume their pre-critique composure, aided by Ricky's decision to lend him a couple of videogames along with a dirty magazine. George decided not to begrudge his friend and was content knowing that it'd only taken him twenty minutes to come up with the story (wasted time?), and he let the dejected tale fall into the waste bin of his brain as he left the Allens' and biked home.

Chapter 3

Ricky and George spent the summer of their twelfth year rummaging around the woods and biking into town and mucking about down by the creek, attempting, at one point, to construct a treehouse, which was abandoned in its early phases—just after they'd constructed a small portion of what was to be the floor—which was no great feat of carpentry, really, as they'd simply nailed a couple of wooden pallets together, stolen from a back alley near d'Artagnan Avenue. The treehouse they had planned to construct was multileveled; it had five rooms: two upstairs and two downstairs (along with a spacious cellar). The idea was more fun than the execution though, and due to time constraints and a lack of know-how, they realized that swinging into the creek via a dangling rope fastened to a hardy tree was a much better use of their dwindling summer days. They played at war and threw stones and splashed teenage girls and occasionally got pushed around by older boys and sought conflict and battle, but only in an innocent and casual sort of way. They packed Gatorade and sandwiches and comic books in their backpacks and spent their days in bliss and bedlam and harmony.

On rainy days, they usually camped out at the Allens' house and watched movies and played videogames and horsed around; sometimes Ricky would draw, and George would stare up at the ceiling, letting his mind roam where it pleased. It surprised him how odd his thoughts could be, especially if he gave them license to roam freely and simply sat around accompanying them on their rounds. Even at an early age, George had begun to separate himself from the incoming flux pulsing about in his brain. Who was he to dictate and filter and censor its flood of imagery and information? Perhaps he should pay attention and submit to its will, and so he did, watching the play of moods and narratives intertwine and develop and then disappear and reemerge under a new guise with a cast of new characters and a development that seemed both fresh and oddly familiar.

One afternoon, Ricky drew what was to be his masterpiece: a strange Daliesque concoction of a spider-like entity, or a dark hand with long and wispy fingers in an arid desert terrain, colors popping and blending every which way. He showed George who told him that it was his best yet. Ricky then showed his parents; his father was somewhat dismissive of it, slightly bored with the artistic preoccupations of his son—but he did his best to hide this sentiment and told him that it looked "very good." His mother, on the other hand, was genuinely impressed, or her performance or show of being impressed certainly surpassed the acting skills of her spouse.

What to do with it now? thought Ricky. He was hungry for praise and wondered what the best avenue was to attain it. He posted it online and received likes and comments and all the apocryphal hype so commonly distributed in the internet age. Ricky's ego swelled as he was further inducted into the identity of "artist"—at least in the eyes of others—which Ricky used as the primary fodder when constructing his own identity, still wholly dependent upon their perspectives and input; he decided to go on an evening bike ride to celebrate the current climate of his feelings.

The night was warm with a slight breeze boasting what Ricky would call "an idyllic temperature." He zoomed around the deserted streets and cut through his favorite park, veering left and right, and dodging abandoned toys and other playground rigs; he was the master of his domain, speeding along lost highways and weaving through narrow pathways. The town appeared suspicious and eccentric when colored under the cloak of nightfall. Empty parking lots with abandoned sofas and quiet suburban streets accented strange and questionable sensibilities. He loved exploring his neighborhood under darkness's livery; high velocities precipitated feelings of invincibility as he pedaled past looming threats and imagined monsters, still viciously susceptible to his mind's projections—"What horrors lurk beneath this darkness?"—a question epitomizing millennia of human fear, fear of the unknown, pushed away by modern living methods or retooled and repurposed as horror movies and adrenaline-fueled activities with tight safety parameters and high profit margins—e.g., roller coasters and the like. Ricky sped down a cement pathway with wilderness encroaching on both sides—and ahead, a streetlight, civilization; he ramped up his speed and jumped the curb and... was hit by a truck, driven by a man named Darryl, who didn't even know what had happened or what he'd hit or what he'd crushed and potentially dispatched, or slaughtered, or exterminated—a doe, a deer, a drunk darting out from God-knows-where—until he'd slammed the brakes and saw Ricky Allen and his busted bike in the rearview mirror.

Two times now! It's no use fighting the Fates. Ricky Allen is dead. The author tried, put his best foot forward and attempted to duke it out with the gods, sync himself to a new timeline, but alas, the gods always find their way, and Ricky Allen wasn't meant to be, at least not in this form, in this story, in this way. It's a difficult situation to say goodbye to a character so rich in potential, so seemingly vital to the tale at hand, but the material has a will of its own, and a writer's duty—no matter how tragic—is always to push forward. And so here we are, Ricky has ceased to be. That is that. We will not describe the tears and sadness and melancholy that gripped the Allens for years to come. Suffice to say that the demise of their only son was a horrible blow, ricocheting constantly in the pits of their souls, refashioning them from the inside out, their trauma marking them in every conceivable way. They would sell their house and move away six months later; they would slowly rebuild a life, and within two years, the pair would have a daughter named June Rachel Allen. Their lives would constantly be marked by Ricky's death, but in some semblance of what could possibly be, the Allens would find happiness—in an off-kilter sort of way. Years would pass, and Mr. Allen would drop June off at school, and Mrs. Allen would pick her up, and the family would dine together and go through their evening rounds, summing up each of their days for the others, sharing anecdotes and woes before surrendering to the couch, hot beverages and popcorn distributed liberally, to watch a movie or some silly TV thing.

"Where the fuck am I?" Ricky was more than a little perplexed by his surroundings. Things seemed to have changed instantly. He was biking along, then boom, nothing. This. And what exactly was this? It looked like an acid painting, everything was melting together, and the depth of the images was unknown. He stuck out his hand, and he merged with the paint, everything liquefying, and he ran with it, keeping some semblance of his form, although he continuously shifted within the fractal world he seemed to be inhabiting. There was no way of getting his bearings, nor any directional clue which way he was moving. All he knew was that he was moving and morphing, and patterns and images—some briefly recognizable, most nonsensical, but all strangely beautiful—rose and tilted and moved both towards him and away from him. He couldn't concentrate and had no sense of time; millennia or seconds passed by without him knowing. He was present to the point of insanity, meaning nothing before or after the imminent visual torrent held any bearing, and he couldn't form any meaningful thoughts—actually, he couldn't form any thoughts, period. He was a slave to it, but not in a distressing sort of way. It felt blissful and rhythmic, like living inside a piece of music. Held captive by its beauty and magnetism, a sensation some might have described as love if love were unshackled from the world of sex and bodies and given a purely visual medium to produce or transmit its spell or sorcery... or maybe it was more like Joy. Yes, yes—not love, but joy. Joy: a feeling of pleasure and jubilation beyond morals and reasoning, exuberance without bounds. This visual onslaught proved to energize Ricky, a flight forward where the destination was both unknown and unimportant; he was drunk on it and held in its clutches for an eternity—or perhaps just a second.

You feel strange and somewhat exposed. You knew the end was coming, but you didn't know it would happen like this. You weren't thinking, really. You were just along for the ride; never feeling threatened or bored by it, you allowed it to consume you. Where are you now? You are unable to move your head, and your eyesight is incredibly blurry. The language centers in your brain seem to be malfunctioning, and your thoughts—including these—are more akin to vague binary notions: happy–sad, calm–upset, scared–serene. You can't keep your eyes open for more than a minute or two, and you constantly feel tired. You don't, or can't, search for orientation; you simply glimpse snippets of your environment as best you can. You cry out when it is too cold or when you feel pain—however vague—and squirm and grip and suck, and you ask for nothing but comfort, although you only know of it when it's lacking or absent; cessation of pain and want your only goal. You think of nothing and are moved by unconscious know-how; you are at the mercy of the world around you; you are warm and held and fall asleep almost instantly.

Two years have gone by; you are a young girl in the grips of an identity crisis: do you prefer yellow or blue? Someone asked you this the other day, and you didn't know. You had never thought about it before, and when the question was asked, you simply shied away from it and hid behind your mother's leg. Why had they asked you this? Was it some sort of trick? You look through some of your picture books and are captivated by what you see. Your mom deciphers the text and vocalizes the tale for you. You half listen and bob around to a tune stuck in your head. You sit beside your father and watch the TV but are restless and begin to sing. You run naked through the house. You chase the dog around and laugh like a tiny maniac. You love everything around you with pure and simple joy. You see possibility and are transfixed by a growing number of things: the sun, the trains, umbrellas, bugs (beetles), your mother's gardenias, a rainbow shot out from an ornamental prism; this is your world, or at least everything you know of it. Life is mysterious and magical, and everything comes to you in full bloom with the volume turned way up; you go to bed each night in anticipation of the next day, dreaming lush dreams that you can't remember. You are Dorothy Gilbert, age two, daughter of Jeanne and Leonard Gilbert. You are alive and well and in flux and reemerging and eternal, or part of you is, but you don't know this. How could you? You are the kernel, of a seed, of a will, from an idea, or a plan, of a destiny, without meaning, or purpose, or plot, or device—but perhaps that isn't exactly true, and you are simply a wonder, beholding other wonders, in a world both terrifying and beautiful, with a cosmic narrative spanning eons and plot devices woven ruthlessly throughout and within, destinies sandwiched together, one on top of another with no end in sight. "What is 'The End'... actually?" you ask, but you ask it rhetorically. The answers don't seem to interest you, but maybe the questions do.

Chapter 4

George is fourteen and has become more svelte with age. He seems to have lost some of the fat that occupied his frame in the early years; he's also done away with his glasses and has adopted the use of contact lenses. He's in the 9th grade now, not particularly popular, but neither is he unpopular; he drifts by in a haze or clutter or flurry that is high school. He has a girlfriend, a girl named Nikki Taylor; she's in the 9th grade too and has a peculiar habit of needlessly tearing strips from pieces of paper that find themselves in her clutches. Each time she puts her writing instrument to use, quill to parchment, she is forced, by some invisible hand, to tear or shred or shave or pluck or peel a hunk from it, robbing or plundering little bits or flakes; her notes contain gashes of varying sizes: some incredibly small, others long and thick—half a page torn out of many. During quizzes and finals and standardized tests, she is forced to give in to her compulsion—allocating another laborious task onto an already stressful game—and she meticulously carves out one chunk after another from each of the pages. Her weapon of choice is an uncoiled paperclip—using its jagged ends, shaving narrow and almost invisible strips; she sometimes eats the evidence. The process is surprisingly time-consuming, especially if the quiz or essay or test is long and difficult and has many pages. She tries to hide her malady and is, for all intents and purposes, a perfectionist, at least in this domain, and it's her saving grace that she's an exceptional and talented student and that her strange kink doesn't have a more dire effect, particularly on her scholastic performance.

The first time George and Nikki met was at school during a storm on a Thursday afternoon; George accidentally walked into her. Not paying attention, head turned, yammering away. She reproached him with pursed lips and a contemptuous glare. But then Tommy the teacher, walking with a self-satisfied mien and a mug full of piping-hot coffee, ran into George and spilled the contents of his cup all over the pair; George and Nikki—each seething with blotchy red burns, smelling of low-end instant coffee—tethered anger to frustration and held it back as best they could; they find affinity in a common enemy: Tommy the teacher, or Mr. Brown, as he's sometimes called.

Mr. Brown had the audacity to blame them for the incident, "The Pileup Near the Science Wing." George played his part, certainly, but Nikki, she remains an innocent and unwilling participant, blindsided by an aloof George, consumed by the chaos of an unavoidable event, and then burned and reprimanded by the idiot Tom.

During the week following the above-mentioned incident, the pair compare wounds and discuss revenge tactics against the insolent Tommy the teacher, or Mr. Brown. George took most of the spill on his stomach and lifts his shirt to display the circular markings around his scorched epidermis. He is unabashed and displays his wounds with pride and is even a little excited to expose himself to Nikki in such an intimate and vulnerable manner. She too received damage along the way, up on her torso, but she only shows George the few small burns on her arms. In an attempt to garner more attention and keep the shenanigans of their increasingly farcical show-and-tell going, she heats a paperclip and presses it against one of her burns, upping the scale of damage; she shows George the lesion, and his reaction doesn't disappoint. It provokes real and unfiltered anger, which he directs towards Mr. Brown, the teacher, and right then and there, Nikki falls... for what? For George... and within a week, the pair are dating.

One of the things George liked best about Nikki was the way her studious and mature nature was counterbalanced by a diabolical edge. Fires slammed against her calm exterior, and George understood that he was sometimes attracted to a fourteen-year-old psychopath. For the most part though, her demeanor was calm and lovable and buoyant, but then something would snap and give a clear view to the demon running amok within, biding its time, now handed the controls—its evil sojourn—directing toxicity at anyone worthy of its venomous spite. And their relationship ran the gamut from love to revulsion for six months, and the breadth of experience that each was privy to was eye-opening, to say the least.

When confronted by a rude cashier at the local grocery store, Nikki punched that bitch in the throat and poured vinegar all over her—vinegar she'd found on the grocer's conveyor belt, directing goods to the now-indisposed cashier. (A serendipitous occurrence placed there by the hand of divine providence? Perhaps.) The old lady standing behind them in line was dumbfounded; such violence erupting amid a modern and supposedly civilized supermarket franchise was beyond her. Who knew that such devils lurked among them? And the old lady trotted off, back to the aisle to resupply her store of vinegar for her pickling projects.

Madness can be a friend to both the wicked and the saintly, and Nikki could also swing the pendulum of her emotional core to the other side, a Botticelli angel, donating more than she could ever do without, dispensing money and goods to the needy and unfortunate; she gave her time—reading to the sick, listening and calling up a Rolodex's worth of friends and acquaintances ranging in age from children to the elderly; each conversation a sort of moral pick-me-up, someone letting them know that yes, someone out there cares, even for you... especially for you: the sick, the lonely, the deformed, the dying. Nikki's dual nature made sense to George, and he likened it to a tall oak tree with deep subterranean roots—a great verve capable of extremes. Weren't the best natures lofty at both ends?

At school, they often ate lunch together and discussed a variety of humdrum and taboo topics. On this particular day, they were discussing natural disasters and global crises, and George told Nikki that if the reverse had been true, and the world were entering another ice age, it probably wouldn't bother him all that much. It had something to do with his aversion to heat, and he found the idea of a gradual warming despicably mundane and tepid for a potentially cataclysmic event.

Six months into their relationship, Nikki and George decided to have a picnic near the cliffs only a short walk from the outskirts of town. They packed an assortment of food and planned to lounge under the blue sky, dozing and chatting and eating away the afternoon until sundown beckoned them back. The grass was long and unkempt, and the spot they chose was completely devoid of people or persons in every conceivable direction. "It's like we're the last ones on Earth," said Nikki, and the pair snuggled up and stared up at the clouds—clouds they sometimes thought looked like cottontail rabbits, and Russian gigolos, and stars from '70s action epics. It was a beautiful afternoon, and after an invigorating make-out session, George fell silent, then asleep, and when he woke up, Nikki was gone.

***

"I don't know anything about anybody," said the detective. "I don't know if I can honestly say I know more than five things about myself."

"What do you mean?"

"I mean that the greater part of the whole is shrouded in darkness and presumably smeared with chaos."

"Ah, I see... and what do you figure we should do?"

"Nothing. We search, we wait, we see. What else can we do?"

Search parties roamed the cliffs, and boats glided along the coastline, all searching for Nikki—some sign of her—a trace or token pointing towards her whereabouts. It was a vanishing act of the highest order. No clues on land, sea, or air. The most probable narrative was drowning, but abduction wasn't ruled out either, nothing was, as there wasn't any evidence to support or squash any of the theories being tossed around. George was heartbroken and felt her haunting presence weighing on him, especially when he was alone in bed or in the bathroom; he'd hear her voice, or his voice would morph into her voice—an internal voice—and his voice (heard in her voice) would ask him how come he let her go, and why he wasn't out there now, searching this very instant, and maybe he should look more closely along the cliffs.

The next day, he went back to the cliffs; it had been two weeks since her disappearance; there wasn't anyone there. A cluster of forgotten debris blew about in the wind, and a section of police tape fell over the cliff's edge. He took a narrow path that led along the crag and down towards the water; it was supported against the rock face and housed a few small alcoves and two large caves that the police had searched thoroughly since Nikki's disappearance. George got to the first of the caves and took out his cellphone and used it as a torch, technology guiding his way. The walls inside were marked by graffiti, seemingly defunct symbols distanced from the rational modes of thought, youngsters and visually impaired vagabonds coated the walls with their uncanny gibberish; these strange, chaotic patterns harked back to the Paleolithic paintings of yore, dipped and repackaged with droll present-day undertones and mescaline-inspired throbs. The delirium of the visuals caused a rush of blood to drain from George's head, and he was forced to sit down. While regaining his wits and, for some reason or other, thinking about a TV show called *Cheerful Nitwits*, he heard something—a shuffle, a whistle, and then, without a doubt, a shriek.

She was stuck against the wall of rock, screaming and clutching a ragged doll. She looked about seven or eight, and her outer appearance was dirty and disheveled. He tried to talk to her, but she didn't seem to register his presence; she kept staring out at the mass of water, screaming, blind and dumb, in the clutches of some inner maelstrom or malevolent state.

Her stupor refused to wane, and George was forced to pick her up and carry her to the top of the cliffs; she put up no resistance but continued to howl during their ascent. He called 911 and sat down panting, watching the young girl as she continued to hurl her voice at the indifferent and formidable sea.

The police questioned George again. Why was he there? Why had he come back? How had he found the girl? What did he see while he was down there? What was he thinking? What had he smelt? He did his best to answer all the questions in a pertinent and forthright manner. He was told that the girl's name was Suzy O'Connor and that she was from a town a few miles away. Her mother had reported her missing a couple of days before, and her sudden appearance at the cliffs in a catatonic state roused many peculiar and, so far, unanswerable questions. He passed by Suzy as he was going through the police station—her screaming suspended, her eyes clouded and obscured—and he noticed her doll again; he saw its raggedness up close and paid attention to its shoddy patchwork and misaligned stitches. For some reason, the doll made him uneasy, and as he exited the station, a cop came running after him and asked him one final question; he asked him what the sky looked like when he found the girl, and George responded without thinking, and he said that it was the color of television.

Chapter 5

There'd been five disappearances over the past year and a half. Katie Cassidy had gone missing first; she was fifteen years old. On October 11th, Katie was at home chatting on the phone with her friend Elizabeth; they'd arranged a meet-up for later that evening around 7 p.m. Katie had eaten with her parents, a traditional roast beef dinner: mashed potatoes, gravy, creamed corn; she left shortly after 6:45 p.m., heading to meet her friend at the agreed-upon coffee spot, an approximate ten minutes' walk from the Cassidy residence. She left on foot but never made it to the rendezvous. Elizabeth waited impatiently, texting angry emojis and hieroglyphs, and then worried inquiries, sipping latte after latte, wondering where her friend was, hoping everything was all right. She phoned Mrs. Cassidy and then wasted time calling and texting friends and acquaintances who had no clue as to Katie's whereabouts. Dorothy Cassidy (Katie's mom) decided to call the police around 10:30 p.m., and the cops came by the house, then checked the coffee shop and patrolled the neighborhood for any sign of Katie. She was not to return, and a missing person report was filed, and a statewide search ensued. The Cassidys were burdened with no knowledge about their daughter, and Dorothy began to see strange occurrences materialize in her once-wonted daily routines. Cracks in the fabric of the ordinary. At the grocery store, an old woman came up to her and said, "You know what, dear? God wouldn't fuck you unless you fucked Him first." She was taken aback by the viciousness of the little old lady, who chuckled merrily to herself as she walked away, not lingering to catch Dorothy's response, and a few minutes later, Dorothy met her again, down another aisle; this time, the old lady seemed to be muttering to herself, speaking in tongues or so low that her gibberish was incomprehensible, mouth slightly open with a lizard-like tongue darting spastically from left to right, spittle exiting the cavity. Dorothy eyed the old lady's cart; she was curious to see what such a vile specimen might eat. She saw stacks of bologna, canned salmon, eggs, and radishes; nothing necessarily outside the bounds of a normal elderly diet, but she was far from reassured of the old lady's sanity, and for days, the episode lingered over everything, even eclipsing her daughter's disappearance, like an actual eclipse, a solar eclipse, with the deranged old lady darting in front of her disappeared daughter, the moon obstructing the sun. She felt that the world was undergoing a sudden and aggressive shift, a change of perspective; it was as if dirt and gunk now clung to the prescription glasses she was forced to wear. Glasses that now refracted and tinted and molded the world in a new and uncomfortable way; horror bled into her dream, and that was just the way it was.

The second person to go missing was Maisel Sinclair. She was eleven years old and lived on the opposite side of town from the Cassidys. She went missing in mid-January, three months after Katie's disappearance; it was the Year of the Rat. She was at home, alone, while her mother went out to pick up a few things from the hardware store. Her father was working. When her mother returned—approximately an hour later—Maisel was nowhere to be found. Edith Sinclair immediately called the police and told them about her missing daughter. She heard about the Cassidy girl on the news, and nightmares swarmed her daytime thoughts even though, on the surface, the two episodes seemed vastly different apart from the vanishing motif. The police came by and questioned the Sinclairs and searched the house, and then they widened their perimeter to include various subdivisions and regions around town. The news broadcast a segment about Maisel's disappearance and showed her picture and a phone number, urging anyone to call who had pertinent information regarding her whereabouts. Calls inundated the line, although none of the information proved to be of any value, a deluge of crazies and pranksters and earnest citizens with useless and cryptic details.

The detective in charge of the Sinclair case was driving in his car, trying to spot some clue or dislodge some instinct that could rouse an answer and spur him forward towards finding Maisel and solving the case. He was listening to the radio, and a pop song by David Bowie was broadcast over the airwaves; he thought back to when he was a kid, and he thought about his cat, Potpourri, and her litter of kittens, and one day, he and his mother had gone shopping, and when they'd come back—all the kittens were dead! A nightmare. Potpourri had killed them all. Fur and blood and the mangled corpses painted a tapestry of carnage in a corner of the living room. Potpourri was irate and scowled and hissed and swiped at anything that came near. She had sensed something wrong in her offspring, some aberration that needed to be undone. The image of the massacre was scorched into the detective's brain and—even after fifteen years on the force—remained one of his most unnerving memories. A base act of instinct? A psychotic feral feline? A genocidal urge to rid the world of her kin? The detective couldn't understand what had possessed the cat. Was it simply its nature coming to the forefront in all its savageness and banality? He heard the snarls and yelps and pithy screams of the kittens, and it drowned out the materiality of the world around him.

Eight months after the disappearance of Katie Cassidy and five months after Maisel Sinclair, Timmy Deluge went missing. He was seven years old and was out with his brother and some friends at a small creek near Plankerton Ave. It was approximately 3 p.m., and the boys were splashing and eating and playing and enjoying the tomfoolery of their Saturday afternoon. At one point, Timmy's older brother, Tizie Deluge, tossed Timmy's hat into the bush, and Timmy, annoyed and more than a little pissed off, went into the thicket to fetch it. When ten minutes had elapsed and he hadn't returned, Tizie went looking for him, but he couldn't find him, and his heart raced—at first, believing (or hoping) that it was just some immature prank pulled by his younger sibling, but then terror tightened around him, a hangman's noose, as no sign of his brother reappeared; he told his friend Derek Riverstoke to go and fetch his parents as he continued to search in vain. The police were called around 4:30 p.m., and the same detective in charge of the Sinclair case showed up. A group of police officers followed by a group of volunteers searched the bush and the surrounding area but were unable to find anything— not even his cap. Tizie was inconsolable, and that night, he prayed for his brother's safe return. Six months went by and no news, and then Nikki Taylor went missing and, a week later, Suzy O'Connor.

Rumors circulated around town, and some supposed a murderer was on the prowl. Others thought some demonic sorcery was at play: a cult abducting the town's youth, sacrificing them in some unseemly manner, excavating riches and fortunes and luck from their heinous and ill deeds. The detective had become obsessed with the case—as anyone would—the case acting as a kind of vortex, sucking in the participant as he or she dived further into its murky depths and tried their damnedest to unveil the secrets governing its core. Suzy O'Connor seemed to hold the answer, although she was unable to speak for quite some time, and when she regained her faculties, she was unable to give any accurate impressions about her abduction, stating only that she felt disconnected and disturbed the entire time. She said she remembered almost nothing except for a sound, like one from a fuzzy TV set, where the signal was constantly cutting in and out. She had no idea how she had ended up at the cliffs and didn't remember George at all. George was seen as a hero among the townsfolk, but there was still apprehension and uneasiness; people didn't trust him. He'd played a significant role in two of the disappearances. Was he somehow connected in a darker and more sinister way? And if so, how? George couldn't figure it out and neither could the detective, but he still kept an eye on him (the detective that is), and he asked George to come by the station every so often to go over some minor detail. George was more than willing to help— as he, too, was sucked into the vortex, unable to let go of the mystery engulfing the town. He would bike to the cliffs now and then and stand by the crag. "Where are you, Nikki? And what the hell happened to you while I was snoozing?"

***

The detective turned on the TV and was beholden to the television for the epiphany that followed. It was a nature show. There was a group of insects, and they were scavenging for food, and it showed one of them acting odd or funny. Going out on its own, away from the others, in search of something. Instinctually propelled forward. The insect bit down and died, and it was revealed that a parasitic fungus known as *Cordyceps* had infiltrated its body, forcing it to do its bidding—to find the perfect environment for the parasite to reproduce, killing the insect (its host) and then proceeding to flourish, releasing a multitude of spores into the air, spores searching for other hosts or insects or prey. An ingenious fungus and a hellish little fiend. The detective thought about the fungus in relation to the kids. How Suzy—the only one to reappear—seemed to have been under the spell of some parasitic entity, something had beckoned her to the cliffs and something within her had overcome it; she had failed to succumb. But was this really what had happened to the kids? Taken over by some parasitic spore? The detective doubted it. But somehow it seemed to be important—the story that is. The TV had escorted him here. Perhaps it was more like a fable, not factually relevant, but important in conveying an underlying spiritual truth, a moral revelation, a structural cipher.

Elements are created through cosmic violence; violence begot the universe. An elderly man in his dream spoke those words to the detective. They were at a hockey rink, sitting, having coffee, not paying much attention to the match being played on the ice. The detective thought he understood or had the feeling one feels when everything clicks and fits nicely into

42

place, but the elderly man put up his hand, as if he could read the detective's mind, letting him know that he hadn't arrived there yet—to slow down, enjoy the ride; the answers were coming. The elderly man told him to pay attention to the fowl, especially the socially awkward ones, and he also told him that life never knew where it was going, but to trust his instincts; they were never wrong—even when they led straight to death. And then the elderly man drank the last swig of his coffee and crumpled up the styrofoam cup and launched it at a canteen worker.

When the detective woke up, he couldn't stop thinking about the dream; uncertain whether it held any importance, but certain of its emotional weight and lingering psychological effect, he sat up thinking about the elderly dream man. He was shaking, maybe because he needed food or fuel or a cold shower to calm his nerves. He sat down in front of the TV with a mug of coffee and flicked on the tube. He was greeted with an advertisement for a sugary cereal geared towards kids; a cartoon rabbit fought valiantly against a diseased goblin and emerged triumphant. The detective looked out the window and saw a young boy walking, lunchbox in hand, head turned downward, downtrodden with slow and stodgy steps. He watched the boy for a moment, then felt a pain sear the inside of his chest, and he heard a high-pitched squeal. He toppled over in his recliner and seized up and lay still. He was left on the floor for three days until a friend and fellow police officer came by and noticed him through the window. The autopsy reported that he'd had a massive heart attack. He was buried four days later, and the epitaph on his tombstone read: "Sometimes, it all seems like it's for the birds."

Chapter 6

Father Tom came to their town approximately one year after the disappearances ended. He was a drunk and a scoundrel and everyone seemed to like him. His church was located just off Main Street and backed onto a lush green expanse that many of the town's kids and families used for picnics and recreation. It shared the street with a variety of stores and shops ranging from hair salons to dollar stores and fast-food restaurants (with one vacant lot reserved as the social hub for the town's numerous winos). Father Tom was transferred to the church but never explained to anyone the reasons behind his sudden posting. If anyone had asked him why he'd come to this bucolic town, he stated simply that he'd needed a rest from the disorder of the large cities and felt a town of middling size (with such beautiful scenery) was just what the doctor ordered—for him, anyway. He conducted his sermons with more fervor than the last priest, Father Jack, whose rhetoric sometimes dissolved into long bouts of mumbled and inarticulate scripture readings, with his pontificated points lost by the wayside.

A rumor circulated about Father Tom three months into his tenure at the church. It had to do with a group of high school girls who'd parked their car one night, drinking liquor stolen from their parents' supplies in a sudden casual assembly near the side of the roadway. He'd passed them on his bicycle and stopped. He noticed one of the girls from his congregation. He said good evening to the young ladies, asked them what they were doing at such an hour; one of the girls—slightly drunker and more brazen than the rest—told him that it was none of his *goddamn* business and to move on and stop harassing them. He smiled and let her know that it was against the law to drink alcohol as a minor unless the drink was not just a drink, a beverage transformed, held up and rearranged to become something else—the blood of Christ, perhaps. He moved her out of the way and sought their stores of alcohol that consisted mostly of cheap rosé wines. He performed the transubstantiation and told the girls that they were now ingesting the blood of their Savior, and he could rightfully sanction their act and leave them in peace. One of the girls asked him if this was not sacrilege—if it were not a blasphemous act done by a rogue preacher. He replied that it most likely was, but at least they could swear to the divinity of their drink if the cops came by. He took one of the bottles for himself and rode off into the night; his black coat trailed, and it looked like an elegant frock blowing carelessly in the bike's wake.

An excerpt from Father Tom's fifth sermon:

"We all judge God. We ask Him why the world is the way it is. Why some entities die and suffer while others—sometimes with heinous and terrible natures—are left to their own devices, free to violate, to sow chaos seemingly without punishment? Disease and degradation run rampant, and man—more often than not—sees a grim and dire future, a world closing in from all corners, ready to devour its prey. Where do we seek hope? Is such a grail an errand for the fool? Where does salvation lie? And perhaps, most importantly, are we damned from the get-go? All these questions are relevant to any soul that dares gaze deeper: where light is obscured, and monsters gather, and the elements are indifferent and hostile. Why then would someone choose this path, face this darkness? Simply put, because they have no choice: one way or another, everyone must take a peek. Hope fostered in ignorance is not the answer; love will not always save you, and time is rarely on your side. The will of God is unknowable, and who's to say that humanity is of any importance in the grand cosmic scale of the universe and, therefore, to God in general? Who knows the scale of God's perspective or His hierarchy of worth? These words are not designed to depress or deter you. On the contrary, its goal is to fix your compass. Realign you in a manner that might equip you with a morsel of understanding and promote a chance at finding a glimmer of grace or steadfastness to bear the burden of that which already lies in wait. We cannot shake our destiny, and all of us still have traumas and battles and deaths yet to contend with. I request that you submit to your nature, be it base or righteous, evil or benevolent, and trust in your instincts and the balance of all things. Change the scale and perspective of your thoughts often, without which we will always be drawn towards the dull and narcissistic. And remember, the game is already over, so relax, and do your best to enjoy the progression. There is nothing to win and, therefore, nothing to lose, just an endless sea of happenings, neither good nor bad—although often incredibly painful. One thing folding onto itself—or into itself—for no better purpose than because it does. The journey God has devised for us is best played out like a joyous howl, or maybe a silent scream."

One of the altar boys came up to him after the sermon and asked him why he chose to share such dark material with the crowd, bless their ears with such hokum. And the preacher responded, saying that in his sermons he seeks a 40/60 split or ratio of truth to bullshit. Most of the time, he'll side with more bullshit, as was the case today, but sometimes he'll scoot over to the side of truth and really let it flow. The altar boy asked the preacher what 80% truth might sound like, and Father Tom said: "God is dead; life is meaningless; the worst is yet to come, but luckily for most of us, the horror is slow to arrive. Tenderness breeds hope, and marijuana stifles boredom."

"What about 90%?" asked the altar boy.

"Words don't matter, only the underlying tones do. He writes His plan in chaos, and ignorance is His gift. And a word to the wise, never try and explain anything. But do it anyway."

A preacher walks into a bar.

There, he sees a hodgepodge of misfits, disgruntled and in need of drink. He enters and eyes his surroundings, looks for familiar faces. "First and foremost, make a good assessment of the milieu with a clear frame of mind," says he to himself. He finds a seat at the bar and orders an Irish whiskey on ice. There is no band, but the music is good; offshoots of old classics from the '50s and '60s merge with more modern sounds, creating an eclectic playlist glued together by the cohesive flow of someone's good taste. Father Tom asks the bartender how he's doing and receives a grunt in reply. The

TV has a baseball game on, but no one seems to be watching. There's a dog running around and a bowl of water somewhere with "mutt" written on it. (The owner's dog? Unclear.) The man next to Father Tom asks if hell is real and then answers his own question. This is a fine establishment, thinks Father Tom, a perfect place for the shepherd and the herd.

It took about seven months for George and Father Tom to meet; the Dilgunks weren't consistent churchgoers. They met at a bench in front of a well-kept convenience store; Father Tom sat drinking coffee and smoking a cigarette; George leaned his bike against a sturdy tree and asked the priest if he'd keep an eye on it while he ran inside. The priest nodded with a smile, but when George came out (three to five minutes later), the bike was gone. George was taken aback and visibly upset. "What the hell happened?" he said, and Father Tom sat calm and still like before, smoking and drinking and smiling. "What happened to my bike, Father?"

The priest looked at him as if he'd just woken up from a long nap. "Oh, your bike—hmm, I'm not sure." Father Tom touched his chin and put on a puzzled expression, a parody of the perplexed. "It was here, now it seems to be gone. A real think-piece-kind-of-mystery, if you ask me."

George's temper began to flare. What the fuck was going on? "I asked you to watch over it." His tone was that of a plea, and his eyes were large with disbelief.

"I got caught up in my mind, kid. Sorry."

George looked around incredulously, unsure of how to vent against an emissary of God. The priest ruminated for a moment and posed a question.

"What did your bike look like, anyway?"

"You just saw it."

"I wasn't paying much attention," said the priest.

George's grip was loosening; he was losing control. Father Tom was calm and seemed to be enjoying the exchange; George was ready to kill him, and George said: "What the *hell* kind of priest are you if you can't even watch over a *goddamn* bike for five minutes?"

"True story," said Father Tom. "I'm afraid there are a lot of blemishes adorning my character and plenty of holes in my way of thinking. And I have a strong tendency to lapse into daydreams at inappropriate times."

George sat down dejected, the winds of anger giving way to the glum reality of defeat. The priest made room for the boy on the bench.

"Don't worry, son. I'm sure it'll turn up."

George walked home and explained to his parents what had happened. They thought Father Tom sounded like an odd fella, and they told George they were sorry about his bike. They could go down to the used bike shop next week and see what they could find. The family ate, watched TV, and went to bed. In the morning, George stepped outside and found his bike lying on the front lawn. "What the H?" he thought.

He visited the church just off Main Street that very day and found Father Tom dressed in his cassock reading in a pew. George figured he was reading the Bible—the most obvious choice—but upon closer inspection, George saw that it was a book called *The Magic Mountain*. He told the priest about his bike and asked if he had anything to do with its reappearance, and Father Tom shrugged and said, "Everything has a will of its own. I suppose it just needed to get back to you." He paused, then added, "And by the way, son, when in doubt, remember, look for the invisible link between all things. The fictions that unite us all."

There was a stabbing not far from the church around midnight on Thursday that week. Father Tom was still working; he heard the commotion and came out. There were seven people divided up on opposing sides of an escalating feud. A man was lying on the ground, still conscious, with multiple stab wounds. The priest went up to the man and knelt beside him. A woman was holding his head and crying, while nearby another man was yelling in a fit of uncontrolled rage, stripping off his clothes and berating the night. The wounded man's head swiveled from left to right, a look of stupor plastered across it. He stopped moving, and Father Tom felt for a pulse he couldn't find. He started doing CPR, and when he pushed against the man's chest, he felt his ribs snap. The ambulance came and took the man who was pronounced dead, and Father Tom took off his bloodied cassock and went to his favorite bar. He stayed until close and got exceptionally drunk.

***

He sometimes didn't like people, and he wondered why he'd become a priest in the first place. But somehow, he knew it was the right profession for him. He needed God, not in the sense that he needed an overarching explanation for the world and all of creation, but more so that he needed an entity or deity or the fabricated notion of one to converse with on a regular basis. It was a chess game he played, and God provided an opponent or teacher or playmate, without which the game—which, at bottom, was the most important thing for Father Tom—would cease to be. Lethargy and apathy would certainly consume a soul like that of Tom's if the game weren't played continuously and with fervor. His upkeep relied on this transaction with God, and Father Tom couldn't think of a more charitable gift than the mysterious dialogue played out vis-à-vis this internal linguistic charade.

51

Chapter 7

The circus came and set up a giant tent on the outskirts of town; its reach extended skyward and many windows were privy to this extension. Circuses had visited before, but this was the first whose scale and grandiosity incited buzz akin to low-grade pandemonium, perhaps because of the famous titular act, hinting at a singular monstrosity occupying the centerpiece of the show, heralding it as the next big event or do or celebration in the otherwise calm current in the lives of the townsfolk. The Yitrahilu Circus was rumored to be a mythical spectacle, a freak show of the highest order, and its central performer (Yitrahilu) was only spoken of or described in words befitting to the indescribable. (The indescribable contained inexplicably in the description of the described.) Cursory suggestions accompanied by an encyclopedia of adjectives sold the circus to the town in flyers and internet ads and local TV promotions, with everyone's idea of who Yitrahilu was—physically speaking—to be vastly different from one imagination to the next. George couldn't wait for the show, and he gazed out his bedroom window, staring at the top of the red-striped tent.

The show was set to begin on Friday—it being Wednesday, a slight wait still ensued. George bought his ticket at a small stand near the big top. A disheveled clown in polka-dot overalls sold it to him without saying more than a few carefully chosen words. His workspace was cramped, not even big enough for him to sit down, and George was undeterred by the clown's lack of enthusiasm. His friend Tim Daniels was going to accompany him, and they searched the internet all week trying to find pictures or hints as to what Yitrahilu might look like. Strangely enough, the pair could find no clear-cut answers. Somehow, Yitrahilu had evaded the internet age and remained hidden from its magic; its myth circulated from town to town, information disseminated from mouth to mouth, expanded and contorted from mind to mind, and yet no one knew its definitive makeup or shape. And the two young lads thought it odd that no modern person had yet captured the creature on film.

The bell rang, and the kids were dismissed, and George and Tim grabbed their bikes from the schoolyard and went to the Dilgunks' house. The show started at eight o'clock. They ate jambalaya and downed orange pop and readied themselves. At 7:15 p.m., they grabbed their bikes and headed for the tent, the sun falling rapidly at their backs. The parking lot was full—the frivolity stimulating and the excitement palpable. Families bought hotdogs and snacks in an enclosure of carnival games and food stands that corralled them together, pushed them forward, a spiral-like trek ending at an entrance. Clowns and fire breathers and dwarfs and strongmen littered the yard; the magicians pulled out bizarre objects from unsettling orifices—some straight out of thin air. A number of incandescent light bulbs hung in zigzag formations along electrical wires, and an antiquated sense of foreboding propelled them onward; sparrows flew in the darkness. No one paid them any mind.

They took their seats and gazed at a lone light sweeping past the deserted ring. A clown entered with a microphone.

"Hello, friends. Tonight you bear witness to a singular act. Since the dawn of man, creatures and myths have haunted the darkest corners of our imaginations. Tonight, in the flesh, you witness a real nightmare. Good luck, and may God have mercy on your soul."

He put down the microphone and exited the stage. A group of six men stood in strange costumes with DIY tentacles; they entered the ring and began to dance, spaced evenly. George could feel the increased probability of a letdown. But then a flicker—like a hologram coming to life— a giant projection attempting the impossible, trying to conjure itself into existence. A beast almost as big as the tent itself, fat and gruesome with one large eye, oval in shape, with an arrangement of hundreds of limbs or tentacles reaching out, far and wide, moving chaotically. It was no longer an intangible hallucination, and its feelers grabbed one of the dancers, who screamed, and a giant vertical mouth unglued from its stomach and bared its teeth, and the styrofoam-clad dancer was thrown into its pit. It bit down; blood spurted out and drenched the first couple of rows. Tim got out his cellphone and tried to take a photo but couldn't turn it on. George attempted to do the same with similar results. People were screaming, some fled, but the exit required a proximity to the beast that few wished to indulge. George watched, and the beast began to grow. It multiplied at a rapid rate; it engulfed the crowd. It merged with them, and they folded into its skin with their arms and legs and faces stuck in the glue of its makeup, still perceptible, moving slowly of their own accord.

George and Tim's turn—the beast is cold; George goes in face-first. Its insides are dark green and composed of various disintegrating masses, conduits link various sectors; George pukes and something stabs him through the cheek; he connects to its circuit board.

"If you glimpse a plane of existence that's marked by chaos, painted by the absurd, and you thereby adapt your psychology to the rules of its unorthodox logic, will you— from that point onward—be characterized as insane?"

George sees a large boulder in a cave with a giant matchstick coming out of its side. A shadow lurks and enters from the rear, composed of broadcast filament like a TV projection made real. It walks up to the match and snaps its fingers, and *poof*—fire. Its face changes in the firelight and a devilish red glow crafted out of twisted flesh wraps around the once-black figure. It eyes George and speaks: "A magician's light?"

The scene fades, and George is walking outside, away from the tent, past the stands and games. Somehow the circus has teleported him, along with the audience, out towards safety; what felt like an implausible denouement has become his reality. He sees Tim and runs up to his friend. Tim's words seem disconnected, but the term "shell shock" hits. George wonders how they made it out alive; it really felt like they were goners for a while. Tim says it would be bad for business to lose an entire audience (especially in these hard economic times), and George concurs, and he relays his experience to Tim who refuses to divulge his own, simply stating that his was wildly different. Others they meet along the way home speak similarly. One woman tells George that she was in some orphanage or hospital or sanitarium at the dawn of the twentieth century, and some nurse with abnormally long and spindly legs chased her, knees jutting out at odd angles, with an obscenely large syringe in one hand; she kept whistling a tune and saying, "Let me take the pain away." Her voice eerily similar to that of her mother's.

The next day, George heard the news: last night, all over town, strange and deviant behavior had erupted from the town's most respected citizens. Orgies in parks, rioting, fistfights, and pseudo-demolition derbies in medium-sized parking lots: Prius vs. Prius. What was going on? That day, the town's mayor, Mayor Purvice, decried the circus and banned any further involvement between it and the town. When George checked his window later that morning, the top of the tent had already vanished.

He called Tim's house and was told that Tim was under the weather and couldn't talk. George, feeling remiss, went out to where the circus had been. Perhaps someone or something was still there. The grumpy clown in the polka-dot garb? He biked down to the grounds and saw that next to nothing remained. Garbage and debris littered the scene, but beyond that, it was difficult to guess that a giant big top—along with all its accompanying paraphernalia—had ever existed here, let alone twenty-four hours before. The only structure he could see was a wooden outhouse, and he stepped towards it, and something moved and came out from behind it. A man? Its contour still too far to make out, dark and somehow otherworldly; it waved to George. He stopped, and it beckoned him forward. A piercing sense of dread cut through the sunny afternoon scene as the dark figure pantomimed friendliness and good-natured joviality. "Come here," spoke the trap. George grabbed his bike and sped off in the opposite direction. When he reached the town square, he couldn't quite shake the feeling of having escaped some hellish fate, and the normalcy of the mundane unbuttoned the stores of food lying in his guts, and he puked on the grass, and then he sat down and watched some kids laugh and swing and play in the park.

Over the next couple of days, things began to normalize, and George decided to write a story about the circus. He thought long and hard about a way to introduce the characters, set up the scene, build tension; and in the end, he drifted back into his usual habits—simply writing and letting it flow out without much thought. He sent the final draft to a literary magazine a couple of states over and heard back a month later, enclosed was a check for two hundred dollars, and George was ecstatic about his first success.

Tim and George got up to their usual shenanigans once Tim recovered his bearings. They pedaled around town with mischief in their eyes, and George took Tim to the cliffs. He'd spoken about Nikki before, and Tim provided speculative answers as to what might have happened, and although George spoke candidly about it to Tim, he continued to be haunted and disturbed by it. He'd seen a fair amount of tragedy in his sixteen years on this planet. His pal Ricky dead, his girlfriend missing, and he wondered if this was the way it was for most American kids, or if he was especially cursed in some abnormal or extravagant way.

Even though the cliffs were ground zero for George, he still liked coming out to them. He was somehow bound to them; they spoke to him, whispered in gusts of wind—and he felt an understanding and calmness there. It also bore blackness, and this, too, seemed to entice George. He needed the mix of beauty and wonder and murk that the cliffs provided. He had glimpsed darkness in the soul of the world and now required a certain amount of its presence in order to keep moving— ever onward, always forward. He sometimes noticed it in the sky, or in the smirk of an old lady at the bank, or in the yelp of a wild dog. It was an important tonal entity to George, and it framed the world in a strange and tragic and beautiful way.

George was sitting at home with his father one night, watching the TV news, when the Yitrahilu Circus was mentioned. The circus had been doing a show somewhere over in the East Coast and someone had tossed a firebomb; the entire tent had erupted in flames. Six people died, and many were taken to the hospital and treated for smoke inhalation and burns. The circus's owner came onscreen, a small balding man with great tufts of hair on both sides of his head; he said he was disheartened by the tragedy but wouldn't allow it to derail his circus. His entire team was already working hard to reorganize and continue their American tour. He said they'd be back on the road within a week. It was later reported that after the interview the owner had gone back to his trailer and shot himself in the head with a .44 Magnum. George's father said nothing. The Yitrahilu Circus disappeared and was seldom spoken of again.

Chapter 8

George caught a bug and was delirious with sickness for the better part of a week. He missed school and remained stuck up in his bedroom. The sickness was primarily concentrated in his head. Strange colors danced around him. He had the discrete sensation of something roaming around in there, chomping on his bits. He had a pulsating headache, magenta was everywhere, and any quick movement resulted in debilitating bouts of dizziness. He spent most of his time wrapped in covers, rocking slightly, sweating, making strange plans, and prioritizing odd and illusory events. His mind was all over the place, and it was very difficult to sleep.

During the second day of his bedridden existence, after a semi-lucid night spent dreaming of death-defying excursions, George saw a strange-looking bug walking up and down his wall around 9:30 a.m. The bug was black and had long translucent wings; its body seemed to be a cross between that of a hornet and an ant. George could muster little more by way of description. The bug seemed content to roam the same up-

and-down trajectory on his wall, and George decided to give it a name. He watched Eric for the better part of an hour that morning; he felt his predictable vertical amble to be soothing, and it set the pace, keeping track of time, or what felt like time, in his current (slightly delusional) state of mind.

While keeping his eyes on Eric, he let his mind wander, concocting weird plotlines full of illogical bends and populated by sweet and innocent personages. Eric's presence, along with the sickness, ignited the flicker that birthed the flames and fed a slew of engaging tales, which George would later pen in the upcoming months. A foray into the uncharted creative interzones brought about by the catalyst of George's seasonal flu and the marching insect. As he watched the bug, he thought about their journey together: the bug's same ridiculous movements up and down, up and down, and his slovenly sick gaze, mouth open, coughing fits every thirty seconds. They were quite a pair. He got up and went over to Eric and decided to add an obstacle to his traditional route. Thicken the plot. He taped a straw to the wall midway in his path. He stood watching closely as the bug approached the hurdle. It bumped into it, paused, not computing, and ran into it again. It stepped back, a centimeter or so away, and began brushing its forelegs together over its head, making strange, atonal screeching sounds. George bent in closer; Eric's panic increased. George took the straw from the wall, but Eric remained fixed, shaking, a ticking time bomb, and then an explosion. The bug's goo shot out all at once; George felt some of the splatter against his face. He apologized to Eric's corpse, knowing nothing more could be done—an apology aimed at vindicating his own sense of guilt. He grabbed a tissue and wiped Eric away and went back to bed.

George's sister, Trisha, is in her room. She's twenty-one, an adult, and she fusses around at her desk in front of her mirror, brushing her hair while surfing the web, multitasking with ease and elegance. She notices movement on the wall, and her first instinct is to ignore it, but the sensitivity of her peripheral vision makes it impossible. She looks up and spots a bug: black and bulky, an abundance of guts stuffed into its armored frame. She lets out a slight scream, but quiets herself and feels angered that her first reaction was vocal. She grabs a tissue and plans to flush the critter down the toilet; she approaches with apprehension, and at the last moment, the bug jumps. It lands on her hand, evades capture. It bites down, and Trisha lets out another scream; this one tinged with the frequencies of pain. George knocks on her door and asks if everything is all right. She tells him to come in, explains the scenario—that there's a bastard of a bug running amok in here, biting down on her flesh. He comes in draped in covers, his closest visual ally reminiscent of the icons of the Virgin Mary. She's shaken the bug off who's now lying dormant on the floor. George kneels beside the creature; he looks at it closely trying to see if it is capable of registering, even instinctually, the looming threat of death. He can't find any evidence to support this claim, and he makes a fist and comes down on the bug four or five times, punching it into oblivion, making a show of the assault. When he looks at his hand, the corpse of the bug is stuck to one of his knuckles, and he grabs a tissue from Trisha's room, scrapes it off, and tosses it in the bin.

That night, George's mother brings him chicken noodle soup and some bread. He props himself up in bed and answers her questions, articulating that he's on the mend, perhaps a day or two more before he's right as rain again. She smiles, closes his door, and he brings out his laptop. He watches a documentary about a wannabe rock 'n' roll star who drifts into occultism and finally into snuff films. In the end, he's arrested and gives up the names of some of his co-conspirators as a form of plea bargaining; the names include some prominent celebrities and influential persons. Not everyone is convicted, and the wannabe rock star is eventually found dead in his cell. Some speculate murder, while others assume suicide; the documentary ends on an ambiguous note.

George follows this up by watching a few highlights from some recent comedy specials and then finds a BBC show discussing the rise of nationalism. He closes his laptop and sits staring at the ceiling, hoping another bug will enter his reality and cure the boredom and monotony of his current predicament.

During all this commotion at the Dilgunk residence, Father Tom was tending to his church and turning around a great many thoughts in his priestly brain, listening to his parishioners: penitents seeking forgiveness, he tried to oblige their desire. He'd listen carefully, taking note of their sins, never trying to separate it from the person he knew to be speaking—supposedly anonymous, thinly veiled, with no audio camouflage. Priests knew the entire gamut of atrocities running through their congregations as well as the faces to pin them to, and Father Tom was not at all surprised at the number of violent, sexual, heinous, and reprehensible acts that happened here, in this quaint town. It did not diminish the town's beauty for Tom; conversely, it expanded it, showed him that beauty could still exist even in cesspools—not that the town was a cesspool, far from it. Darkness and sin lurked everywhere, and violence and mayhem hid behind every human heart, and the general vibe of the town was still strongly situated on the moral high ground, or so Father Tom thought... sometimes.

Eight-year-old Suzy Jenkins came to the confessional one day and wished to tell her sins to Father Tom. He opened the dialogue in the traditional ceremonial way and asked the child to go ahead and reveal her wrongdoings. The young girl said that she'd killed eight hedgehogs, twenty-three squirrels, six dogs, and twelve cats—not to mention entire colonies of ants, bees, and hornets. ("*What the fuck*!?" thought Father Tom.) When the priest asked the young girl why she'd felt the urge to destroy and decimate these creatures, she said because God had told her to. Father Tom didn't know what to make of that and asked her how she knew it was God, and she told Father Tom that God lived in her mouth and spoke to her in dreams ("*Hmmm... batshit little monster...*"). A fly landed on Father Tom's eyelid, and he blinked furiously to get it off. Then he told the young girl to come and see him the next time she was entrusted to perform any violent action; he'd help her decode the true meaning and perhaps find a less wrathful message contained within.

During his next service, Father Tom looked through the crowd and spotted Suzy Jenkins, the wunderkind of destruction, eight years old and already a strong predilection inclined towards the psychotic. She was dressed in her Sunday best and looked like the archetype of a sweet and caring third grader. Although she had openly confessed to the atrocities and exhibited an eerie calmness while doing so, Father Tom still saw an innocent and good-natured soul nestled within this tiny killing machine. He held out hope that with the proper guidance and penance, her future could still be bright and prosperous. He made it his mission to keep an eye on her; he would do his damnedest to steer her away from future misdeeds with bloody implications.

Suzy came to see Father Tom a week later at his house. It was located in a subdivision called Little Acres just south of the church. Suzy had come to discuss another violent message she'd received. God had spoken, told her to sacrifice her next-door neighbor's cat, a Maine Coon named Tulip. If she did this, He said, she'd reap a great reward, and He'd also cure one invalid living within the town's radius. Father Tom thought this sounded crazy ("*What the fuck is wrong with this kid?*"), and he asked her what would happen if she let the feline live, and Suzy said, nothing—except God would be awfully disappointed in her. Father Tom shook his head and laughed and said there was nothing to worry about. God was disappointed in them all, all the time; that was His default mode. He told her she should get used to it and live courageously with the guilt of having disheartened God; it was the natural way of things. The sacrificial nonsense had dried up long ago, a thing of the past, a barbaric time when the populace lacked the fortitude to bear the burden of collective chagrin. She smiled, and he seemed to have convinced her; she put down her knife. He walked her home, and they talked about school and butterflies and favorite flavors of ice cream.

When Father Tom got back to his house, the garbage bin was tipped over, and a raccoon was plowing through his trash, making a real mess of things. He shooed it away (which took some effort as his attempts were generally met with disdain and mockery by the furry creature). It finally wandered off, and he wished he still had Suzy here, in full Colonel Kilgore mode, ready to dispatch that little son of a bitch, before he'd redirected her path from the violent to the downcast. Well, next time, he thought; there was no shortage of violent humans with homicidal whims to champion into doing his bidding; he'd come by one soon enough, and then that little son of a bitch would meet its grisly end. He lit a cigar and sat on his veranda and watched the black sky above, dead stars shining therein.

It'd been a week since he'd gotten sick, and George finally made his way downstairs to resume his seat at the table with the rest of the family; he took his first few bites of his mother's beef stroganoff and was happy to report that he'd finally gotten his taste back.

Chapter 9

George's father, Walt, was tired from a long day at work. He was a company man as men in those days were sometimes referred to as. He also seemed to not like people all that much—although that wasn't entirely true: sometimes he liked them very much and other times, well... he hated the lot of them. It depended mostly on how many assholes or dicks or cunts he met in a day. A day with one or two cunts wasn't bad, but a day with eight or more was downright intolerable. Nothing spoiled a day, or a mood, like too many cunts. He decided to take the long way home that day, decompress along more scenic vistas—typically a point-A-to-B style driver. This decision proved to be a fruitful one, and he began to feel better almost immediately; he rolled down his window, allowing some of the newly arrived spring air to creep in. He saw a young couple sitting at a picnic table, and an insane idea formed in his head that he was unable to shake. He pulled a U-turn and parked the car—down the road and out of sight. He grabbed a scarf from the back seat and draped it around his head—placing his sunglasses on last—a rip-off disguise, a purportedly invisible man, nothing but a movie cliché.

He grabbed the handgun from his glove compartment and tucked it into the front of his pants. The urge for sudden violence deadening all of Walt's civilized tendencies. His movements felt detached from the person he was. He walked carefully up to the couple, a silent sneak, and the boy was still smiling when he pulled out the gun. He paused. And then he shot them each in the face before they had time to really register his presence or even mutter a quick "hello." It had all happened so fast. He felt good about what he'd done and was happy to kill without motive or reason. There was something cathartic about senseless violence and myopic worldviews and chaos and death. He needed a couple of killings that day, and he was glad to kill those two lovebirds seated there, in broad daylight, at that goddamn fucking picnic table. He got in the car, tossed the gun back where he'd found it, unbound his face, and drove home.

That night during supper, Walt Dilgunk was in a wonderful mood. He joked with his family, ate heartily, asked his daughter, Trisha, and his son, George, how school was going. He made love to his wife and even took out the garbage without being asked to. Balance seemed to be restored all at the paltry price of killing two nobodies. He felt good and wondered if killing wasn't the answer to all of life's quagmires.

He saw the killings on the news the following night and deduced by the vague details that no one had witnessed him do the deed. The police were calling on the public for support, and Walt felt good about his prospects of getting away with it. Oddly enough though, he didn't seem to care much if he got caught. He'd somehow lost the ability to give a shit over the last couple of days. (Was this apathy or stoicism?) He started to think a lot about suicide around this time. He wondered about the intricacies and details, about whether or not to leave a note. He seemed to have come to the end of his character development and just wanted a way out, a sound exit strategy, nothing more. In the end, he decided against the note, and he drove his car off the town's famous cliffs at breakneck speed.

When they retrieved the car from the water, they found the gun in the glove compartment and searched the Dilgunk residence and found traces of blood on a scarf that matched that of the picnic victims; and George and Trisha and Jill (mom/wife) were surprised, but only slightly, that their father/husband was a homicidal maniac. Almost no one came to the funeral, and George missed his father a great deal.

Summer came and went, and George entered his senior year of high school, fatherless, morose, a little depressed, and very horny. He wondered how he'd get a date for the prom but figured he had a good eight or nine months to come up with a solid plan or a reliable solution.

George's mom, Jill, began volunteering at the hospital around this time. She needed something to get her mind off all the recent craziness, and she looked at the hospital as a possible place of redemption; she dove right in, a capable worker, and this proved to be an excellent strategy, and she met a whole host of interesting sorts. Some without arms and legs, others without properly working hearts, some wheezing with respiratory problems, but all with their own brand of biological malady uniting them under the hospital's galvanized roof, an island of misfits and rejects all in need of a spare part or two—or, at the very least, a lavish retooling of an old morsel. Jill started by volunteering four hours a week but upped it after her first month to twelve; she was grateful for the hospital and the joys and sorrows she was able to witness and, more often than not, share in, in this labyrinthine center full of dramatic and engaging corridors.

She met a man in his mid-fifties who was in the hospital because of a ruptured spleen. His name was Gordon, and he was a kind, white-haired man. They chitchatted for hours, and Gordon told her about his life: a widower, contractor, and world traveler—and Jill told him about hers. He listened attentively and made all the required gestures of shock and understanding and even held her hand during the really unseemly and traumatic bits. They were bonding, and after a week, when Gordon was getting ready to go home, Jill Dilgunk gave him her number and told him to call her and stay in touch. Gordon nodded, a flirtatious and knowing smile cropping up on his lips. They hugged, and he left towards the exit with a slight hobble in his step.

It hadn't been long since their father's death, but both George and Trisha were happy for their mother, content that she'd found some healing in a new friend or companion or whatever Gordon was—someone who could divert her mind off last year's woes. Gordon would come by and eat with them, frequently going for walks with their mother, and he was always friendly and jovial with the pair—asking Trisha how college was going and seeing how George's writing was coming along. He brought back normalcy into their household, and everyone was grateful for that.

High school was also beginning to eclipse the craziness of George's family life. George's interest in school hadn't miraculously increased, but this being his final year, decisions had to be made, and a lingering sense of the approaching end dogged him through many days. He eyed his classmates differently and wondered what would happen to them in the upcoming years. Jocks developing opioid addictions, nerds becoming upper-middle-class professionals, most presumably blurring seamlessly into modern life via college or school or some job that immediately made them part of the larger whole. Who would die first? And would anyone care? George sat twirling a pencil around his thumb as he watched Ms. Monahan, his twelfth-grade biology teacher, discuss cell division, and he wondered what life might have in store for him, what insanities lay ahead.

He decided to ask Leanne Wilcox to prom. She was in two of his classes, and he thought his chances would be greatly improved if he asked her before the Christmas break, try and beat the rush. She wasn't the prettiest of the graduating class, but she was kind and thoughtful even in small and subtle ways; he felt that she was his best candidate, and so he fitted her with his favor and waited for the right moment to pop the question as his courage waned and waxed over the upcoming days.

He was walking back to class from the washroom in mid-December when Leanne approached, a nervous glint in her eye. She asked him how he was and what he'd been up to, awkward questions of little importance posed as she got closer to the meat of her query; after a long detour, she popped the question. And can you believe it, dear reader, *she*... asked him. She wondered if *he* wanted to take *her* to the prom, and George enthusiastically said, "But, of course," and they each beamed at one another, a prom-bound duo. As George took his seat back in class, he thought of how sometimes, and generally in odd and unexpected ways, life works out.

Prom night proved to be a surreal event; George was at home getting dressed in his suit following his cap-and-gown ceremony. He was a dashing seventeen-year-old man-child; he chatted and took photos with his mom and sister as Gordon worked the camera. They went out to his father's gravestone, and he left his grad cap leaning up against it, and he spoke awkwardly in drawn-out sentences to the supposed resting place of his dad.

That night at the prom, George's pal Tim approached him, passed him a plastic cup filled to the brim with punch. George, having danced up a storm with Leanne, was thirsty as hell, and he downed the lot of it in one swift go; Tim held a pernicious smile on his lips, and he told George that the punch was spiked; he was under its spell too, along with Eddy and Bo. George was worried, but Tim assured him that everything would be fine: it was only acid after all.

I'm never going to make it to the end... I guess. The walls leaked phosphorescence, and one girl's face was a thing cut out from Dr. Moreau's thought process. Acid didn't morph reality, it transmuted it... whatever that meant. George saw his teachers grow great tusks and swirling banners come alive to reveal hidden dimensions amalgamating with locker-room portals to create infinite elucidations of what could possibly be. Everything was distorted and blue. But only for a minute, because then it turned orange and yellow with a bassline of green pumping through, and George attempted to dance with Leanne but just ended up standing there, staring at her, saying, "A man is a man is a man is a man..." right on through to the end of one song and into the middle of another. Leanne left without George, and he ended up alone outside, wandering around. He had passed one of modern life's most traveled milestones and was too high to think anything of it.

The night sky proved to be the ideal overhang to blur through his rambling midnight voyage. He stopped at someone's garden and stared at the chaos and asphyxiation and growth contained therein; then he looked up and contemplated the nothingness so vast and cold and diabolical, and then he looked at the orderliness of the houses, the row upon row of manicured lawns and evenly dispersed mailboxes. Wherever he focused, perceptions of ecosystems drew out of his brain, and he decided to lie under an oak tree and rest his eyes for a minute. When he opened them, the sky sang a hymn in the key of ozone and lustrous colors broke in through its dawn chorus; the crickets made their sound, and George walked home. His mother asked him how his night had gone, and he kissed her on the forehead before going to bed.

***

There's a bug on the wall that goes up and down and up and down in the attic. There are eggs cooking in a pan, the smell of toast and bacon, and the steam of the dishwasher. George sleeps upstairs, and his mother sits reading the newspaper in her robe. Trisha has gone to pick up a dress from a friend, and the alchemy of the house and the connected mojos of its inhabitants daftly intertwine and each passes through the center of a design in momentary harmony, headed, as is always the case, back towards the cryptic and disorganized, towards unruly parallels and unseemly perpendiculars. But the break was nice, and the pause gives hope.

Chapter 10

Walt, the father, is circling the drain and about to plop smack down the middle of the well and into the Great Unknown. He's been dead for a while but can't gauge any exact figure. Memories of driving off a cliff, weightless and plummeting, are long gone. He's just been running in increasingly smaller circles, ready to finally get to the center of the pit. And then he's off—down he goes.

He sees a group of rabbits in a dimly lit forest, and a wolf is chomping at their heels. Walt runs and notices he's part of the rabbit clique. A furry critter on the run, he looks back and sees one of the rabbits being torn to shreds in the mouth of the beast. He hops left and separates himself from the group. Every bunny for himself, and he slows down in a thorny patch. He makes his way through in no particular rush. He sees a cave ahead and enters. It's dark, but there's a flicker of light coming from some unknown spot, keeping his journey visible, and he continues on as the cave narrows, which is not much of a problem for Walt in his current and compact incarnation. He hears a voice that asks him how his performance is going. It also asks him if he'd like to move on to the next chapter, keep the pace brisk and pleasing. He thinks of an answer. And all of a sudden, the wolf from before leaps out and devours him. It is extremely painful, and he feels his flesh pull and tear, and one eye escapes its socket. And then it's over—or he thinks it is, but is it? And then he's lying still, immobile in the bushes, outside the cave, a cadaver it seems. He can't move, and he's being devoured yet again, this time by tiny insects, working through him, tunneling and repurposing him as raw material. He is a buffet lying in wait for his eaters to finish. He has plenty of time to think as he's being consumed and wonders why his mind seems undisturbed by all this rigmarole and all these alterations. Before he knows it, he's whisked off; he's no longer a rabbit, but a speck of something attached to a worm or a maggot—burrowing underground. What a weird series of events? thinks Walt, but he is pleased by the seemingly stress-free nature of the sequence, although he'd have liked it more if pain weren't such a prominent factor, a godhead in this strange reality. The digging continues, but it's hard to make anything out, and then he starts to see glimmers of light—and hands in front of him... and a steering wheel. He's driving on some backcountry road; it's night, and his headlights illuminate sturdy trunks in a coniferous forest on both sides of a slanted roadway easing constantly to the right. He seems to be traveling along another spiral-like path, and this time, when he gets to the center, the wolf is there, and he runs over it (on purpose, no less), and he chuckles to himself before everything goes black, and once again, the scene resets.

A man is sitting at a desk across from him. He is normalcy incarnate. He sits staring at Walt as one tabletop lamp intrudes upon the space between them.

"That was the test," he says.

Walt nods. "The test?"

"Yes, that was the test. People get confused about that part. They think the part that came before was the test. The life lived out there, down among them." He gestures downward with his finger, taps the table. "The job, the karma, the choices, the regrets, the sins, the death, the money, the charity, all of it: not the test."

"Not the test," repeats Walt.

"Exactly. Preparation. Everything that happened before, when you were down there, all of it: preparation. The test is the test is the test. You prepared your entire life for it; all your decisions and instincts and talents put to use and graded and combined, and now you've been judged and are waiting on the prospect of atonement or, at the very least, advancement."

"Did I win?"

"I'm afraid there is no winning, but prizes are awarded. Rights are given, and you, sir, have not played badly... not great, but not bad either. If you see here—"

He pushes a piece of paper towards Walt. The number 68 is circled.

"Your score reflects an above-average run. You evaded the beast but then were eaten not long after. You made decisions that demonstrate cunning but also a self-destructive urge. You're vengeful and patient. We have decided to allow you to return for another round of preparation. We think you can do better. We think you should prepare more... before you move on."

"More preparation?"

"Yes, exactly. We knew you'd understand. I'll leave you to it. You will return soon. You will remember nothing. Good luck."

Walt is back, and he's got six legs—and a shell. He seems to have been demoted to life as an insect. But maybe this is a promotion of sorts. Perhaps preparation in this form will allow him to move quickly up the ladder, onto the next realm or phase or whatever is next. His lifespan will be significantly shorter. Death is already creeping in. He doesn't think this though; he is most assuredly an insect with insect instincts and little to no psychological profile. No recollections of anything prior, including the Dilgunks or his mischievous testing out in the mysterious "There," are present in Walt—if this can still be said to be Walt. The insect moves on, directed by an immemorial will, guided by the mechanisms within; he's got sustenance on his metaphorical mind, and he scours the terrain in an erratic search.

It's a clumsy movement that finally does him in. He slips climbing up a rock and falls on his shell and can't turn himself over, easy prey as a bird swoops down and picks him up, chews him a couple of times, then swallows the rest of him whole. The scene returns to the rabbits and the wolf, and he escapes using the same method—this time, he doesn't go in the cave though. He doesn't remember anything about any of this, and all alterations and actions are supposedly instinctual, happenchance, or results caused by excess preparation. He goes down a ridge and finds a creek, refuels, and eyes his reflection. Across from him is the wolf, on the other side of the water. Will it jump in, swim over, chase the rabbit? The wolf stares at him, and he, the rabbit, shits out little pellets and decides to hop away, back to where he came from. The wolf stays put, and when he gets back to flatland, he sees a path and takes it, hops for a while, and hears a sound, looks left—a boy... and the barrels of a shotgun. Bang. Game over. The rest of the episode happens along the same lines as the previous playthrough, close enough that we can skip over most of it; the only memorable tidbit being that it's the boy he runs over at the end and not the wolf.

"That was the test," he says.

"The test?"

"Yes, the one and only," says the man. "You'll be happy to hear that you've received a good score, not a great one, but certainly a good one." He passes him a piece of paper with the number 65 circled. "You were patient and evaded the first beast and worked your way around smartly, but you took the main path and were negligent of the dangers of traveling in plain sight. We think you need more preparation..."

This game, or anti-game, the game within a game, materializes yet again and is played over and over, eternal recurrence for Walt. Sometimes he's an insect, or a bird, once he was a microbe, from time to time he becomes a person—all in the name of potential advancement—the preparatory stages, then he's flushed down the pipe and enters via the rabbit hole, and from there the divergences ensue. It takes him many incarnations and attempts before he is given the green light; he doesn't know this though; in fact, he's been at this for eons, and our story only catches the tail end of his timeline. He gets an impressive score of 85 one time, and he's told he can pass along to the next phase. The interlocutor shows him to a door, and there he goes through, off on another journey. So long, Walt, you old scallywag.

Chapter 11

Tim tells George about a beautiful girl in his first-year anthropology course with huge breasts. She wears glasses and embodies a nerdy sensuality that Tim finds alluring, and most classroom days, he is forced to stifle his hard-on when he looks in her direction.

They have both decided to stay in town and take up their studies at the regional college. George sees the frugal and thrifty side of his personality emerge, and he decides to live at home for a while. His mother is content with his decision, especially since Trisha has moved away, pursuing accolades elsewhere in the hopes of setting up a fine beauty shop one day, currently attending a hairdressing academy and bringing out pork-laden plates with overly seasoned eggs to truckers and bureaucrats in a big city, hustling for tips, one state over. George has decided to study English and still has hopes of becoming a writer. He rarely articulates these aspirations to anyone outside his closest circles, but once he uncaps a couple of cheap American beers, generally at the college tavern (having acquired a fake ID), he preaches from the mountaintops and proclaims himself a god with a felt-tip pen. He cuts down idols: he says Joyce is a hack, Bolaño is a god, and Beckett is a perv—when, in fact, he admires all three. His showmanship pays off, drunkenness is mistaken for confidence, and he quietly sneaks the nerdy, big-breasted girl into a bathroom a couple of hallways down. He loses his virginity in an odd three-way while humping away at the fleshy freshman as he and she mold their frames to accentuate the reach of their inanimate porcelain cohort. At one point, his knee slips into the toilet, and he continues on, a display of eccentricity and purposeful focus allowing him to come and pull out and kiss and caress the girl before she leaves—paths forking; she goes her way; he stays stationary. He looks at himself alone in the mirror: penis out, pants around ankles. Someone enters, he turns, but he's too drunk to see them as anything but a blur. He pulls up his pants and walks home, the journey taking him more than an hour; he passes out, forgetting to have paid his tab and leaving his jacket presumably draped around a chair at the college bar.

Tim pays George's tab and grabs his coat for him. Even when George relays his tale to Tim, he's neither angry nor overly envious, perhaps a tad, but no more than is customarily so, a genuine moderate, or a good lad all around.

George's hangovers are atrocious but short-lived. Thank God for his youth, and he's back at it again with Tim and his other classmates and a random assortment of strangers; kids excited to partake in the adult world of legally sanctioned drugs and beverages, celebrating their inebriated freedom by whoring themselves out to one another and puking out on the grass or, for the more mature and less alcohol-oriented ones, by socializing in polite and civilized circles, discussing, arguing, regurgitating, and opining intellectual debates and theories that have plagued mankind—or provided the fodder for masturbatory thought—since classical antiquity.

Most of the classes George takes are focused on reading and analyzing texts, rather than on writing, the exception being a course taught by Mr. Mickelson; it's a beginners' writing course, and George is eager and nervous to partake. During the second week, they are tasked with writing a short one-page story and reading it to the class. He rips out the one-pager in two days and is excited by his story. When class rolls around, and it's his turn, he coughs a few times, dislodges some phlegm, and begins to read. Mr. Mickelson thanks him, a lukewarm reception; most of his classmates seem bored. When asked about their opinion, one girl comments on the strangeness of its structure, its overly fragmented form, although she does praise the tone and wordplay. George feels slightly defeated but not overly so. After class, he goes to the school pub to meet Tim and Eddy. They drink, leaning at the bar, it's roughly 5 p.m., and a girl from his class comes over and tells him she liked his story; her name is Amber Holmes. He thinks back and remembers Amber; her story was about a lost dog—or was it a cat, he can't recall—who joins a roguish band of wild animals and eventually usurps them all, becoming the leader, only to be run over right at the precipice of this victory by a red convertible. Amber had a flair for the tragic in condensed form. She was also quite pretty: a longhaired brunette, curvaceous, who cocked her head to the right and jutted out her hip when she spoke. He thought he should get to know her.

George spoke to her again three days later, and she invited him to the town's oldest theater to watch a horror movie Thursday night with her and her friends. The movie was a

European slasher film from the 1970s that George had never heard of. Pink and lavender and crimson streaks, an unorthodox palette, to say the least—the film was gruesome and bold and stylized to the point of gimmickry. George loved it and told Amber so. She and her friends, Wendy and Renee, asked if he'd like to accompany them to the diner and grab a bite; George accepted, and the foursome entered the eatery, describing the beauty of a particularly clever murder scene, one that was bathed in mauve, and involved a glistening meat cleaver and an aggressive zoom lens.

During their meal, Wendy told him about a coming messiah. A Black man who'd personify and deify all the best and most alluring traits of mankind, an Adonis of the spirit riding a White Whale, one who'd purify the souls of the unclean and wash away the nihilism of the day. He'd stand towering above the masses, and his style would usurp his message, and time would be a kind and benevolent friend, a witness to a type of inverse entropy, a future with the prospect of faith.

George liked Wendy. She said weird things—unexpected things. She was herself... perhaps to a fault, but because of this (or, perhaps, in spite of this), she fostered a spiritual brawn and an innate strangeness; it was her supreme light, a faithful guide, and she probably thought nothing on it, when, in fact, it was her most enduring and defining trait. A precious rarity among humanity, a true-blue individual, and George was annoyed that he was already smitten with her.

Amber apologized for Wendy during their walk home. George laughed and said it was fine, but Amber wouldn't let up. And she told George that Wendy was a unique type of person, one who preferred winter to summer, east rather than west; someone not accustomed to general and popular tastes; someone who could be brilliant but also foolish. This talk about Wendy only seemed to solidify George's longing for the girl, and he wondered why Amber was so keen on talking about her. Perhaps rivalries had erupted between the pair before; George mulled this over while walking Amber home.

He kissed Amber and went home and looked up Wendy on the internet. She was strikingly beautiful, and although George had just made out with Amber for the first time, he seemed to have repositioned his romantic interest elsewhere—in the direction of her closest friend. That week, Amber invited him over, and they slept together; the sex was fun but forced, lacking a certain spark or *je ne sais quoi*; he wondered if she was aware of this too. They went to a party together the next weekend; they entered holding hands. She introduced him around, and he ended up in a circle with Wendy and Renee and some others. George's heart beat in an arrhythmic fashion; his physiology reacted to Wendy, and that night, after too many beers and whiskeys and wines, George kissed her, and Wendy kissed him back, and they went into a bathroom, and she bent down and sucked him off. They were both dazed by the whirlwind of passion and exposure, and George told her he liked her, maybe more than liked her. She smiled, and then she kissed him, and then she left the bathroom. The next time he saw her—a week or so after the party—she was kissing Brad, one of Eddy's friends. They were dating, started to a couple of days after the bathroom incident. George hadn't told Amber what had happened but had kyboshed their relationship anyway. A few weeks later, Amber was dating a soccer player named Gregory. An outbreak of genital herpes had infiltrated the school's dormitory; one wing in particular, wing C, was especially contaminated with one in three students supposedly infected by the disease. College life was really something, thought George. And life went on, and over a beer at the college tavern, Eddy told him that he had chlamydia and downed a couple of doxycycline pills and said not to worry, that it'd clear up within a week or two.

Not long after, closing in on the Christmas break, George and the rest of Mr. Mickelson's class were tasked with writing a longer story, somewhere around the five-thousand-word mark. George, as per usual, began instinctually and coerced the words out without much thought. His story centered on an old bogeyman living in the attic of a now-abandoned house. The house had once been a fashionable Victorian-era home, with the bogeyman specifically choosing it because of its partitioned layout, symmetrical adornments, and lavish interiors. He was bored and stuck there, forever beached on this hallowed ground. He decided one day to burn it all down, which proved to be an easy task, and he fried right along with it. He couldn't be killed—but suffered serious burns—and so he lived on, on the same patch of earth, directly beneath the sky and the stars, and he got tired of his solitary plot and its lack of walls and interiors, and he decided to build a new house from scratch; he was, after all, a magical (nightmarish) entity and could therefore summon a whole assortment of materials at will; he mixed and matched and used organic and inorganic matter and created an interwoven tapestry of animals and humans and bricks and mortar and fused it all together, a living and breathing network of macabre design. He would be the parasite living within its whimsical realm, tending to his house's (and host's) needs, providing it nourishment and upkeep, all the while making it his very own humble abode; its excretions used in the garden, benefitting him, the bogeyman, with everything repurposed and reused. A perfect zero-waste system. He was the mite living atop the hissing cockroach, and he loved his house and found it to be a true and dignified friend as well as an above-average shelter.

When he received his story back from Mr. Mickelson right before the Christmas break, it was riddled with notes, and he was told that his story was both repugnant and boring (the actual text contained more descriptive passages regarding the grotesqueries of the house). George wasn't surprised, as he'd begun to realize that he and Mr. Mickelson had rather different takes on what constituted good literature. So it goes, thought George, and he filed his story away among the ever-growing pile of pages accumulating in the drawer of his bedside table.

Chapter 12

The snow had accumulated since early December, and by the time Christmas had rolled around, the town was shaped and transformed by its usual seasonal dressings. Multicolored lights wrapped around rooftops and swayed between lampposts, and wreaths hung in decorated doorways, symbols of the eternal and cyclical nature of all. Kids tossed snowballs and went skating on small ice rinks etched out with boards a foot high, outlining their perimeter. George was exceedingly fond of Christmas; it brought about so many memories and feelings, a nostalgic takeover for the eighteen-year-old freshman; so many emotions were pinpointed and centered around this day. A day about coming together, family and celebration, giving and communion, but then there were its darker components, rifts developed because of the proximal nature of its revelry, families at each other's throats, tempers flaring, drunks emerging; the holidays blistered with emotional residue and a heightened sense for the dramatic. George's sister was coming up and bringing her new boyfriend (Willard) to meet their mom. His mother was preparing the usual feast: turkey, stuffing, cabbage rolls, mashed potatoes, gravy, salads, and beets. Trisha and Willard arrived shortly after 10:30 Christmas morning, and after a brief introduction, they gathered around the tree and opened their presents. Willard had brought wine and dessert, his contributions for the day, and Mrs. Dilgunk—kind and benevolent caregiver—had bought Willard a small gift. The morning went about its merry way, and the foursome sat down at noon for a holiday lunch, cheerful and full of grace, the good-natured Dilgunks and Willard—the new addition—dug in and stuffed their faces, then sat down on the couch, put on a Christmas movie, and uncorked Willard's wine.

***

As the Dilgunks and Willard lie lethargically on the couch watching the traditional annual run of holiday specials and movies, George spots a cockroach running along the fireplace. He's too lazy to get up and squash it; he sees its presence as a minor nuisance or irritation, something he thinks could be said for Willard too, who's coming out of his shell more and more, much to George's annoyance. Willard doesn't seem to be a bad guy, but George can already tell by the few things he's said that there will be no fruitful transaction shared, no blossoming friendship born. George doesn't feel superior to Willard; in reality, he's beginning to come to terms with the fact that most people simply don't interest him. They bore him, and he presumably bores them, and if he doesn't, well, he doesn't really care. He begins to miss his dad more and more throughout the day and feels alone, surrounded by his mother, his sister, and a stranger. He wishes he could tell his father how he feels; the murderer inside him would surely understand.

They go to church that night, their annual clerical outing. George fantasizes about gigantic disasters, ones which could actually destroy the planet—no rinky-dink nuclear war or flood or famine; he wants planetary destruction on the grandest scale, Earth shattering into millions and millions of pieces, its complete and utter annihilation as a celestial body. He spots one of his classmates from college, Chloe. She's a vulgar and vocal activist, calling out and casting stones against anyone she disagrees with, trumping up charges of moral turpitude under the guise of such claims as cultural appropriation, misogyny, racism, and ethnic privilege. She constantly seeks out a supposedly worthy foe, someone who's uttered (or stuttered) a phrase or an action that she regards as unbecoming, and she wages war against them, usually online, via a community known for keeping their tirades under two hundred and eighty characters. George has met certain folk he would classify as racist and misogynistic too—an ugly bunch of ignorant assholes, to be sure, generally proclaiming their hateful opinions without much coaxing or cajoling. But Chloe, along with many of her generation, seems to have tweaked the requirements and qualifications for even the most lurid of identifiers: for example, the Nazis—no longer a swastika-clad group of rabid anti-Semites, but now inclusive to an array of conservatives and liberals or, really, anyone whose questions and opinions grate against the overly awoken sensibilities of certain trigger-happy pseudo-intellectuals: people (like Chloe) who were presumably bullied and have rearranged the game to put the proverbial shoe on the other foot; or people whose narcissism finds its perfect mask and stage, hijacking the narrative with a tenuous performance of outrage and vic-timhood (But what about those who were actually violated? Raped and beaten and mistreated? Shouldn't they receive their vengeance? Their just deserts? Have their monster hanged, drawn, and quartered for all to see? George certainly thought so, but perhaps this was just to appease his more barbarous impulses—target a worthy tyrannical foe and watch him be chopped in two—George being something of a sadist after all.); or perhaps they are the other ones—good-natured and loving citizens who've simply watched too much TV and embedded themselves inadvertently in an online community with extreme and conflicting views. George did not know and, really, he didn't care. He felt sorry for many of them, some of whom had truly suffered, and looking at Chloe, he wished her well, but he just wanted her and her moral crusade to leave him the fuck alone; he wanted nothing to do with them or their so-called battle (and truth be told, he wanted nothing to do with the opposing side of it either, some of whom he found truly vile). He wanted to be left alone, to write, to create, to follow his own thoughts and unearth the little magic he felt he could reach, not in the domain of politics or sociological progress, but alone, along a solitary path, deep in the core of his own being, however trite and clichéd that sounded. He supposed it was a quixotic quest; a similarity shared between him and Chloe, each searching for a type of wholeness, a delusional journey—one in the artistic realm and the other in the sociopolitical.

In many ways, George found that humanity was almost always alike anyway, regardless of gender and skin color and culture and socioeconomic status. There, in the trenches, humanity found its common thread, its true color—love, money, hope, fame, fear, sexuality, violence, legality, morality, justice, creation, all used in the service of their will, of their ascension. All blind and ignorant to its bidding, its scheming. Everyone clinging to the false hope of achieving some phantom progeny, some echo of a legacy, when no control was ever truly given, no escape possible, at bottom an inherently rigged game—for the benevolent and psychotic alike. Even for those who were aware of it, there was nothing to be done. Best to push on, always forward and ever upward—what choice was there?

And George knew that he was just like them—and probably worse than most of them—but he didn't dwell on it; it was what it was. What was he to do? But being a helpless hypocrite, he couldn't stop himself from judging and was constantly irked by the self-righteousness of those who purportedly stood outside or above the ubiquitous pettiness of human volatility—self-described as the charitable and the just, but more accurately dubbed "the pedantic and inessential"—people whose actions and willful ignorance (and often their abrasive conduct and capricious rants) had them shackled to mankind's most ignorant and preposterous ideologies, deluded by wordplay. This, along with the gross amnesia of humanity, was what George found most disagreeable with its current state. He was also disturbed by the modern lackluster view of sin, forgetting the impor-tance embedded within it, the concept of the all-guilty and the infinitely corrupted. Born broken, born into this. Redemption its ultimate mirror, its other half, and necessary to the function and fruition of one's soul, a loop that couldn't be avoided on this corporeal plane, whether it all be illusory or not. And he was sick and tired of those scrutinizing the trends for the next big witch-hunt; ready to burn someone, anyone, for whatever reason, so long as the mob gets its fill, popularizes its ham-fisted designation of good and evil, pats itself on the back, and performs its self-congratulatory circle jerk.

It really came down to the fact that he was tired, tired of himself, tired of the others, tired of the hoops he was forced to jump through and would have to jump through, each and every day, for the entirety of his future. The world hung thick, and it was difficult to garner the energy to continue, let alone dance to the beat, smiling and invigorated, all hunky-dory. He hoped insanity would come soon, a happy madness to offset his melancholy, but he knew no such hero was galloping his way. He was naturally inclined towards endurance for better or worse, and he would bear the burden of his life regardless of what came to be (or the monster he became); it was just who he was. George stepped out from the church at the end of Father Tom's sermon and watched two young brothers attack each other in the parking lot's lamplight. One brother (age 8) punched the other (age 6) in the face, and blood spurted out from his nose, and George noted the hypnotic beauty of the red soaked up by the snow.

"It takes all sorts." This line echoed around in his head during the drive home. Said by Father Tom at some point during his Christmas Mass. A cog in the universal wheel, morality nothing but a way of dividing humanity into teams when in fact their actions, both good and evil, were more alike than different. Futile moves to advance the human plot, which the cosmic game cared little for. Indifference seemed to be the defining trait in the cosmos, and if not indifference, well then, the code was indecipherable; God's perfectly woven tapestry was an obnoxious atonal barrage of hokum to the human mind, or at least to George's, anyway—but the fact that he didn't believe in the freedom of his will seemed to soothe him. The acceptance that control was not within his grasp opened up the world in some ways. He made peace with this idea and found solace in it. It helped him to reconcile the disappointments that continued to accumulate.

When they arrived home, they uncorked another bottle of wine, set out some snacks, and sat around the fire. They chatted about the service, and Willard spoke about himself, and he asked them, in turn, polite but slightly probing questions, and under the spell of the wine, George perked up a bit and told them that he was tired and set off for his room. There, he began to write. He wrote for a few hours, heard footsteps climbing the staircase, and glimpsed the light extinguish beneath his doorframe. He tap-danced along the keys of his laptop and was shocked at the ease with which the story flowed out of him. He felt like a common receptionist taking dictation from some other, some creative force in possession of his fingertips. He'd heard of the Spanish term *duende*, described as an earth spirit who helps the artist see the limitations of intelligence, the one who forces them to confront their mortality, the smallness of their being, the scythe-carrying porter known as Death; a battle ensues between the pair and primes the conditions necessary for the birth of an ascending work of art, usurping conscious effort in favor of a kinetic and immediate (and sometimes unendurable) connection—intense, visceral, strong, and willful. God as the inversion, God as entropy's other, God as the destructive creator.

He went to bed around 2 a.m. and slept a beautiful and deep sleep. His dreams were both vague and evocative, and when he woke up, he went to his computer and tilted his head and titled his story. He called it *Hokum's Pass*, and then he went down to join the others for breakfast; the smell of coffee reached him at the top of the staircase, and he smiled— thinking how wonderful life could sometimes be.

Chapter 13

Christmas night, Father Tom had a strange and disorienting dream. He dreamt of a magnificent light, best described as magenta or pink, but in reality, under the delirium of the hallucinations or visions, the color was truly indescribable (and sometimes he even remembered it as bluish—it shifted around), off the charts, never before seen in all his life. The dream was just that, a landing strip of light embedding itself in his noggin. It felt like his brain was morphing, bubbling up, but in a manner befitting an upgrade. God had seen fit to equip Father Tom with some new mental hardware whose powers were yet to be known. Upon waking, Father Tom felt energetic but somehow faint, too. It was like running a long race and being exhausted but also exhilarated by the noise and hubbub and crackle of the finish line. He made himself a cup of coffee up in his apartment (he'd moved into a smaller dwelling, forfeiting his lease on the house in Little Acres) in a tenement next to the church. He smiled to himself, looked in the mirror and heard, for the first time ever, a voice address him directly, a foreign voice from inside his head. Something *new* was in there. Holy shit!

It communicated with him, told him not to be afraid, giggled and laughed, told him she was a friend—*she*: who the hell was she? Father Tom asked her questions, all without opening his mouth. And he asked her if she was a parasite. She replied that she was, so to speak, but that that was a disparaging way of looking at her. She was there to help him, an illumination crafted specifically for him, devised for a special purpose that she was not yet ready or capable of disclosing. He asked her if she'd always be talking to him in this manner, and she replied that she would be, at least for the time being, until their objective was complete. He asked if she was God, to which she replied that she preferred this analogy over that of the parasite—but that neither was exactly correct, although they both were somewhat appropriate. Was she an alien, a fallen angel, a deity, a monster by design? In a way, she said. Strange, thought Father Tom, and he sat on his couch Boxing Day morning, drinking coffee and chatting inaudibly to the newfound entity taking up residence inside his mind; he began to wonder if he'd gone crazy. She replied to his query and confirmed his diagnosis, but she told him to embrace it, and perhaps—to quote an old country song—it'd keep him from going cuckoo or mad. But he thought not, insanity was knocking at the door, and the entity in his head laughed, and Father Tom liked her sick and fucked-up sense of humor. Welcome to your new mind, thought Father Tom; or was it she who thought that? It was sometimes difficult to distinguish the thinker from the thinkee.

He went to the grocery store to pick up some provisions. He needed the basics: meat, cheese, bread, and a children's cereal called Influx Residue (it contained little marshmallows that crackled and popped when milk was poured over it).

The being in his head congratulated him on his choices and asked him to grab some hash browns and bacon and some frozen pizzas, too; he obliged and paid the total up at the checkout counter, dealing with a friendly young maiden who recognized him and wished him a good day. He went for a walk in the snow-laden landscape and picked up a coffee and chatted with the she in his head as he went along.

"So, what's the point of all this?" asked Father Tom.

"You don't know?"

"Not for certain," and he caught his own lie and figured he might as well come clean, given that she, or it, or whatever the voice was, was most likely aware of his distortions and factual inaccuracies. "Actually, I don't know jack shit. I'm like one of those lost dogs that picks up a scent... goes in one direction... but then catches another... and follows it... and so on and so forth. It's a very chaotic and frustrating racket. Intuitive by design... but I've never been able to get a solid foothold or figure out what the hell's really at play—not consciously, at any rate."

She said, "Well, let me explain it like this. There's a layer of chaos enclosed like a dome over your current order—the supposed 'here and the now.' But there's also a sentient and all-knowing entity residing above that, guiding and combatting the other. In a weird way, they work together, and the higher one occasionally breaks in, often hiding, sometimes in plain sight, sometimes in the minds of a very *chosen* and select few."

"And I'm one of the few?" asked Father Tom.

"You're a prime host."

He noted yet another reference to the parasite, and she paused, and the airwaves of his brain went quiet for a brief second. He was reminded of former times, and then she began again: "I need a certain robustness of spirit and mind. It's like certain people qualify without knowing they qualify, and only a handful are lucky (or unlucky) enough to be seen as good candidates based on certain criteria or incidents or traumas or experiences that make their heads ace contenders for us."

"So I should feel honored?"

She laughed. "I never said that."

He thought about this for a moment; he still seemed to have his mental independence, to move his mind where he pleased—separate from her—but sometimes it was as if she hijacked his channel, and his thinking went all fuzzy and screwy-like, and then she'd overtake him. But then she'd stop and give it back, and he was free to go on thinking, just like before, until another interruption or chat or conversation ensued.

"But that's what's really going on?" asked Father Tom to the entity in his head.

"Not really, but it's a pretty good story anyway."

It was about a week later, on Sunday, after his sermon, he was leaving the church, and he felt woozy. He asked the lady in his head what was going on, and she said that she'd tricked him. Hahaha, she laughed. *What the fuck?* thought Father Tom. He went down on his knees and curled up in the snow and passed out without being able to come up with a witty retort.

He woke up in the hospital. Groggy and deranged, high on whatever medicine they were pumping into his system. He tried to talk to the voice in his dome but received no answer. What the hell was going on? A doctor came in, and he moved his hands to his head and noticed that he was all bandaged up; the doctor explained that he'd passed out and fallen over; an ambulance had brought him to the hospital; they'd done some tests and discovered a tumor in his brain; they'd removed the mass and were performing more tests—but the prognosis looked good, and he'd most likely be able to go home in a couple of weeks. He asked her how long he'd been in the hospital, and she said he'd been there for three weeks already.

"So that little son of a bitch was out to kill me," thought Father Tom, "I should have known." Was it Satan's spawn, or some gimmicky cosmic asshole trying to upend his timeline, or, simpler still, some creature munching away ceaselessly, carelessly, and uncontrollably on another, just because? He was happy he'd averted the potential deathtrap and thought he'd be more careful about trusting random female voices emanating from inside his mind from here on out.

It took him two months before he was finally able to go home. His left eye had developed a twitch from the operation, but beyond that, there seemed to be no lingering effects. The townspeople came in droves to see him in the beginning but then thinned out as time went on. George waited awhile before going to visit; he let the rush pass and went a month into Father Tom's tenure at the hospital. He asked the priest how he was, and the jolly follower of God proclaimed that he was well and on the mend. He praised God and told George he got lucky, had a new lease on life, and that each new day was a gift to be cherished. George thought Father Tom was pandering when he said things like that, but he let the recovering priest go on uninterrupted.

"Were there any symptoms before you fell over?" asked George.

"I heard a *voice*."

"Reeeaally?"

The boy was intrigued.

"Yup, and I thought it might be the voice of God, or some omniscient entity, a divine presence coming down, out of the darkness and to my aid. Turns out it was a malignant tumor."

"What'd it say?" George hunched over and leaned in towards the bedridden fellow.

"Oh, a lot of bullshit mostly, but some of it seemed to reek of truth. It felt like she was privy to my subconscious, unearthing pearls that might not have been ready to dislodge of their own accord."

"Hmm," said George, "sounds like quite a trip." He leaned back, slightly bored at the offered victuals of Father Tom's tale. He tried not to show this though and kept his eyebrows raised in mock interest.

"It was definitely something," said the priest, "and it's certainly given me a thing or two to chew on."

The two friends sat together and chatted some more; the priest asked the young man about his life and his writing, and the sun shined in and reflected off the many metallic surfaces of the hospital's sanitized room.

When he was discharged, Father Tom took a taxi home. He sat on his couch, poured himself a whiskey, and lit up a joint. Father Tom owed much of his good fortune to dumb luck and perhaps the grace of God, and he was happy to be back in his humble abode once again.

One thing he found odd was getting used to the solitary voice inside his head, as opposed to the multiple voices he'd grown accustomed to (and even missed a little). It hadn't been long with her, maybe a week, but the effect of having a cohabited mind was a strange one and had ingrained a pattern or habit or knack for mental dialogues that was difficult to get rid of. He asked himself if he should go for a walk, and no one answered.

He walked to the outskirts of town and kept going. The rolling hills and farmers' fields provided good and solid terrain for his meandering. He saw a chicken farm he'd once been forced to visit. He was asked to perform the last rites for the dying patriarch of the Dursley clan (the farmers in charge of the poultry farm); they lived in a house out back. He'd been given a tour upon his arrival by Jonathan Dursley, the current chief of operations, and glimpsed the atrocious living conditions of the mite-infested and hairless chickens, dying and squawking and laying eggs, one on top of the other, a simple and brutal life. The farm had been shut down numerous times by various inspectors, but somehow the farm had *always* resumed production and kept going. When he looked at the chickens, he noticed their eyes, ferociously stupid and filled with fear. Their life was brief, horrible, and terrifying. They certainly got the short end of the stick, and he thought about their few consolations: a fleeting existence with limited awareness.

When he got back to town, he passed a fast-food restaurant specializing in fried delicacies. He couldn't help himself and went in and bought a bucket of chicken—subjecting his mouth to the juicy, well-seasoned drumsticks. He sat on his couch and finished off the few remaining pieces he'd taken home, thinking of the consolations of humanity: their affinity for dualism, fictions, charades, and sham morality.

Before going to bed, Father Tom resumed his old nightly habit of speaking with God. He thanked Him and told Him he thought He was a cocksucker, motioned a thumbs-up at the ceiling, and then quietly passed out under his duvet. God did not respond, and the slumbering priest dreamt of horses and circuses and a dwarf with no name.

Chapter 14

Right after Christmas break (just around the time Father Tom entered the hospital), George returned to class, submitting his short story from Christmas night, which he had elongated over the rest of the break, and whose true form was now closer to a small novel than anything else. He saw the glee in Mr. Mickelson's eyes as he handed him his assignment. *"Another animal ready for the killing floor..."* George was weirded out by the intensity with which his professor stared at him.

"What's this joker's problem?"

George would find out two weeks later when his assignment was returned to him with a big flunking F on full display—with the added addendum of "come and see me."

"What the *fuck*?"

When he went to see his professor, he spotted him in his office reading some pages of a manuscript, and George knocked lightly to gain admittance.

"Come in, sit down."

George was a bit nervous; he was also a bit annoyed. A failing grade seemed to be overkill, particularly for this story, which George held in very high esteem.

"You know... I couldn't even get past your first paragraph," said Mr. Mickelson. "There's something about *your* writing that really grates on my nerves. An underlying tone of barbarity and chaos whose structure makes me want to gouge out my eyes."

George was surprised by the honesty of the confession, but when he thought about it, it made sense. He smiled. Perhaps being the worst was akin to being the best in some ways.

"I've decided to pass you—not because you deserve it, but because I can't read another one of your goddamn stories. I genuinely despise your writing." The professor said this while looking away from George, perhaps at a misaligned screw or a dirty picture taped to the underside of his desk; he wore a vexed look. "They make me ill, they do." He paused. "Do you understand? Everything you hand in this semester gets a D regardless of merit. That's it. Now, get out."

George left with a slightly victorious feeling, even though his win was won on the grounds of repulsion.

Today was a good day, thought the young scribe.

***

Hokum's Pass (an excerpt):

I thought that life was only sometimes complicated, that its inner rhythms were generally simple and unclouded. I was living under an overpass with people the townsfolk sometimes called the Children of Lesser Variation. They were misfits and degenerates who'd somehow seen the wayward beacon of hope and self-actualization and thought it to be located beneath a giant slab of rock ferrying cars above. Most of them I didn't like much, and the few I did, I still didn't talk to. They were ragged and dirty and vile, not unlike myself. I was here for now and saw it as a respite before moving on. One night a rat bit me, and I blamed the boy sleeping next to me for no real reason. I kicked him as hard as I could; he barely moved, but in the morning the group expelled me, and I wandered down the expressway with nothing in my pockets.

A woman offered to buy me a sandwich outside the grocery store, and I ate nine-tenths of it and then gave the remaining bits to a dying squirrel. It had attempted a colorful jump from the grocery store's roof to a nearby tree; it failed and fell, its guts opened up to its left and to its right. It didn't seem to like the ham or the cheese, or maybe both. I watched it for a few minutes; it stopped moving, and a young girl holding her mother's hand pointed at it and said, "*Ewww!*" I pointed at her and said the same thing; her mother hurried her along. I looked at the sky and counted thirty-two clouds. I wasn't sure about my accuracy, so I asked someone in the parking lot; they told me that that sounded right, and then they got in their car and drove off. I picked up the squirrel and placed it in the rubbish bin. I was a good citizen and wiped my hands on my jeans, leaving behind streaks of red.

At the far end of the parking lot, I saw a group of eight skateboarders and went over to them. When I got there, I didn't say anything, and they just stared at me and asked what I wanted. I said, "Do a kickflip." One of the boys told me to fuck off, another one performed the trick; I told them that there are thirty-two clouds in the sky. They seemed confused. I said, do a shove-it. No one moved.

I tried to ignore the passage of time, see all time as equal, night and day, and not change my habits regarding the external phenomena. I was preternaturally adept at believing my own lies. I slept when I was tired, ate when I felt like it, but routines could surface at any moment; one had to be vigilant. I liked my life, and I assumed the others enjoyed theirs as well. Life was the accumulation of one overall feeling fed along an immovable timeline. I had a beginning, middle, and end somewhere, although I wasn't exactly sure where the demarcations were. I rarely tried to remember my past or where I came from or how I started; I favored a simple "flight forward" philosophy.

I slept in a park, in the sand, using my shirt as a buffer. A woman woke me up and asked me my name. I told her I was the chief-commander, and she said, "The commander-in-chief?" and I said, "No, you blubbering fool." I left the park and realized I had forgotten my shirt. I looked in the trashcans for a substitute to no avail and ended up bullying a twelve-year-old into giving me his. It was black and had a picture of a duck and was at least one size too small. I wandered around aimlessly and found myself on a path in the woods by a creek leading to a bridge. A woman told me about a cheap hotel she wanted to take me to with bedsprings so squeaky we'd have to make love on the floor. I declined and told her I was abstaining from all rigorous physical activity. Then I realized she wasn't there, and I'd probably just made her up or had a vision—an ecclesiastical sighting. I looked up and counted thirty-two clouds again. "Time is irrepressible and irresponsible," I said to myself, but I forgot to pronounce the *e* and wondered who Tim was, and then I decided to go looking for him.

I dreamt I was back in olden times in the Wild West. A knight approached me, and I shot him in the cheek. Dreams liked to superimpose timelines and use delaying tactics and anachronisms so no one could get to the meat and potatoes, or heart, of their true meaning. Understanding was a difficult thing. I woke up in the woods and followed the path and ended up in a neighborhood bordering the creek. I looked through the windows as I walked by, stopping for a while to investigate any illuminated frames that piqued my curiosity. A woman was arguing with a man; he hit her and left the frame; she stayed, stuck to the floor, crying. I tapped on the window and tried to comfort her, cheer her up a bit. I gestured a thumbs-up and contorted my face into a big grin, and she screamed, and the angry man came back and gestured at me to leave. I punched the window and left. I saw him holding her in his arms as she cried; he was trying to comfort her. I kept walking and watching and looking through the windows. I wondered where Tim was.

I saw the hospital and decided to go in its direction. I spotted a station wagon driving erratically. The vehicle stopped in the middle of the parking lot, and a man stumbled out. He looked like he was drunk. I jogged up to him and saw that he had something sticking out of his eye. It looked like a steak knife. He mumbled to get help. She stabbed me, he said. I laughed; I don't know why, but I became giddy, and I ran into the emergency ward; I yelled: "There's a man outside with a knife in his eye, and she stabbed him. Yes, she did." I waited eagerly with the rest of those in the waiting room for the man I'd just announced to take the stage; it took a while for him to make it to the automatic doors, but when he did, the whole room went wide-eyed, and I clapped, and someone else gasped, and I said, "See! See! He's got a knife in his eyeball."

I decided to wait for the man and asked the nurse behind the glass partition how he was doing every fifteen minutes. She asked me to leave the fifth time I went up. I asked if he'd lost his eye, and she called security. They said I was a bona fide pest and that I smelt bad.

I sat in the grass and looked at the starry sky, thinking how time had conned us, and I tried to come up with an escape strategy for its ruse. I heard that all learning was remembering which meant that all knowledge was already known which might mean that everything that was going to happen had already happened because somewhere at some time someone would have lived or learned or known that thing, which meant that they were actually just remembering it, like one communal mind of one macrocosmic being, each individual a metaphorical synapse, reversing the amnesia; and if someone could remember or know the entirety of all knowledge (the past and the future, forwards and backwards (God)) or even just remember their own supposedly accumulated stores of knowledge or experience (mini-god), they could, theoretically, untether themselves from time because if they knew their orbit—even if they were forced to exist in it, continue along the same line and live out all the same events in exactly the same way—they would (hypothetically) be unstuck mentally because they would be able to see the entire shape of the structure, even as they were forced to live inside of it. Freedom from the shackles by way of an increased field of vision. The eyes of God in the body of a man.

I fell asleep outside and dreamt the world around me folded itself into a ball, and I was stuck inside of it, and it turned into a giant balloon, which began to rise, floating upwards with beautiful projections adorning its outsides for all the onlookers below to see. Inside, I was alone and cold and tired, but I continued to rise, higher and higher. I bumped into other balloons up in the sky, and I kept going, and I escaped the atmosphere, and I didn't stop. There I was in the magnificent expanse of space and loneliness, and I was thankful for my craft and the rising action heading towards some unavoidable climax.

The sun pierced my eyeballs, and I woke up suddenly to a frightful and beautiful day. I turned and noticed I was in a large park, but I couldn't spot anyone else or even any cars. I sat and let my eyes adjust to the landscape. I saw a squirrel and wanted to give it food; I looked up and saw a plane and wanted it to crash. I went over and looked in the trash; I found a half-eaten pizza in a box on a bench. I sat down and ate and threw two loose pepperoni at the squirrel; it ran off without taking either... maybe it was saving them for later. One can never know anything.

(End of excerpt)

Chapter 15

It was during the winter months, as George retouched his novel, that strange parallels from his writing began to surface in his life. Instances presupposed in linguistic tirades as distraught descriptions started to crop up in the world around him, and it became increasingly odd and difficult to ignore the coincidences. He once believed that creativity or writing or fiction did not feed reality, that it was a separate mechanism designed to decompress the practitioner, a relaxing and calm and meditative art; or perhaps he thought it was a game, like solitaire, played alone with the hope of murdering time, but this, too, appeared to be false—a red herring, and so he kept going along the railways of these thoughts, seeing where they led, and he arrived at an idea: maybe, just maybe, it was reality channeling itself into existence by way of the creative act—a delivery system—an indirect route into the world, forecasting future events waiting to be summoned; the unconscious prefacing the upcoming timeline, delivering its own interpretation of what was just ahead, conjuring what was to be—in a month, around the corner, or in a year's time.

He wore his mask and paired it well with a baseball cap and zip-up hoodie. He blended in respectably enough with the surrounding student body, but inside and underneath, boreholes full of questions were dismantling his terrain. What the hell was writing, and where did it come from, and how could a throwaway line written years before keep coming back to haunt its creator? What entity told him the words, and why was he compelled to write them down?

When George had finished and was happy with the final product, he decided to send *Hokum's Pass* out to the publishing houses. What did he have to lose, anyway? He received a rejection letter followed closely by an acceptance email. Hurray! George was going to be published under an auspicious house banner—and it wasn't just some rinky-dink short story this time. A real winning moment for George and he celebrated by getting blackout drunk at a pub called the Lion's Den.

***

Tim asks George about his book at bars and at cafés and acts as a good friend, using it as a means of leverage to bait the interest of random girls a stone's throw away... or within hearing distance... an icebreaker... for the two of them... just two keen lads in search of a lively and passionate fuck. George and Tim agree that not many folks their age seem to have books out in the marketplace (even though his book isn't coming out until late summer or early fall), but do people really care about books anymore? Will such a thing impress the masses? Or the girls at the bar, for that matter? And surprisingly, the answer was yes. Not because they were necessarily interested in the book itself—but because of the mystique surrounding the term *author*, the writer as magician; and that mask (referring to the writer's mask, or even the word "mask," which in itself was a type of mask) intrigued them, or piqued their interest, even though they probably didn't frame it that way. And when they asked him about his opinion, about his thoughts on writing, George described it as a very passive activity. He said he considered himself a receptionist—nothing more—taking dictation from somewhere or something, presumably his unconscious; but even that, that fucking word, *unconscious*, strange and somehow regressive and vague, and perhaps it was the combination of those features that George found so appealing and unorthodox in its layout, that particular combination of letters and sounds, beginning with the antagonistic prefix "un," denoting absence or reversal—the antonym. And even though it was a common household word nowadays, he still loved it because words—even overly used ones, saturated ones—when paired or placed in the right order or context, take on a new and potentially redefined glow.

George's publisher called him up and asked if he wouldn't mind taking a look at the ending of *Hokum's Pass*, maybe jazz it up a little. The ending he'd originally chosen had the unnamed narrator simply vanish into the night after another long and dysfunctional day. The publishers asked if he might be interested in swapping it out, maybe adding something with a bit more bite or spice, a more virile and potent ending. George thought it over and decided he'd write an alternate take that night, no plan, just sit down and see what happened. If it turned out well, he'd send it in and exchange it for the original finale.

He wasn't sure where the idea came from, perhaps a Dennis Hopper film from the 1990s or a reinterpretation of his favorite author's death, but he decided to have his hero perform a bastardized (or westernized) version of seppuku in the subway. After the unnamed narrator sees an old flame or girlfriend, he trudges down to the subway and goes and stands at the farthest end of the platform. He kneels and places his shoulder against a brick wall and unsheathes a bowie knife and waits, watching the timer as the next train is said to be approaching in less than a minute. As he hears the rumble of the tracks, he readies himself and digs the knife into his guts, cutting from left to right; he does his best to succeed in his own disembowelment. He plans to fall forward, hoping that only his head reaches out past the platform and onto the path of the approaching train; with his shoulder and body securely fastened next to the brick wall, the train will come and decapitate him, and he will be dead; he will have killed himself, but in a manner befitting a samurai or warrior or someone with more respect or honor or clout than is usually afforded to misfits and bums. When the train hits him, its velocity sucks his entire body onto the tracks and under the train, and he is crushed and splattered and ground up by the metallic meat grinder. The story ends with him dead, but death—in this story—doesn't immediately kill the consciousness of its host; the narrator continues to live, slowly fading away over the course of weeks. He lives and rethinks his life, stuck in little chunks to parts of the train that the cleaning crew was unable to clean off; he rides around the city in the same loop over and over again, thinking to himself how strange life is, watching the daily life of commuters and subway workers as the volume of his thoughts is increasingly muted, decaying into silence; until finally, they cease altogether, and he's gone and disappears, and his exit, although barbaric and violent, is also gentle and meandering and slow.

His publisher loved the new ending.

Chapter 16

Father Tom was getting back into his usual routine as spring descended on the town. He was back at the church, doing sermons, sometimes sharing the duty with another priest, Father Kirk, an affable and older clergyman. The pair got along well enough, and Father Tom was thankful for Father Kirk's help as he recovered from his illness.

One day, while out enjoying the crispness of the spring air, Father Tom, having already sipped a couple of whiskeys that morning, went for a slight and stumbling stroll through the woods. He was still obsessed with his experience with the talking tumor; he couldn't entirely rid himself of it or simply shrug it off. What a weird experience, thought Father Tom. How many people have talking tumors? Is that a thing? One had to wonder if others had had similar experiences but kept it quiet for fear of being inundated with questions, or thought of as insane. Perhaps he was insane—but now he felt fine (or back to normal, at any rate), so had sanity returned just like that? Tough to say, thought the priest.

He continued to walk, sobering up while taking big lungfuls of cool air.

Sitting on a bench along the woodland path was Lucy, a dwarf that Father Tom knew only by name. He sat down next to her.

"How are you, my dear?" said the priest.

She looked at him, annoyed; he had obviously interrupted some important inner dialogue. She did not answer his question.

"Is everything all right?"

"No," said the dwarf. "My dog's run off."

"Oh—I'm sorry."

They sat in silence, and Father Tom raised his eyes and saw a peregrine swoop down towards the forest floor.

"He took off in that direction a few minutes ago." She pointed a shabby-looking stub of a finger east, and Father Tom scrutinized the woods for any sign of movement.

"I'll tell you what, how about I go take a look and see if I can't find the little critter?"

She smiled and wiped a tear from her cheek. "Thank you, Father."

And like that, the priest had a mission: rescue a lost dog somewhere in this labyrinth of tangle and growth.

The dog's name was Tartan. A strange name, thought the priest. He yelled and clapped and went further into the bush. He could no longer see the path or the dwarf or the bench; he was now slightly confused as to his own whereabouts. "Tartan!" he yelled. "Where are you, you bitch?"

It was getting dark. How long had he been out there? The priest was getting worried... but like most mysteries, the answer was right under his nose or, in this instance, right under his boot. He felt a difference in the malleability of the soil and realized he'd just stepped on something soft with lots of give. He took out his phone and used it to light the gooey mush beneath his boot and saw the corpse of a dog. It had been mauled badly, torn to shreds, really. A wolf? A coyote? Hard to tell. Father Tom took a picture as evidence, not entirely sure why. Surely he wouldn't show his findings to Lucy, a mere word or description would suffice, but the practice of keeping evidence was always a good one to follow.

He looked around, did a one-hundred-and-eighty-degree turn, and did not recognize anything at all. The sun seemed to have set, or the darkness from the impeding branches obscured enough light as to make the forest damn well impossible to navigate. He'd lost cell service, but Father Tom kept his phone out to light his way and heard strange growls and roars, and when he placed the light close to the ground, he saw mounds of insects crawling and devouring and munching away on one another.

He continued on, coming to terms with the fact that he'd genuinely lost his way. Now walking for the sake of walking, in God's hands he trusted, praying on the off chance that God was listening. At times like these, Father Tom wished he had his talking tumor back.

Then he saw her, a child roaming the woods, a familiar countenance—was it Suzy? Suzy Jenkins, the psychotic eight-year-old turned ten, wandering around the woods in total and obscure darkness? Yes, lo and behold, it was.

"Suzy?"

"Father Tom? What are you doing out here?"

"I should ask you the same question. I'm completely lost; do you know where we are?"

She looked at him in an amused way, as if he'd just told her some silly joke. "We're about fifty feet from my backyard. Look."

And she pointed behind her, and Father Tom could make out a vague light coming from what he suspected was her back porch. The child took his hand and escorted him out of the woodland, and he was surprised by how much light there was once he'd exited the thicket.

Suzy smiled and said goodbye, and she promised she'd come visit him soon. He watched her as she reentered the woods, skipping as she went along.

Father Tom decided to call Lucy; he telephoned a friend of his whom he thought might have her number. The gentleman did, and he gave it to the priest without much fuss. When Father Tom called Lucy and told her about Tartan, she began to cry, and she asked the priest if he could describe the state of her dog—or, if he'd taken any photos, could he please send her one... just to be sure it was definitely her mutt. Father Tom hung up and begrudgingly sent the photo to Lucy. An hour went by before she replied via text, acknowledging the dead dog to be her own. Father Tom felt bad and shook his head, wondering why he kept getting into these weird and semi-horrific adventures in this godforsaken town. He poured himself another glass of whiskey and lit a cigar and stared out the window, watching the cars and trucks pass him by as the sleet struck their windshields at odd and irregular angles.

Chapter 17

The four months leading up to the publication of George's book were some of the happiest of his life. It was a time of transition, a time when the future had a definitive and bright glow; a happiness best described as a particular moment, not too far off, where something of definite goodness *could* be fostered or nurtured, an exact and exciting and prosperous— not to mention distinct—period, different from anything that had come before it. A transitional period of repose, thought George; a tightrope walk dogged by mild anxiety—but mixed with excitement, with potentially ripe and mesmerizing futures, just off, at the end, beyond the verdant pastures.

Other than telling Tim and his sister and his mother—and the few gals he and Tim met at the bar—George didn't speak much about his book. It wasn't something he specifically tried to keep secret, but he found that when he vocalized his feelings or ideas concerning it, they always rang flat. To speak of it seemed to limit it. Sometimes, words had a way of diminishing things in the same way that they could sometimes elevate them. And George held this ridiculous practice of assimilating syllables into phrases as akin to a religious rite or prayer. He saw the way these empty vessels dispersed beauty and horror and sadness and was wowed time and time again by both the simplicity and difficulty associated with the act. How could he properly explain this without sounding like a fool or degrading the craft? So he mostly kept his mouth shut regarding his favorite pastime. He'd also begun writing his second book around this time, and this he spoke of with no one.

The book was to be a strange journey mixing genres and tones freely with an emphasis on the cosmic (particularly its more terrifying aspects) but also spaced—rather nicely—with some mild (and some sordid) adventures and salted, just so, with a healthy dose of violence and love and melancholia. The process of writing his second book was markedly different than what he'd encountered writing his first. His first book came out seemingly of its own volition; George felt like he didn't have to do very much to egg it on or conjure it up. The second book still seemed to follow the rules set up by the first book, but somehow the process had evolved—like a relationship trying to sustain itself beyond the initial intoxicating phases, when both parties were privy to the strengths and weaknesses of the other, requiring a more subtle and conscious effort to keep the game afloat, but in light of this (or perhaps because of this), the process and the relationship took on a more complex and robust body, expanding and growing, becoming more powerful and meaningful and therefore requiring a different approach to coax it onward, to keep it moving, to keep it interesting.

During this period, he had a dream, an epiphany, or a narcissistic nightmare. He dreamt that he was the embodiment of the world, of all of humanity, its all-encompassing will.

He saw himself as a disgrace, angry and embittered, unable to fend for himself, cortisol levels on the rise, staggering with stress. He snapped at and murdered anyone entering his path; motives were moot; he hated them all. His was a wolfish persona—predatory and hungry, stalking with a voracious appetite. But then an answer seemingly arose from no-where—an antidote, a moment of truth: he knew what he must do, or he did it instinctually, because something within him forced his will—the All-Will—to abide its bidding; perhaps it was something outside (but also inside), the noumenon, or God, or the unknowable entering in and taking control; or perhaps it was always planned this way, waiting to occur at this time in this manner at this exact place. Anyway, George began to walk slower, talk slower; he appeared to be an absolute idiot to most people—if not to everyone around him. But he sensed a change, a calmness akin to happiness overtake him (two synonymous states, to be sure), and when he woke up from the dream, he began to slow himself down, almost to a trickle. He began to walk unhurried, loosen up, and from this small shift he felt better; he sensed a peacefulness, as if he could fall asleep anywhere (sleep being comparable to happiness too). He figured that those with personalities like his—those that could be said to border on the evil and vile and creative—were highly encouraged to slow the metronome of their habits to the smallest common denominator, a worm-like crawl, a lazy shuffle forward. This was a strong elixir, perhaps more encouraging and altering than the publication of his book, which allowed him to enjoy to the fullest degree the time he had before him.

***

"It was amazing that the same philosophy could in one instance create and in another destroy; in other words, prioritizing one set of values, in one case, could be good and, in another, evil. It was not enough to pick a philosophy or ideology and stick to it, one had to have the wherewithal to understand when to use it, and when to scrap it, or repress it, or pocket it and save it for later. One had to conjure the musician, carefully picking their notes, searching for harmonies and melodies lurking in the mystery that could break on through and diversify or strengthen elements of the landscape, always expanding by means of creation and destruction without claim to perfection or end. One should accept the duties of the constant gardener (a perpetual state of becoming)—and one should be wary of movement for the sake of movement."

—spoken by the wolf in the dream

Father Tom was also having some weird dreams around this time. He dreamt of the woods and the dog and little Suzy Jenkins, and his dreams had a way of mixing all these elements together while adding something new or extra; like one time, a romantic interest from Father Tom's past stalked the woods, and when he saw her, she was eating some animal, feral and wild—and then she came at him, *him* being next on her menu. She was dressed elegantly with blood encrusted on the contours of her face and splattered across her white dress. That dream frightened the hell out of him, and he checked the lock on his front door when he woke up in the middle of the night. He wondered what his subconscious was playing at trying to rile him up like that.

Father Tom went about his usual duties and was visited by George one afternoon as he was going over a sermon he was set to perform that Sunday. George looked different to Father Tom, perceptively altered, but not in any one physical way. His vibe or aura—to use the hippie lingo of the day—seemed different. Father Tom asked him how he was doing.

"I'm good. How's everything at the church?"

"Oh, pretty good," said the priest. "Same old humdrum happenings. So, what can I do for you, George?"

"I brought you a copy of my book." He took the book from beneath his arm. And, for some reason, Father Tom thought it was a snake—only for a second though—and the hallucination was too brief (or odd) for it to be registered properly; he was old and slow, and his mental process only assimilated rapid images gently or, in other words, poorly, which gave him plenty of time to discredit it. And George said, "I got a few early copies, and I know you like to read, and I thought you might like to check it out."

"Thank you," said the priest. "That's awfully kind, son." He took the book from George; its cover displayed a scantily clad woman with the title of the book obscuring her nipples. "I'll start it tonight."

Father Tom opened the book that evening. He sat on his sofa with a glass of whiskey and lit up a joint; it was raining again. Father Tom was instantly struck by the irreverent tone of the book: acerbic and forceful. He read a great deal of it that night. He was amazed at George's talent; he was also a little shaken by what he supposed the boy had incurred as experience or trauma in order to pen such a thing. He seemed to be a normal enough kid, but upon reading his book—although fantastical and fictional—Father Tom couldn't help but speculate certain things about him, and he felt as if he *really* knew him, or at least knew him better, but perhaps that was just the lie of literature.

He had trouble concentrating on his duties the next day. During confession, his mind wandered off, and he was forced to ask the repenting sinner to begin again, right from the top. When he got home, he fell back into his routine from the night before and picked up George's book, *Hokum's Pass*. He finished it that night, and the ending—about death and suicide and lamentations and honor in an unkind and cruel existence—touched Father Tom, although the book also codified some of life's more ambiguous consolation prizes. What a poetic and horrific finale, thought the priest. He wondered what the average Joe might think of such a book. Too weird, too unforgiving, he wasn't sure, but he praised the publisher and George for articulating some rather ugly truths in a frank and winsome manner. He looked at the clock; it was just past midnight. He grabbed his bike and puffed at a joint as he pedaled around the city. He eyed it differently. He saw two bums huddled around a fire set up in an oil drum and found the scene both romantic and sad. The world was strange and arbitrary yet had the potential for great beauty when focused and aligned through the proper prism. A spectrum of its finest attributes could be displayed through the perceptions and articulations of a few, artists of a rare breed, giving voice to colors unknown, uncensored, and unconcerned with modern trends, following their own fancy and recklessness.

When he saw George next—a few days after he'd finished his book—Father Tom couldn't help but pat him on the back and ask him the most sophomoric of questions: how had he come up with those ideas, that story? George shrugged, not entirely sure himself.

"A mystery, a gift from God, a creature captured and procured, taking up residence in my head; I don't really think anyone knows where this stuff comes from, Father. I'm glad you liked it, though. It's a strange little tale, not to everyone's liking."

Father Tom laughed and told George he was proud of him.

"Thanks, Father," said George. "But I really can't take credit. I'm just the receiver, articulating the lies, scribbling the maze."

Father Tom nodded and thought back to his talking tumor. Life was quite a ride, he thought, and he thought that George was quite a kid—a unique breed, and he wondered how he'd fare in life. Would he become an ordinary citizen, a famous writer, a criminal, a nobody, a priest, a drunk? Time would be his ultimate judge, just as it was for the rest of them, and the priest stood thinking, staring up at the vaulted ceiling of the gun and ammunition store.

Chapter 18

Father Tom bought his first gun. He wasn't sure why or what possessed him at this junction at this time to go ahead and buy one—but the town, for the most part, was full of them. People had them for hunting and self-defense; an eccentric duo even had a knack for playing "William Tell" during their lavish and flamboyant parties. It started with a drunken slight. Someone had accused the madam of the household of lacking any vigor or "balls"; she retaliated, grabbing the hand of her husband and escorting him to a china cabinet in the main dining hall where she opened a drawer and withdrew an old M15 pistol and placed it in the hand of her hubby. She distanced herself a good twenty to twenty-five feet, back against a brick wall, and told the crowd to shut the fuck up and placed a cantaloupe on her head. She told her husband to take aim as the spectators stood around, aghast at what was unfolding in front of their eyes. The husband did as he was told and fired the pistol; thank God he was a crack shot, and pieces of cantaloupe sprayed attendants in the immediate vicinity along with Mr. James, an elderly man who was hard of hearing, too drunk to have yet noticed what was taking place. He licked a bit of the fruit's nectar that had stuck to his mustache and then continued chatting to Dorothea Knickerbocker, even though she wasn't paying him the least bit of attention.

Two weeks after his firearm purchase, Father Tom heard faint murmurs of a potential pandemic, started overseas and making its way across the globe; the virus had a flair for extinguishing the lives of the elderly and the immunocompromised. Father Tom was not worried, but as the weeks wore on, the virus arrived on their doorstep; first, infecting a few, then trans-mitting to a growing cluster of the town's populace and, eventually, its scope expanded, the virus touched almost everyone. A month after the first reported case, one hundred and sixty-eight people had died in their town due to the outbreak. Grocery stores wore barren shelves. Schools closed, and mass gatherings were prohibited. All church services were postponed, and Father Tom found himself sitting at home, drinking, reading, watching TV, and cleaning his gun. To break up the monotony, he decided to visit certain families from his congregation, see how the people were faring. He went to the Dilgunks' house on a Wednesday, the streets nearly empty, the town on lockdown, and Father Tom thought of how boring and sad life looked when it halted its movements.

He knocked on the door, and Jill Dilgunk opened it, proud mother and kindhearted widower; she presented the priest with a cup of coffee, and they sat down in the living room, chatting about this and that. He asked about George and Trisha, and she mentioned that Trisha was back (from the big city) for now until things got back into their usual orbit. Father Tom asked if George was around, and she said that he was out with his friends. He finished his cup of coffee and thanked his hostess and proceeded towards the exit. Father Tom told Jill that if she needed anything—anything at all, not to hesitate and that he'd be happy to pop by again if she liked. They parted on good terms, and Father Tom walked around town, nodding to the few citizens he passed, stopping to grab a coffee and a paper and see the current figure of the rising worldwide death toll.

As he sat at the café, Father Tom saw a large beetle climbing up the wall. The café was essentially empty, just him and the beetle and a waiter hiding in the back room—only resurfacing every fifteen minutes or so for the scheduled top-up, edging the coffee towards its rim. Father Tom walked over to the insect, fascinated by its size and opulent glow, the sheen of its shell. He thought it beautiful with a majestic aura and was sure that he'd never seen anything quite like it in all his life. He went behind the counter—there being no one to witness or stop him—and grabbed a mason jar. He coaxed the bug into the container and tightened the lid and paid his tab and left.

At home, he emptied the container into an old aquarium he'd once kept for hermit crabs. A strange creature that he'd purchased on a whim and whose death resulted in an empty glass vessel prepped and awaiting its next occupant. He scattered leaves around the base of the aquarium, hoping that this was an acceptable standard of chow for the coleopteran. The beetle walked about, munching on this and that, and otherwise went about its typical insect life. Father Tom sat in his chair and stared at the bug.

The news said that because of the protective measures enacted by the state and the country as a whole, the spread of the virus was minimized—although not without its casualties— and due to the gradual slowing of the virus's momentum, life was steadily resuming its former rhythms. Father Tom had been off from the church for a little over a month now, and the church still hadn't given him the go-ahead to return and preach from the pulpit. He had drunk quite a lot during his time off—even putting on some considerable weight—and over the past week, he'd seldom left his flat, opting for a quiet and drunken existence, just him and his bug, each contained within their own cell. News of the virus's containment and dwindling spread should have brought joy to Father Tom, but his gloom was not lifted, something was stirring in his depths, and his fatigue and desperation seemed to be at an all-time high. During the morning when the church was set to reopen, Father Tom loaded his shotgun and fetched the beetle and dropped it down one of the barrels; he returned to his chair, put both barrels of the shotgun into his mouth, and that was that. The neighbors and those below on the streets heard the shot and rushed up to his apartment. There was nothing left of the top half of his head. The sight was ghastly; one was able to see all of Father Tom's bloodied mandibular teeth.

The funeral was held at the same church where Father Tom had worked. Many of the townsfolk were in attendance including the Dilgunks. Father Tom was hailed as a devout believer, someone who took his faith seriously, and someone who could always be counted on in times of crisis. Tears were shed in droves for the cassock-wearing priest. George was deeply saddened by the loss of his friend, and feelings of guilt at not having visited him during the last few months circled his insides. The last time he'd seen the preacher was at the gun shop, which tainted the entirety of that encounter because of its foreboding and macabre nature. George had been there with Tim, preparing for a hunting trip with him and his father. His talk with the priest had mostly centered on his book, and George wondered if that chat had any bearing on what had finally happened to Father Tom. He supposed not, such ideas were the stuff of vanity; whatever was eating at the priest had presumably dug its heels in long ago, with the addition of the month-long quarantine not helping matters. In reality, no one could know why Father Tom had done what he'd done except for Father Tom, and George was not ignorant of the fact that both his father and his priest—in some ways his father's surrogate—had each exited this life through violent spectacles orchestrated by their own hands. Sadness gripped the boy whose traumas and guilt continued to accumulate, piling on more and more with each passing year.

George was reminded of an allegory—he thought by Pascal, but he wasn't entirely sure—of a chained group of men, wandering and waiting around, stalked by an invisible hand that hacked them to pieces seemingly at random. Someone among the chain gang would scream, and the others would look, and there was their companion, in the throes of butchery, split open and lopped apart. Such is life in its bleaker times or views or hours, thought George.

After Father Tom died, the Dilgunks stopped going to church altogether. Over the past few years, they had come to think of themselves as Christians, but in reality, they were dilettantes, merely a fan of the man, their friend, the priest, not the tradition, nor the faith. His sermons, along with his presence, were magnetic—enough for some people to rekindle emanations of hope and joy. Not that the preacher was necessarily a good man—but he made people feel comfortable; and somehow, that was enough.

George's book was set to come out in one week. He didn't think he could take all the hubbub and vainglory. He wanted to be alone, far away. Give himself time to think, to rummage around in his head, and try and find some peace with the events that had accumulated so far, perhaps even pen another few chapters of his next book, who knew? He told his mother about his feelings, and she reminded him that they had a cabin, only a few hours away, around a beautiful lake, waiting on an inhabitant, ready to cater to him for as long as he liked or needed. He asked if it'd be possible to get a ride up there. She agreed, and they left the next day. Riding along Highway 51, George and his mother sipped coffee and watched the coniferous trees sway even and just; and when she dropped him off and drove away, George uncoiled himself on an old musty mattress and had a long, rejuvenating nap.

Upon waking, the sun had already gone down. The cabin wasn't large—one floor with a partitioned bedroom and bathroom, the kitchen and living room bleeding into one another. It was a comfortable space teeming with memories. His father had brought him up here years ago with his sister. They had gone swimming and fished, and life seemed simple, if not good. Other memories of the four of them, gallivanting about, were numerous. But that one stood out in George's mind for some reason.

He stepped out onto the back porch and flicked on the light. He rolled himself a cigarette and eyed the lake. Crickets conducted their soothing song, and George turned around to face his shack, and he saw the graffiti on the back wall. "Is That All There Is?" scribbled in large letters, spray-painted, no doubt, by some first-time tagger. He smiled and decided to roll a joint, and he extinguished the outside light, sitting on the porch in complete darkness, inhaling the weed, happy as a pig in shit.

Chapter 19

He dreamt of a cherry blossom tree beneath a vibrant pale sky. Such a dream was rendered cinematic by the low-angle tracking shot performed by his mind's eye and its trusty wide-angle lens, pushing in, as it were, towards the seemingly gargantuan *Prunus*. George awoke to a peaceful and sunny day; a lakeside peek at nirvana, only briefly—as it were— each illusion destined to collapse, time's disastrous journey forward, inventing even as it destroys, and sometimes destroying the perfect illusion in favor of a foul and cancerous one (and vice versa), although no one really complains when it goes from bad to good, but the other way around—*pshhh...* forget about it.

Life: an orgiastic maze, the good and the bad of it, constantly changing its layout, dominating time and space while the peon stalks about in the darkness, or the drudgery of the unknown, courting failure and defeat until time opens up, calms it down, allows the shifting and breathing of the landscape to act as its guide; he or she intuitively follows it forward, a gut feeling prodding them onward, acting exactly as they are supposed to act, swallowed up and repurposed for the world (or maze) anew: again and again and again, sans end.

These are examples of the queer thoughts inundating George's mind that morning while he sat on the back porch beneath the words "Is That All There Is?" drinking coffee and smoking a morning joint and penning another tale. Such mornings were the very definition of perfection for George: solitary, quiet, vulgar, with a tinge of the psychedelic.

By 11 a.m., he'd begun to get hungry; he opened the fridge—he had store-bought provisions with him. He thawed some meat sauce in the kitchen sink, and he tidied up the cabin; he sat on the couch and read a bit of Houellebecq's *Atomised*. He closed his eyes and readied himself for a nap.

His dream took him face to face with Father Tom; only *he* had no face—or no head, at any rate. His tongue was still there along with his lower jaw; they acted as his new pinnacle, shortening his stature by a good eight or nine inches. He was truly grotesque; his voice was guttural, and he lacked the pronunciation that typically accompanied the practiced oration of the priest's former speech. He tried to say, "Do not be afraid," but it came out in one long and disjointed glottal howl. The priest shook his jaw and motioned upward, and some paper and a pen appeared in his hand. He wrote the words, "Nice to see you again, George."

He explained a strange scenario, that he and God had teamed up on a mission; there was evil lurking in the woods, and George's timeline had brought him here to undo that evil. He wrote all this down at a furious pace (a goddamn cursive wizard); George nodded, reading as the headless priest worked. He wrote about a cabin in the woods, not too far, where an entity had set up shop. This entity was an abductor and killer, the epitome of evil and vileness, a corrupting agent towards all that was innocent and good—and George was tasked with putting an end to it. God needed a true and sturdy hand, and Father Tom told Him he knew just the boy or kid or man-child to do it: George, age nineteen, holy crusader— or perhaps it was God who had picked him or created him specifically for this act, and Father Tom was chosen merely as the messenger; facts and sequences were confusing in the heavens, just as they were on Earth. And Father Tom wrote that he was sorry to put this burden on him, but that he was— by his very nature—the right candidate: a wolfish boy, both cunning and smart, and not averse to hardships or violence. George interrupted the priest with a query that diverted the conversation; he asked him why he'd killed himself, why he'd forsaken them. The priest wrote down that he didn't know... that it'd just happened... that he was sorry... but that they must accept events as they unfold, unfair or not. He told George that they must focus, prepare, remain on task. He wrote that George should go this afternoon. Go see for yourself—all the evidence would surely be there. The priest wrote that the address was located in the wall at the bottom of the *t*, and then the dream faded to black, and when George woke up— understandably flustered—he went to the back porch and looked at the graffiti; he eyed one of the *t*'s and saw a small hole near its base. He pinched at it and got ahold of a small rolled-up piece of paper. When he unfolded it, it read: 57 Cherry Lane.

He ate lunch and mulled over the dream. What the fuck? thought George. He was unsure what to do; the dream had absorbed itself into his psyche differently than any he had ever had before. He felt as if he should at least make the trek, see what was out there; if nothing else, it'd be good exercise on a fresh and beautiful day, and perhaps satisfy some curiosity—which could also, potentially (depending on what he found), shatter his reserve of sanity. Wasn't the universe an odd and mystifying place?

He cleaned up, grabbed his backpack, tossed a hammer in, and took a nervous shit before departing. Then he struck out in the direction of the supposed monster's den, wondering just what the hell in the hootenanny he was doing.

He knew where Cherry Lane was; it wasn't an entirely remote spot but certainly a spot with nothing much going on, fairly isolated terrain, spread out with huts and cabins of the lower grade popping up every now and then, camouflaged in the foliage, set down all willy-nilly-like. The walk was quite enjoyable, and he hummed a tune as he moseyed through the woods.

It took him less than an hour to get to Cherry Lane, but it took him almost the same amount of time to find number 57. It was well hidden, way off near a strangely shaped inlet. It was small and had a dock almost as big as the hut itself. He went up to the door and knocked. No one answered, and the sky was orange, and he tried the door, and it gave way without much fuss. Inside, there were markings all over the walls; they appeared to be burnt, blackened by soot and carved upon, signs etched into the wood. The carvings or markings were odd, shaped as pictograms, hieroglyphics of some kind or other; they covered every square inch of the cabin's interior. There was a cot in the corner and a desk full of ink and paper. As George approached the desk, movement caught his eye, and he turned to face the cot, and a beautiful young woman emerged from under the covers in a tattered negligee.

"Who the hell are you?" said the woman.

George stuttered trying to find his bearings.

"I'm s-s-sorry." He whirled around, ready to head for the exit.

"No! Wait. You're here for him, ain'tcha?" She stood up, and one of her breasts fell out. She came close to George; her breath was rancid. "He's in the cellar—making his song." She motioned downward with her pinky finger, giggled, and then she exited the cabin, her dirty bare feet pitter-pattering away.

George stood stunned and eyed the hatch. He took off his backpack and grabbed the hammer. He quietly opened the cellar door and slowly descended the steps.

He heard a peculiar sound, like an organ but flatter and more muffled. There was no light in the cellar, except for small glints of sunlight that shone through between the cracks of the floorboards overhead. He could already tell that the cellar was the hut's locus; it was two or three times larger than the floor above. There was a shape, far off, moving in the corner; he supposed that was where the sound was coming from. The reverberation or acoustics of the space disoriented him and provided very little navigational support. Through stark and minimal beams of light, he caught glimpses of the creature hunched over what looked like a cross between a bagpipe and a piano outfitted and stretched with rawhides and skins. It hugged and prodded the instrument and made it acquiesce to its motions and pressures; the instrument emitted strange and surreal soundscapes. George approached.

"Hello," he whispered.

It jumped up, went berserk, and George saw the flash of tentacles, an oblong head, no eyes, big incisors; it lunged forward, its dirtied white frock coming at him—its scream comparable to the high-pitched wails of a child. George tumbled back, and the creature fell on top of him. Its slithering skin and centipede-like limbs clambering to pummel him, stab him, enter him. He was still holding the hammer, and he swung it as best he could, catching the creature on the side of the head. It jammed a tentacle into his mouth, and George bit down and swung again. The creature screamed and retreated, and George rose up and began smashing the instrument as the creature wailed. And then he turned, hammer in hand, and walked towards the beast...

When he came to and regained his wits, he knew (even in the darkness) that the creature had been defeated, decimated, its legacy a foul stain in its subterranean lair.

He strolled back in a daze, and when he got back to his cabin, he stripped naked and fell asleep on the floor. When he woke up, he went to the bathroom and flicked on the light. Blood was all over his face, even embedded in his teeth from when he'd bitten down on the limb or tentacle or whatever the fuck it was. Gross, he thought. He showered and threw his clothes in the firepit. It was just starting to get dark; he felt strange and empty and unsure how to proceed, but not caring much either, one way or another. *Whatever will be... will...* Oh, fuck that shit. He sat back on the porch, naked and unashamed, and turned his attention to his recreational drug habit. He realized he hadn't written much that day, and he grabbed his laptop, eager to get back to work.

The coming days blurred together, slowly coalescing into a routine. George would eat breakfast, drink coffee, smoke, write, nap, and continue this cycle until nightfall when he'd find a sudden urge to venture for a walk; carrying a flashlight, he'd slip out and into the woods. Although he tried to keep his thoughts away from 57's cellar, the event itself seemed to have emboldened him, and his midnight walks were somehow both calm and refreshing, contrary to what one might expect. Time passed, and he stayed at the cabin for three weeks, and when his mother came to get him, she said he looked awful, as if he hadn't rested at all. He laughed at this, not sure how else to reply, and she told him she had good news: *Hokum's Pass* was a bestseller, and its dark and provocative tones had lit a fire under the established literary pantheon (or so she was told). "Congrats," said Mom.

Chapter 20

Surprisingly enough, a bestseller didn't mean shit; no one really gave a tinker's fuck about books anymore—actually, a lot of people did, just slowly, over time, never all at once; the longevity of a great book was like a slow virus, its popularity won gradually, the richness of its audience amassed over generations. Such a book was kept alive because of its originality, its ferocity. Books were the medium of the individual—ripe with the intricacies and errors of their makeup, sometimes hitting the target of genius square on the noggin, but in such an odd or unorthodox way that no one knows of it for quite some time. George was nonplussed about the whole thing; his mind still focused on giant bugs and dead priests.

He did a couple of interviews over the phone and a few in person and then talked to his publisher and refused to do any more. They were annoyed but couldn't do much; his book was out and selling well, and he wasn't contractually obligated. So it goes, they concluded.

Life got back to normal for George, and he kept writing; his sister returned to the big city; his mother kept busy. George dropped out of college around this time. He'd gone on his last day to see Mr. Mickelson, gave him a copy of his book, signed:

Go fuck yourself.
George

He felt this gesture might have been overkill, but so had their meeting when Mr. Mickelson had dropped his writerly advice on George, branding him the worst writer to have ever walked those dim scholastic halls. Fuck that prick, thought George, and he went out and met Tim at the Lion's Den, both fellas in need of a pint.

By this time—roughly two months since life had resumed its former bearings and Father Tom had killed himself—the town seemed to have recalibrated to the oddities that had come its way. The overall changes were small since the end of the outbreak, slight shifts in degrees that could have a larger impact—but slowly, over time. George's stock had risen considerably since the publication of his book, and he found himself being courted by some of the higher-ups and socialites of the town: a woman and her husband in their late fifties who'd once toured the world with a famed and experimental dance troupe, performing everywhere from Paris to Timbuktu, were among those whose curiosity he'd piqued. Their names were Elden and Gertrude Somovar. They phoned George's house one day and asked if he'd like to come and dine with them at their home, discuss literature and dance and the finer things in life: he accepted immediately and wrote down their address. Afterward, once the thrill of the surprise had faded, George regretted his decision; he was venturing out into an evening of unknowns in two days' time with two strangers who could turn out to be full-blown wackos or, worse yet, pure and unadulterated bores. Goddamn you, pride!

When he knocked on their door—a large black monolith with a devious door knocker and a strange, horrific bas-relief— George was in low spirits, already annoyed at having to come and dine with strangers, and now more so because of what he suspected was awaiting him inside (their fucked-up door being an ominous sign).

The door swung open, and a small man in a double-breasted suit of antiquated origin greeted him and beckoned him in. There stood the madam of the household in the entranceway— a trim fifty-year-old woman in lavish dress, mauve and low-cut, showcasing a great buoyant display of cleavage. George had worn a pullover and quite enjoyed the stark contrast between his and his hosts' outfits.

"Come in, son. Would you like a drink? Wine, perhaps?"

George agreed to a glass, and they sat in an ostentatious living room full of animal heads pinned to walls and old-fashioned oil paintings; velvet coverings hung from various points, and a large bookcase, piled high, defined its westward contour; the house was like a decadent Parisian mansion lifted from a misanthrope's nightmare.

"Supper should be ready soon," said Elden. "Do you like duck?"

"Yes," replied George. "A grand meat if you ask me." His cadence aimed at kindling an air of posh irreverence.

"Splendid, my boy! We shall dine in fine fashion tonight. I must admit that we are very keen on having you here—to pepper you with little questions regarding your wonderful new book. What a treat! A true delicacy and conceived and concocted right here in this fair town." He smiled at George, exhibiting some rather strange teeth, tiny and crowded as if more were added to make up for their miniature stature.

"Please, let me ask you: what made you write this tale?"

The madam leaned forward, Gertrude's half-a-century-old bosom darting out, eager for the reply.

"I don't really know, actually," said George. "I just write and see what happens. I've never been good at planning it... or explaining it for that matter. I never really know what comes next. Every time—"

"But wasn't there a code," interrupted Elden, "a purpose, a secret message hidden somewhere in it? For the Order... for the Order of Nonnus' Dionysiaca?"

George started to laugh; he couldn't stop. What the fuck was going on? What the hell was Elden talking about? Life had become so goddamn odd that this new turn—the appearance of a presumably loony cult or group, one with connections to his book—only added a small stick to the weird, accumulating bonfire that had become his existence as of late.

He told them no, whatever they saw or thought they saw had not been intended or consciously put there. Gertrude was upset, started talking loudly and quickly in some foreign language, pointing her gnarled finger at her guest; George's laughter ramped up; his giggles couldn't be stopped, and soon Elden was standing and asking him to leave, apologizing for the misunderstanding. George continued to chuckle, cheered on by the merriment of their discomfort, and he left the house in far better spirits than when he'd first arrived. Cults and monsters and plagues: the twenty-first century was shaping up to be just as fucked up as any of the previous ones; a superimposition of olden times transmuted with the flair of iPhones and the internet—but at its base, in its heart, as medieval and superstitious and mysterious as ever. God bless this demented haven!

Two weeks later, while bopping away to Gordon Lightfoot's hit song "Sundown," he saw in the newspaper that a foolish cult—twelve members in all—had drunk hemlock and perished by a ravine just outside of town. His world was one of destruction. What the hell? thought George. Everyone he touched (even peripherally) died—and it wasn't just everyday regular death, but the imminent and suicidal kind.

He saw the names of Elden and Gertrude Somovar and wondered how it could be, all these deaths, so frequent, so common, the dispatch so swift. Was this his talent? Not writing, but some kind of proximal death wish visited upon acquaintances and loved ones and friends? Was he some kind of New Age killer? A spiritual hitman? Would Mr. Mickelson hang himself next? Blow his brain out like Father Tom? But what about his mother and sister? Tim? They were fine, but there seemed to be a trend, a common thread of fatalities outside the norm of what most people would accept as pure coincidence. These were strange and disturbing questions. Was he some kind of murdering *Übermensch*? Was there some dormant power laying waste to those around him without his conscious consent? Was he causing them to kill themselves or put themselves in harm's way? Or was he a schizoid with narcissistic tendencies and paranoid delusions of grandeur? Perhaps...

Or perhaps this was life. Typical and mundane, grandiose only because of the limited perspective of the human mind (his mind), unable to see the larger picture, a pure and tragic tale only because of the abysmal height the *Homo sapiens* was capable of attaining, gravity's fault or a dreamer's dream peaking too early, nothing more. Was it all verbiage? Was this despair? And then he remembered the girl, in the bed, above the musical monster—with the one breast hanging out—

beautiful and familiar. The girl from 57 Cherry Lane: Suzy O'Connor, the girl who'd suddenly disappeared and then reappeared at the cliffs—the one with the strange doll and the piercing scream.

Chapter 21

Jill Dilgunk had long ago separated herself from her hospital chum, Gordon—over a year, in fact—and she now lived for her children and an accumulated reserve of hobbies ranging from crochet to archery. She was constantly learning, tossing her mind into books and movies, joining literary clubs and cinema soirées; she went to bingo twice a week and volunteered at the middle school just down the street. George was proud of her, keeping busy, and she seemed happy so long as she didn't slow down too much. George came in late one night and saw her on the couch, her gaze inward, her hands still, a halfway knitted sock lying next to her, her mind uneasy, her eyes not healed. When she noticed him, her face changed instantly, and the mask of congeniality and kindness resumed its place. She was happy to see her son, and this shook her out of wherever she was, deep inside, with the accumulated stores of wounds and demons running amok.

"How was your night?" she asked.

"Good, thanks. Just hung out with Timbo and had a few pints."

"How's Tim?"

"Same as always."

He rummaged through the fridge as they continued to chat. She helped him put away the leftovers, said good night, and went upstairs. George ate quietly on the island in the middle of the kitchen; alone and ponderous, he looked out the window and saw a cat wandering the yard, hunched low, ready to pounce, stalking some unfortunate prey.

He thought a lot about Suzy O'Connor in the coming days— the girl from the cliffs and then again in the woods. One thing that didn't add up was her age; by all accounts, Suzy should have been thirteen or fourteen; the girl he saw was closer to thirty, if not older. But her eyes, fierce and defiant, ringing with the same intensity he saw that day, six years earlier, at the cliffs. His acceptance of what was possible in this world was changing day by day; cults and monsters—the fabric of the rational subdivided into what he thought could be and what actually was. He decided he should go back to 57 Cherry Lane and inspect the surroundings further. He asked his mom to drop him off at the cabin the next day; he readied his supplies and expected to be gone for two weeks.

The drive was scenic and calm. Fall was well underway, but the leaves had yet to turn, only the slight cooling of the air hinted at the approaching shift. The hymn of decay poised on each branch; an immaculate dance of death by each leaf, showcasing a natural harmony that found grace even in its downfall. George loved this time of year and anticipated the coming hues with great zeal and enthusiasm.

His first night there, he unpacked and sat on the couch in a mostly meditative state. In the morning, he set out for 57 Cherry Lane, bringing with him his hammer, some food, and a flashlight, among other supplies. He ventured into the bush, and when he got there, it looked just as when he'd left it.

Inside was brightly lit; sunlight was cutting in through empty window frames. No one was hiding under the covers this time, but the rest appeared to be the same. The markings on the wall, stark and frightening in an atypical way, somehow conveyed the uncanny and grotesque—an alphabet devised by a madman. He pulled out his phone and started taking photos. Most of the letters or symbols appeared to be of heads or faces, animal and beast, swine and ape, contorted in a miasma of renditions. But there were pairs, almost identical, and a pattern was forming. He thought they were all black and white, but upon closer inspection, many appeared to be rendered in color, coated thickly with rich dark oils and contrasted sharply with opaque whites; they sang a tune or created a song—but a discordant one, in a constant battle with its prescribed order.

He opened the hatch and lowered himself into the cellar. He switched on the flashlight and admired the studs posted up against the crumbling concrete and mud; he saw the decomposing heap in the back; the stench was atrocious. When he got near, he saw the bugs, the maggots eating. The thing was melting away in a fit of its own juices—blood swirled in a colorful mix of dark (almost pitch-black) browns and deep purples; George tucked his nose under his shirt and tried to slow his breathing and resist the temptation to gag.

His focus had been on the dead creature, but as he neared, he saw that the instrument—bound in skin and smashed to bits by George at an earlier hour—was trying to reassemble itself. He eyed it closely and noted a slow wheezing coming out of it. Its keys were attempting to reorganize themselves, still poorly placed and jutting out; its legs were busted and its main component swayed slightly—half engorged with air—a mess, but one that was attempting the impossible, a resurrection towards its initial form, a basement reanimation. He continued his exploration and was again surprised at just how spacious the cellar was.

He walked around the perimeter a couple of times and didn't find much. He checked the ceiling and then did a careful sweep of the floor. He snagged his foot on something and then repositioned the light to find the outline of another hatch just barely visible. He used the hammer to pry it open and then lifted it and shined his light to reveal whatever corruption lurked below. The only thing he could see were wooden steps leading ever downward, nothing more. The light was unable to pierce much in this echo chamber of tenebrous gloom, and he gripped the hammer in one hand and the flashlight in the other and descended the steps at a slow and careful pace.

The steps continued for a long while; downward and downward, the same march—a never-ending cascade. He shined the light behind him to see if he could approximate the distance traveled (had it been five minutes or an hour since he started?), but the light was swallowed up in the blackness, and he was left perplexed with only his will and curiosity to push him on. Down and down and down he went.

And then—out of the blue—he hit the ground, a flat surface, dirt; he almost tripped from the surprise. He knelt, grey soil, chalky. He swept the flashlight around and again had trouble piercing the murk. He supposed he shouldn't go too far, keep to the stairway; he only had a bit of water left, and the probability of getting lost seemed especially high. He yelled to see if anyone was there, and the reverberations caught him off guard, disturbed him—he felt like he must be in some giant chasm with ceilings one hundred feet high. He couldn't see anything, but his mind's eye concocted a blueprint, proliferating visions of gargantuan floor plans made up of otherworldly rock. There was boundlessness in the sound, and he felt like he was in some underground stadium—alone?

And then he saw it, or he thought he did—or maybe he just heard it—either way, he ran. Something was coming down the stairs at a surprising speed, a full sprint, yelling and growling, its weight shaking the entirety of the staircase—a debauched maniac in pursuit. "I'm gonna fucking kill you, you son of a bitch!" yelled the gruffest voice imaginable, and George took off. He ran into the darkness, the voice gaining on him. "I'm gonna gut you like a fish, you fucking imbecile!" His lungs were ready to burst, but he kept going, as fast as he could, the voice still gaining—his heart thumping against his chest, and then he caught a gleam of something in the blackness, some shimmering artifice tied to the corner of his eye. There, to his left, and he ran for it: a glistening metallic staircase, golden and spiraling. He thought of nothing but escape and climbed as fast as he could, choking down mouthfuls of air, dizzyingly ascending.

The climb seemed much shorter than the descent. He arrived at a hatch and smashed into it with his head and his hands, flinging it open. He jumped through and closed the doorway; a padlock and chains beside it, he locked the hatch as quick as he could and waited—but nothing banged against it. Where was he? He looked around—bright blue wallpaper with cartoons and clouds all strewn across its walls, immaculate finish carpentry. The room was small, very comparable to 57 Cherry Lane's main floor, structurally speaking. George took a minute to catch his breath, and he took in the strange details of the place. A holstered gun (like an old Wild West memento) and a bandolier were lying next to him. He grabbed them and unholstered the pistol, cocked the hammer back—and, right on cue, his pursuer burst through, sending splinters every which way, shattering the hatch, busting right past the padlock, and George fired on reflex, and its head exploded, and blood and brains shot everywhere—the walls, the ceiling, George, all covered—and it fell, tumbling back towards the pit wherefrom it came, a headless ragdoll in motion, returning to the ground floor some thirty seconds later with a dull thud.

Chapter 22

He exited the main den and found himself in a vast expanse of desert. Sand packed tightly, sprinkled with cacti, a glorious pink sky, and the entire landscape bathed in the hue of salmon. It was bright—too bright, considering where he'd just come from. He squinted and tried to see any monument or waypoint which he could venture towards; there was no way he was going back down that godforsaken hatch if he could help it.

He kept the gun in his hand; having commandeered the bandolier, he took a bullet and loaded it into the pistol, making sure all six of its chambers were secured with ammunition. He saw what he thought might be a tower, blackened and hazy due to the heat; he couldn't see exactly what it was, but it was the only decisive marker in an otherwise barren and monotonous terrain. So be it, thought George, and he headed off in its direction, dragging his feet ever so slightly across the sand; he took a sip of water, noting that his supplies were almost gone.

He seemed to be keeping a decent pace. The black smudge he'd originally oriented himself towards had, in fact, turned out to be a large monolith, black and foreboding. He wasn't yet able to tell much about it; perhaps it held a doorway at its base; either way, it would provide shade and a spot to rest. He fired random shots from his pistol, blowing off limbs and torsos of the scattered flora here and there, noting that he was quite an ace with the gun—procured just an hour before in that strange infantile room. He tried to spin it around his finger like he'd seen the cowpokes do on TV; unfortunately, the gun kept getting caught and falling to the ground. He decided that he'd rather be a crack shot than some dilettante showman anyway, and he fired at a cactus some twenty feet off and blew it clean apart. He smiled, and in light of his grim prospects, he was quite enjoying himself.

When he got near the monolith (which took a while), he tried to discern the time, looking first at his phone, which wouldn't turn on, and thus, with no alternative, he tried to use the sun as some form of timekeeper—the shift in degrees marking some sort of approximation as to just how long he'd been out strolling in the desert. He guessed haphazardly that he'd been out walking for at least three or four hours, his tiredness catching up with his thirst. And then he arrived, and the size of the monolith was extensive, towering some ten or eleven stories high; a fat cubic base erected in the middle of nowhere. He couldn't see any door, and he sat with his back against it, taking a reprieve from the sun's harsh light in the shadow of the beast.

He noticed that his thirst was going away. And much to his surprise, he actually felt good; leaning up against the giant obelisk, he watched the sky, and the formation of clouds dazzled him. From time to time, he shot his pistol off, but mostly he just sat there—straight-legged—tossing grains of sand at his shoes.

Nightfall fell upon the scene, and George kept his station. He wondered what he should do. Go back? Face the evil beneath the earth? Try and find his way back towards that wooden staircase housed under 57 Cherry Lane? Fuck it, he thought. He was just too goddamn lazy; he knew it. Even in the face of probable death, it just seemed absurd to waddle all the way back to where he'd come from (the beginning)—might as well continue in a linear and forward-thinking fashion, see where he ended up. Probably dead, but one never knows.

He fell asleep, and when he woke up, head tilted back, he saw the moon directly above him, a strange sight, whole and haunting—pointed to by the tip of the monolith. He then centered his gaze, parallel with the horizon, and had a jump. His legs were gone! Actually, they were there but transformed; he appeared to have woken up under a new guise, the black encasement of a bug replacing that of his former skin. A new outer shell? Was this to be his new being? His new normal? "*Wake up, goddamnit!*" He had spindly little bug legs—eight in all—a hardened back with tentacles slithering about and pincers jutting out from the edges of his lips. When he tried to speak, his voice was shrill, a polyphonic mess, and he screamed with panic, no longer capable of such luxuries as English—although his mind kept up the habit... for now.

He saw the gun next to him; it was no longer of any use.

"We are the rippable, zippable ragdolls!!" For some reason, those words came out of him. Was it his prolonged exposure to the sun or his new bug brain? The words appeared in his newfound entomological tongue, and suddenly a door dropped from the monolith, and an entrance materialized twenty feet away, out of the blue, leading inside to the belly of the structure.

Inside, the walls were a glossy black, reflecting any bit of light they caught, and the moment George entered—crawling on his many legs, no longer of the bipedal rank (he was more adept at maneuvering in this manner than he originally thought he'd be)—he saw a great staircase going around and around, ever downward, with beasts like him, hundreds in fact, scattered across at various points near the edges, going down or coming up, climbing along its walls, scaling, a descent (or ascent), a hive of movement, and George supposed he should get going. Up or down?

He decided down was his best bet; perhaps he could converse with one of the many creatures as he descended, try and find his way home (wherever that might be). He approached a blob-like creature, oozing bodily fluids; it appeared like an obese man who had set upon himself, eating his own rotten flesh (and by the looks of it, he'd started with his feet), and halfway through had conceded defeat (the flesh too filling), thereby leaving limbs with twisted and stick-like protrusions branching out as poor makeshift substitutes at various nooks and recesses; he seemed to be the most human of the creatures, so George approached with caution and aired his query (voicing his new alien tongue), hoping the monster's jargon would be comprehensible: "Do you know where we are? And could you help me get to where I'm going?" The obese half-digested man-thing let out a growl and lunged forward; its jaws opening up to reveal a deranged mouth housing an array of pointed teeth; it chomped down on one of George's tentacles and rolled off, a surprisingly nimble exit, munching away at the stolen chunk of meat. George fell, shocked at the sudden display of violence—not to mention the sharp pain of losing one of his appendages—he tumbled along the staircase, past blurs of monstrosities gnashing fangs this way and that, furnishing him with rogue kicks as he fell past. Eventually, his momentum carried him towards the abysmal center, and he plummeted down into the darkness, falling for what felt like an eternity. He seemed to prefer this mode of travel; everything was a blur, and he couldn't quite make out any of the grotesqueries adorning the inhabitants of this structural conundrum. He hummed a tune in his head, and he moved his limbs to the beat, dancing in free fall, and all of a sudden, his back began to jitter, and he began to chaotically twirl in the air. *He had wings!* And he didn't even know it. Although it took him a minute to organize himself—disentangle and coordinate his efforts, proliferate all his grace of movement—and like that, the bug halted, floating in midair. George hovered, batting his wings as fast as he could, and once again, he looked around, oriented himself, and posed the questions: what the hell am I, and where should I be going?

An opening hung above his head—a hallway—a rectangular highway pointing forever towards infinity. George decided to buzz in there and make a go of it, change his direction, so to speak, pursue the horizontal plane for a while.

He flew into the passage (his aviating still clunky and juvenile), and he continued forward, the single-point perspective an odd optical phenomenon in this never-ending corridor. And then the lights went out—vanished. Pitch-black. And all of a sudden, something rose from the floor, a television hoisted up on top of a pillar. God's private show. George was hypnotized; white noise appeared on the screen; he halted his movements. Color bars and an audible hum—and, finally, a face—but only the eyes and nose and mouth, everything else... missing. The mouth spoke these words: "Congratulations. You have found the egg. Congratu— Congratulations. You have found the egg. Congratu—

Congratulations. You have found..." It continued in this glitchy fashion, and then its screen splintered, shattered right in front of George; sparks shot out from its back, and its antenna warped and bent. An escape attempt was underway; the television was cracking apart, readying to expose its interior, an orgy of microchips and plastic wires in primary colors. George saw a gnarled claw break through, and then again—everything went black, and when he came to, he was draped under something. Captured? He kicked furiously, and the pupil of his left eye constricted from the light, the blanket lay on the floor, and George recognized the interior of 57 Cherry Lane. He got up and sat on the edge of the cot, allowing his eyes time to adjust, contemplating what the hell had just happened.

And God was he thirsty.

He found the bathroom and drank greedily from the tap and looked at himself in the mirror. He was back to normal—sort of. He had a beard, long and tangled, growth that had seemingly been left to its own devices for years. His eyes were different too; great crevices hung around their outer edges; hardness not known before—angular and crow-like—appeared and colored the countenance of his face. How long had he been down there? He unearthed his phone, which turned on, and he saw that he'd only been gone a few hours, but somehow—physically—he seemed to have aged more than a decade. Perhaps it was just the dirt and the beard. But perhaps not.

Before leaving 57 Cherry Lane, George decided he should destroy it. He remembered that coming here had supposedly been due to the request of a celestial entity, prompted by the hand of God and headless Father Tom. He wondered, upon reflecting on his journey, if it had not been some trick, a devious ploy or deception to get him here, orchestrated by some devil; or perhaps it was a genuine mission, a godsend, and this second outing—devised without the supposed interference or guidance or consent of any heavenly force—had been a mistake, urged on by a curiosity that had ultimately eaten up a good chunk of George's youth. He found a jerrycan outside and poured gasoline throughout the hut, starting in the cellar and working his way to the front entrance. He lit a match and watched the flames eat away at the house. It was a divine sight.

When he got back to his cabin, he showered and began chopping away at his beard. Hacking at it with a pair of scissors, then using his trimmer to lower it even further, and then, finally, he went at it with a razor, dispatching the final minuscule hairs. He had a new scar above his lip, a rather nasty one too. He supposed he should call his mother in the morning, prolong her arrival, tell her he needed another couple of weeks. That would give him enough time to grow some hair back, allow for some camouflage, distance the change somewhat by offering a distraction and covering up the scar. These were strange times.

Chapter 23

So what to do now? thought George. He had three more weeks of seclusion, a face that had aged a decade in a few hours, an uncanny glimpse at the governing chaos hidden (potentially) below every hatch and deck and, not to mention, the beginnings of a mustache, still in its infancy, pubescent at best. Time was on his side—or perhaps his greatest foe; it was difficult to tell where it stood and was probably best viewed as a governing directional force, amoral and ever-present, practicing its own strange laws, relative, but relative to what? To the here and the now? But what if the here was different than the now, plunged far off—the here wound to a different mechanism, a different speed, a smaller loop, even though it was spinning on the same downward sloped cylinder, circling towards the center, the abysmal hole, nearing the drop, the plunge, the drain. All George knew was that wherever he'd been—presumably the same locale as Suzy—had caused a drastic acceleration in the span of only a few hours; the depths of the underworld were not forgiving towards one's appearance or skin.

He thought a lot of God as he sat on the back porch. A man who appeared to be in his early thirties, tighty-whities, shirtless; he sat thinking of the Absolute, the original paradoxical Yahweh. He thought about his experiences: the tragedies, the comedic elements, the puzzles too big and too complex for anyone to dare grasp their overarching schemes. He thought about what he'd experienced in *that other place*: his transformation, his pilgrimage, his gift or prize cloaked in a TV—a monster within. Had he absorbed that thing? Was it metaphorical? Had it been there all along? Was it a warning? A message? Nonsense? A prophecy? An example of the absurd?

Or was it a reflection, pointed at him, whispering a secret... Was he evil?

Presumably not, or not entirely, possibly it could even mean the opposite, an ascension of sorts, a good omen—a higher height requiring a lower depth—a prize to reflect its opposite, to reestablish equilibrium. He didn't know much about any of this, but one thing was for sure: he felt good, better than he had in a long time, and it'd only been a week since he'd returned from 57 Cherry Lane, and the future never held so much promise.

He seared a steak on the stove, turned down the heat, and drenched it in butter. He had potatoes baking in the oven and a nicely chopped salad on the side. He ate and leafed through a book he'd found, a biology book describing various illnesses and conditions. He found the photographs fascinating and was reading about arthrogryposis when he heard a rustling outside. He paid little attention to it and continued to eat his steak. Whatever lurked out there couldn't possibly compete with what he'd faced just a handful of days before. A stronger man he was, no doubt, and he cut into the meat and savored its sapid flavor.

That night, his dreams spun him back into that dreadful underworld of yore. He was no longer an escapee who'd won or been cursed with its prize; he was stuck in the monolithic prison like the rest of those creatures, acquiescing to the mood and volatility of his surroundings. He picked a fight, singling out a praying mantis with a goat's head; it dripped black mucus.

George was brutal; he instantly went about lunging with his pincers, using his tentacles to fend off attacks and gain advantageous positioning. He succeeded in dismembering his adversary, picking it apart limb by limb—but the others had him cornered; and it didn't take long before they charged (an attack), and the rest of the dream was a slow-motion agony as he was eaten in vivid detail by the hungry mob.

He woke up suddenly, a noise and a window ajar; he eyed his milieu in search of the threat, saw nothing, and went back to bed, and then he heard it again—that strange instrument from the basement, the monster and the organ, he recognized the tune. He jumped out of bed and listened carefully; it was coming from the bathroom. He grabbed a butcher knife and readied himself outside the door, preparing his attack. He pulled the door open, and there it was, that same creature from 57 Cherry Lane, with that same fucking instrument, now in his goddamn bathroom. He jabbed at it.

"Wait!" cried the bug.

George halted.

"I'm a friend. I'm here to—" And George swung... fuck its speech, cutting a chunk off its back; the creature screamed, exposing its huge mouth and hideous fangs; painful grimaces flashed across its animated countenance; George stumbled back, and the creature slammed the door and locked it.

"You cut me, you bastard... We need to talk, *okay*? Calm yourself, amigo. You rogue killing machine," said the voice inside the bathroom.

George slowed his breathing. In a daze, he walked to the fridge and grabbed a beer. "So, what do you want?" asked George. "Why are you here?"

... To make amends? Negotiate a ceasefire?

"For you. Did you think we were done, pal? We're just getting started."

George took a sip of his beer. "What the hell are you on about?"

"I mean, that you and me are buddies, partners, compadres, amigos. Wherever you go, I go, and vice versa. And we still got a few things we need to get sorted, settle the score, so to speak—can I come out? And promise you won't swing that goddamn knife at me again."

George put the knife on the counter and agreed to the bug's request. He relaxed and took another swig of beer.

"Come on out."

The door opened, and the creature walked out. Its bulk and gait somewhat comical once the initial luster of fear and disgust had washed away. The creature took a seat, and George stared at it, wondering where the hell it had learned English.

"Thanks. Been a long day, you know. Say, you got another beer, champ?"

George grabbed a beer from the fridge, twisted off the cap, and set it in front of the creature now seated at the dining room table. He watched it with curious eyes as one of its appendages grabbed the beer in a surprisingly dignified and gracious manner. It gulped down a few mouthfuls and set it back down.

"Much obliged."

"So, what did you want to talk about?" asked George.

"Well, you remember all those strange adventures you've been having as of late?"

"Maybe."

"Well, it seems that you and me are linked, buddy. See, you've been tangled up with me in one form or another since day one, and it seems that we need to strengthen that link, cultivate that bond. It's time we merged, partner. 'Tis His will, as they say."

"Whose?"

"God's or Bog's or whoever you think operates this big ol' clusterfuck of a machine."

"And what are you, anyway? Some sort of retarded demigod? A demented musical demon?"

"Well, there've been plenty of names for me over the years—but I suppose I'm best seen as an emissary of a higher power. Not good or evil per se. Necessary to the scheme... you know. A capable entity, without scruples and such."

"So, what now?"

"Well... unfortunately, this next bit's a bit messy. You just chill, hombre, and try and keep quiet."

One of the creature's tentacles shot out and hit George in the cheek; it felt like a giant leech sucking at his marrow. "Just relax now," said the creature. "It'll all be over soon."

The bug approached, and its other tentacles stabbed into George at various points. It stood as high as it could, shaking and convulsing in some orgiastic dance—raring to go. And then it chomped down, opening its mouth as wide as it could; it devoured him in two quick bites. Blood and guts painted the cabin, and the bug lay down and digested George. It dozed off and dreamt of pink deserts and circuses and young writers and cheap, greasy meals.

When the bug got up after what felt like a long and restful sleep, it went back to the bathroom and checked itself out in the mirror. It looked like a cross between the Toxic Avenger and that actor nearing the end of his metamorphosis in *The Fly*. Remnants of George were visible; the bug and its meal were amalgamating into a single being—although it was quite a disgraceful concoction infused with lechery and digestive overtones as the two beings competed, digested, and fucked each other into this new and paradoxical state. To make matters worse, George the bug (or just George as we'll go about calling him) opened its mouth, large and wide, and ate the skin-bound instrument it'd left near the tub. Was this part of its gastrointestinal alchemy? Various animals and objects coagulating and mixing in the cauldron of its gut, forcing a new being to the fore?

After two days in which George lay supine on the floor, he recognized his mind coming back into consciousness. His thoughts were once again operating the head, and he felt as if the bug had lowered its position, a subservient entity, the Sancho to his Quixote. He felt it in his neck, near his collarbone, its opinions and ideas funneling upwards towards his brain, but not occupying the commanding post. A fascist creature this was not—perhaps it wasn't all bad, thought George, but then he saw himself in the mirror, and he glimpsed what he supposed was the final product of his metamorphosis: a bulky mess of man and bug stitched to-gether, an abomination in every regard. He had his arms and legs back, although the skin was lumpy and one arm was far longer than the other. He carried bulging muscles on each of them, but they bent in and out at odd angles, not conforming to typical human physiology. His legs, too, seemed to be suffering from similar developmental oversights. And his back had bones protruding out, webbed with skin, like tiny rickety wings. He had protrusions on his side—little bug legs, three or four inches long, jutting out near his ribs. His penis was larger, with a heftier girth that zigzagged outwards. And then there was his face, worst of all, one eye lower than the other, clumps of hair missing, part of his lip gone—exposing long teeth and no gums. His mustache was still present and had thickened considerably. It was night, and he went out and sat on the porch with a beer and a joint. What the hell was he to do?

His mother came to pick him up two weeks later; she honked the horn, and George came out without much ado. He opened the passenger-side door.

"Hi, Mom."

"Hi, Son. How was your trip?" She turned and took a good look at him; her face changed. "What happened to you? You look terrible. It looks like you haven't slept in a month."

George said nothing and just stared at his mother.

"Well, let's get you home. The Petersons are coming by tonight. Is that okay? Can you handle that?"

George nodded.

"Good, we'll fix you up a nice meal and then have an early night. Get you back on track, young man."

George said nothing as they drove; he listened to David Bowie on the radio and wondered how in the hell his mother hadn't noticed all his deformities, his bug-like peculiarities. But when they entered a gas station to grab a snack and a coffee, no one paid him any mind. His lesions and distortions invisible to the common man, or at least negligible, anyway, and when they got back inside the car, his mom said, "And by the way, Son, I didn't want to bring it up—but I like your new look... has a gentleman's air about it... a real mature and masculine tone."

And at that, George let out a hearty and high-pitched roar. And his mother laughed, too.

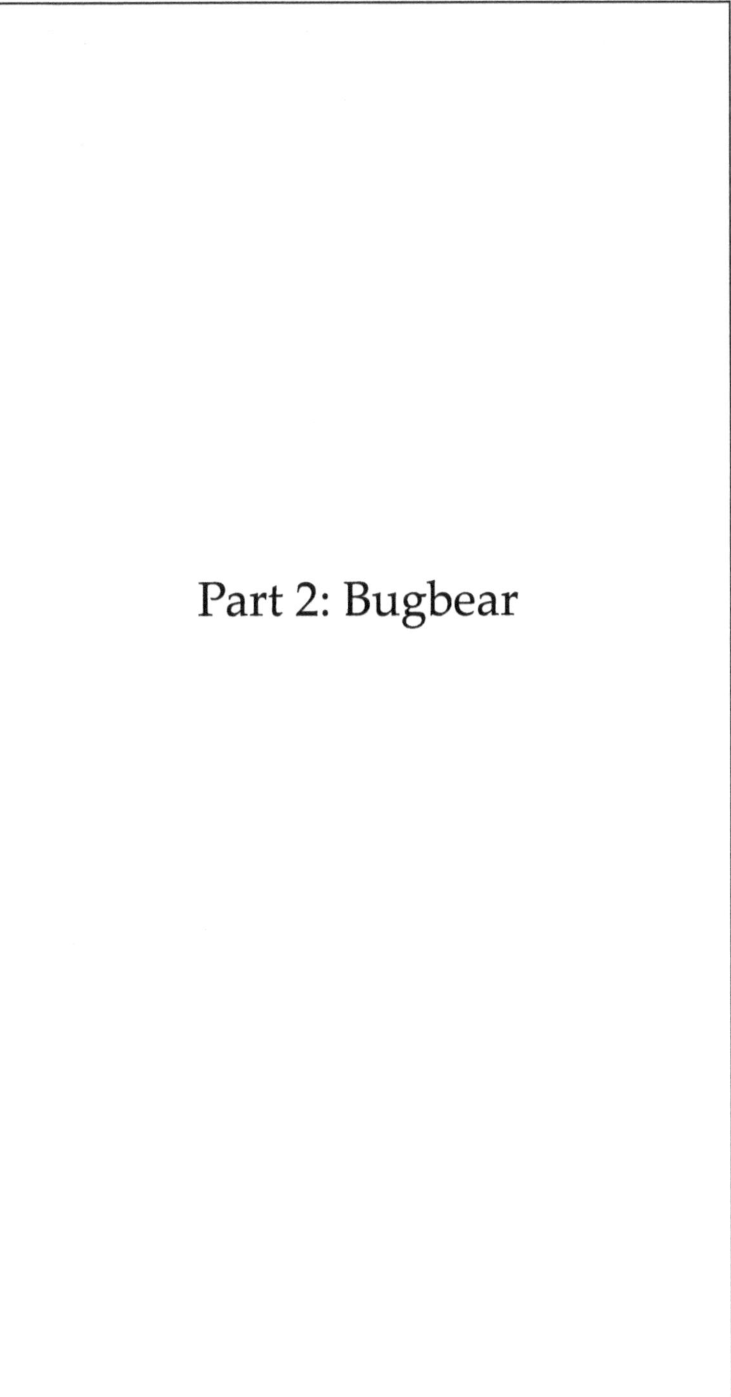

Part 2: Bugbear

Chapter 24

Fade in. Black and white. A remote island off the coast of God-knows-where. George is seated in the front row of what seems to be a theater. Walls with holes, cracks appear, and the wood is unevenly spaced. Upon closer inspection, the walls are built with a variety of boards and branches (you can still see the bark on most of them), tied and fastened together or nailed haphazardly, and one is hard put to compliment the professional nature of the carpentry. There is a small stage where a play or farce or some theatrical tomfoolery is taking place. A man wearing a bonnet seems to be mimicking the actions of a child; he smokes a cigar, and this is obviously played up for laughs. Next to him, another man, dressed as a woman, scolds the childlike figure, a large wooden spoon in her hand. She chases him; her large limbs flailing about, and she succeeds in landing a good smack every now and then. George yells, "Cut," and the characters break, and their illusions shatter, and they focus their attention on George, the monstrosity, as he patiently lumbers about and lights a cigar of his own.

"Good work, everyone. That's it for today."

That night as George sleeps in his tent near the ocean, he envisions going back to civilization, away from these creatures, these *actors*. How had he ended up here, adrift and so far away from everything he knew? He remembers that he wanted a change and that one change had led to another change—and that that then led to a cacophony of change that multiplied and proposed other changes that endlessly mixed up the batch that was the sum total of his life and that led him away—way out here—to this remote hellhole. How much time had gone by? Had he been out here five years? Ten? Twenty? And more importantly, what was he doing out here? What goal had directed him here in the first place? It seemed hard to imagine that he once even had a goal, any goal—a goal as ordinary and mundane as doing ten push-ups in the morning: could such a goal be the precipice by which a man encounters his undoing? Was the repetitious act, however humdrum, the means by which a man is able to blind himself and push on, losing touch with reality or his initial presupposed destination? Repetition being the ultimate tool wherefrom an individual could reinvent or reinvigorate or distance or destroy and deceive the entanglement that comprises the Self, or at least its current (receding) incarnation. Had he repeated some action so many times that he now ceased to be what he was? Had he succeeded in destroying himself through blind endurance? Had that been his goal all along? All he knew was that he needed a new one, another change to add to the list of changes, a new repetitious act to veer his ship elsewhere. Time for a new beginning or, better yet, a lavish end.

There was a girl in the hallway; what the *hell* was she doing there yapping away on her cellular? Even here, in this far-off place, the modern tentacle still attached, its reach exceeding far beyond any boundary.

The commune was an unusual place; it acted as a home for an assortment of characters, lowlifes, and amnesiacs from dissimilar walks of life. They all ended up here through various circumstances, called forth from a variety of trajectories for supposedly different reasons. Jacque, for instance, a navy captain from some distant country who'd washed up ashore on a sunny Tuesday and decided to stay, never relaunching his boat out into the open waters. He told the others that he was waiting to be rescued, and if no rescue ever came, just as well, one spot was as good as any other.

Jacque was smitten with one of the Laura sisters—siblings from the UK. Their accents thick and their speech verbose. They were longtime residents, each with a hefty ass and a penchant for parading this hardware around in scantily clad, frayed denim shorts. They were popular with the men and often had the pick of the litter when it came to sex or fucking or just sleeping (and cuddling) with, and Gisele Laura, the eldest of the pair—known for her bleach-blonde hair and opinionated rants—was the general of the duo, adhering to a more regimented lifestyle than her younger, dark-haired counterpart. She was often the deciding voice between the two, governing their lot; she used her active and demanding mind to plan for their future, navigating the social spheres of the commune with a general sense of ease and entitlement.

George sometimes slept with the younger sister, the dark-haired one, Jeanette Laura. Jeanette often practiced a method of randomized lovemaking in which she would go out and have sex with one or more of the men and women of the commune, usually ones she wasn't particularly close to or fond of; and after having her fill, she'd return to George, and within a week, the cycle would repeat. But George didn't mind, in fact, he secretly encouraged it, planting hints that he needed a day or two alone, that the time had come for her to flee the nest for a bit, do a lap of the island, see what else lived on out there. After about a year of this routine, Jeanette ended up shacking up with an American named Vince who'd come to the island after hearing about it on an online forum on a now-defunct website called Little Lotus. He became the *new* George, her navigational North Star, and George was folded into the mix of strangers and guest stars—sleeping with her every third month or so, as routine or chance would have it.

What seemed to be pushing George away from the island—this place of refuge—was primarily his ability to see the curves coming; he knew all the patterns and the predictions and the contradictions of the island and its inhabitants. Even when someone new came, he was able to watch as they ping-ponged around; the ingrained rituals of initiation—although never forthrightly organized or spoken of by the islanders—were carried out and always to the beat in the same manner or whim. Some inner organizational mode was dictating the rhythm here, the ends by which every individual donned their role, played their part, wore their mask. And it seemed that the time had come for George to set sail again, away from this group and this setting. He needed to jumble up the dice and have another turn, venture back to the mainland and see what was happening (what was going on in the lives of the ones he knew and loved?), go home—or to some far-off corner where the air and food and culture were once again new and refreshing. He needed the antithesis to this horrible paradise, and so he commandeered Jacque's boat and ventured off in the early morning hours—when the sun had not yet risen, and only the lapping of the waves and the distant moan of aquatic life bid him farewell.

On the boat, he enjoyed himself immensely, especially at night, out in the open air among the calm and placid and blue. He even admired the storms and the disturbances and the ruckus caused by the rollicking winds and the blackened clouds; it all afforded him some form of joy or ecstasy, some injection of pure pharmaceutical mastery. What big teeth you have, thought George as he watched the waves bury themselves into one another during a particularly destructive stretch amid horrid skies. The waves excited, dipping and rising, an ornery battalion of drunken muscle crashing into itself (or onto itself) and then repeating the scheme over and over again.

Were they laughing? Playing? Was this the jesting violence of Mother Nature? Of the gods? Were they nothing but oafish fools or blind invalids, ignorant or indifferent towards their colossal strength? No, they or it or she or he was the genuine article, the real deal—violent and sacred, and of a different frame of mind. Beautiful and breathtaking and insane.

"Now, George, you sit down now. Please go back to the main area with the others."

He was starving; he searched the ship and found a fishing rod. He deployed it on a calm morning, and in no time, he caught himself a fish. So hungry, and without gentility or embarrassment, he smacked the fish against the bow of the ship and went about clawing it open, eating its innards and meat without any attempt at distinguishing the parts. Polite culinary conduct held little importance out here, alone with only the watchful eye of God to survey him.

"Please, George, go back and sit down now."

For a while now, he'd noticed it. He could see its great shadow beneath the waves. Its size cosmic, black and distorted; it fanned out with its width comparable to three or four football fields. It glided beneath him for hours and days, and George's anxiety only subsided once he began to suspect that perhaps this monstrosity was a good omen, a disturbing beauty below offering guardianship among the waves. The water refracted its blessed image.

Then he was caught off guard—a gust of wind and a low-flying flock of seagulls—one of the birds hit him in the face, another in the leg; and disoriented and distraught, he flailed about until he hit the edge of the boat and fell into the icy depths.

Splash.

A bucket of water in the face. He was strapped to a chair—Mrs. Arnett watched him closely, peeking over her bifocals.

"I'm sorry, George, you were being very disruptive again."

The walls were grey, barred windows, large bald and shorthaired men, Mrs. Arnett in her white gown holding a clipboard. He, George, harnessed to a chair dripping wet, some youthful assistant holding an empty bucket whose former contents had been tossed, drenching George, bringing him back, back here—to the now: Asylum #8, Tower 2.

He returned to the main room, a giant gymnasium with only one entrance fitted with a metal cage, requiring one to pass through two consecutive doors requiring two different keys. The inmates of this particular cell numbered around the low fifties and had plenty of space to move about. The open nature of the setup had various stations scattered about including a television area where rows of chairs were placed on a dusty rug facing an ancient thirty-two-inch screen. Other areas included a tetherball station where one inmate, Sally Joe, hung around—all alone—for three to four hours daily. She'd stand there, unenergetic and redundant, only batting at the ball every few minutes or so, but if any of the other inmates approached or tried to play or requisition the game for themselves, she would erupt in a volley of tears and shouts. The Laura sisters were seated in another section where the inmates could draw or doodle or create with erasable markers on a movable whiteboard, and George was walking around the gymnasium trying to dry off; his path arcing along the largest loop he could muster, following the contours of the walls as he glimpsed the TV and saw some mascot or kids' television personality dressed as a giant lizard bounce around to the applause of those seated in the front row.

George continued his lap, shifting his eyes beneath the fluorescent mise-en-scène and the drab decor: "I need to get the hell out of here," he thought.

Chapter 25

George had been conducting a series of plays for the staff and their families that grew to include the local gentry along with noticeable and prominent figures and stewards spearheading many of the campaigns and committees of the town, hoping to bring about a brighter and more moral order for its inhabitants. When George was admitted, it was no secret that he was an author, and one of some notoriety and renown. His treatment was discussed among the medical minds as they reflected on which form of therapy would best suit George and his psychosis. They concluded, with the input of George, that he should continue to write and express himself. And as a means of growing and articulating the social web and bonds of the asylum, he should stage a play, write a scenario, and perform it with the help of the other inmates.

The first few plays that George put on were mostly comedic in nature. He kept the dialogue minimal and the action brisk, using silent cinema as a reference point or template (namely ripping off Charlie Chaplin and, to a lesser degree, Buster

Keaton) and then infusing these sagas with an omniscient voiceover that he performed or narrated for each of his shows. This allowed him the opportunity to go off-script if any of his actors goofed a line or went into some raging fit of lunacy.

The first play was an immediate hit with the staff, and the inmates all seemed to have a good time, except for a girl named Tina, who cried during the entire run of the show. George knew she would be trouble, but he was forced to include her and opted, in the end, to cast her as an inanimate object, a part he wrote specifically to keep her stage presence slight—giving her two unimportant lines of dialogue—and thus fulfilling his requirements to the loathsome lass.

The stage they performed on was of sound and professional design—an actual amphitheater, no doubt. The asylum, with its many wings and corridors, was privy to a whole slew of amenities. Although George spent most of his time in his cell or the large and spacious gymnasium/common area, he was sometimes escorted around the grounds for various meetings and appointments. He once visited a doctor's office at the opposite end of the hospital and rode in a small vehicle through underground passageways, took two separate elevators, and spotted a rather sizable manmade waterfall constructed in the main cafeteria of an opposing wing. The accommodations weren't awful, according to George, and once he'd acclimated himself to the routines of the asylum, he even grew to enjoy it... for a time. But then, as the years wore on, the drudgery of confinement and the compulsory socialization with the condescending staff and the insane convalescents forced George's hand: he decided to plan his escape. His will bound itself to this goal, and a plan began to surface, edging him towards his freedom, although the plan was still somewhat clouded and murky and juvenile, as the zygote or beginnings of most plans typically are.

The inmates themselves were mostly kind folk. Insane, yes, but so was George, apparently. None of the inmates in George's wing were overly violent—the odd scuffle or unorthodox tackle, sure, which could happen anywhere, especially when people were forced into such close proximity and for such long periods of time. His best friend at the asylum was a man named Will Brighton. He was a jovial lad a bit younger than George, attentive and even-tempered; he suffered from fits of paranoia and constantly fidgeted about, generally repeating his words two or three times in succession, namely focusing on the ends of his sentences to espouse these repetitious redundancies, creating his own brand of echo or reverb. He was cast as the lead in one of George's plays, and George used his tic as a device, writing a character who'd accidentally fallen down a well, and through Willy's odd bit of vocal reiteration, he was able to simulate the sound of being stuck inside that long and narrow vertical prison.

Willy had left the asylum a year ago. The doctors had pronounced him cured, and George was happy for his friend. He hugged him on his last day and saw him exit the cage at the far end of the common area; Gisele Laura leaned against him and fixed her left slipper all the while. And then, three months later during a weekly assembly, George and the other inmates were told that Will was dead. They left it at that, but George found out later, from his sister Trisha, that Will had killed himself, cutting open his wrists in his attic, slicing long and deep from his elbow to his palm.

George was numbed by Will's death; he took it calmly, never making a fuss of it in front of the other inmates or staff, but inside it tore him apart. It acted as the wind driving him over the precipice, down towards the exit. The devil be damned, he thought. He was getting out of there one way or another.

The play he wrote next was more complicated than any he'd yet attempted at the asylum. Many moons progressed over the time it took to write and conjure and rehearse the play into being. He was able to keep the staff away; he'd gained enough trust and momentum to keep them at a distance so long as he not excite the other inmates too much and keep the vulgarity to a manageable level. He promised wholeheartedly to adhere to these criteria; lying to the faces of the staff and swearing on the name of the Lord, he crossed his fingers and thought this indiscretion negligible in light of the sins to come.

The play was to center on a war, a longstanding feud between two families: the Meatsmiths and the Ballyhoos. The play was set in modern times and was about how one incident—a small shove between the eight-year-old Meatsmith girl and the ten-year-old Ballyhoo boy—could spiral out of control; first with the kids, then with the parents and the school, then with legal action, and then dividing the community up based on secret ties and friendships and hidden agendas, and then the incident gains fuel; it escalates into a drunken brawl and, finally, into an all-out battle between the factions culminating in an over-the-top finale where the Meatsmiths and their supporters meet up in the street and face off with guns and axes and machetes against the Ballyhoos and their gang on Pumice Avenue. It wasn't the most original play when outlined in such broad strokes, but in its minutiae, George was able to infuse it with lines and moments of genuine poetry, or so he thought. He was never one to overcomplicate his plots; he kept it simple and was able to infuse the time-honored structure of simple stories with strange ornamentation without losing his audience's attention or trust. He also made sure it was either funny or violent or sexually exciting—on some level—at intervals of five minutes. And George outfitted the actors with papier-mâché weapons that took weeks to make, and he was proud of the final product.

***

The night of the debut, lineups outside the theater tell George that word of mouth has spread; a packed house is expected. People are turned away due to the limited number of seats; a VIP section is set up near the front of the stage, reserving the best seats for the most important guests. His plan is underway; the play begins; everyone takes their seat...

Everything goes according to plan, they've made it to the final scene: the climactic battle. George has instructed the inmates to don the philosophy of the method actor, to utilize and extend their rage and excitement to the audience, allow the final confrontation to spill out amongst the gathered crowd; and right on cue, as the battle begins to attain its height, the actors start attacking those in attendance. First, one of the Laura sisters bites a young child; she's smacked in the face by its mother, who she, in turn, smacks harder, whereupon the lady's wig falls off, and it is revealed that she is a bald aristocrat; people laugh but not for long; the inmates are on a tear and heading violently in their direction.

During the ensuing chaos, George hunts for the main guard and his ring of keys. He sees him with his baton out smacking a fat man called Turk who's currently wrestling with a prominent town lawyer. The whacks don't seem to be doing much, and Turk pummels the lawyer with his large rotund fists. George, meanwhile, sneaks up behind the guard and hits him square in the jaw; the guard goes down—a glass jaw, no doubt. He struggles to get the keys loose; he must hurry, more guards are surely coming. Aha! He's got them; he unlocks the door without anyone paying him any mind as the violence of the inmates overshadows his escape. In the hallway, he runs—not overly sure which direction is correct—and he sees a set of elevators and gets in, swipes the stolen access card, and presses the button for the main floor. When the doors open, he's met by a large group of security guards who decide to beat him senseless.

His plan is foiled, but he's had a good run.

He is placed in a straightjacket in a padded cell in an unknown subbasement, and he understands now that only a miracle can get him out. He spends his days dreaming up weird ultimatums: death or exile. He wonders if he pleaded, would they just kill him and end it on the grounds of mercy—but then a miracle occurs. The asylum goes bankrupt, no longer supported by government funding, and George is released on a technicality as nowhere wants to take him, and after only three months of being stuck in a straightjacket, he is released into the world anew. Ready to breathe in the air as only a newly released maniac can.

Chapter 26

Which direction should he venture in? Left? Right? North? East? In actuality, he doesn't know how to orient himself vis-à-vis any direction (Where the fuck is north?); it's three hundred and sixty degrees of confusion and uncertainty. He walks on ahead; forget about directions, he'll follow the road. It is certain to lead somewhere, deduces George, and he pats himself on the back regarding his sound logic and embarks upon yet another journey, the pavement his oracle showing the way—some way—off to somewhere, in the distant unknown.

He meets a man sitting on the side of the road; he asks him what he's doing there, and the man replies that he's waiting—been waiting for quite some time for a friend of his, supposed to have shown up ages ago, but he's never turned up, not even once. George finds this odd and asks why he doesn't abandon his mission, say to hell with it and go and do something else, or go off and seek his friend of his own accord. The man, who George can now see is rather old, rubs his whiskered chin and smiles with only half of his face and says, "Well, gee whiz, never thought about it like that. You think I should go?"

"Yes," replied George.

"Well, where are you going?"

"Don't know."

"Can I come?"

"Sure," said George, and the duo set off, and they followed the path together, chatting amicably to one another about this and that, each forgetting proper introductions, just a nameless old man and a recently released inmate rambling down the road in search of something that neither was yet aware of.

When they got to the edge of town, the old man stopped in front of a store; he gazed at its window display. It was a vintage store specializing in what appeared to be typewriters, or maybe not... perhaps it was a clothing store with an abstract window dressing—honoring the tone of the store rather than prioritizing a typical, mundane, and straightforward exhibit. The strange thing about the display was that it had insects and bugs morphing into typewriters. Some stuck against the window, sullying the main pane, while others were displayed on tiny shelves installed at varying heights. What was the store trying to say? Was it something beyond the power of words? (The visual offering a more immediate attack on one's sensory perception.) Was it the high-fashion formula of marrying the grotesque with the beautiful? Was such a combination the height to which anyone working within the realm of beauty should (if they could) aspire to? George had a sudden need to write, and he asked the old man if he had a pencil or a pen and a piece of paper. The old man unbuttoned his coat and tore out a piece of paper from a small notepad he'd kept in his jacket pocket;

he handed it to George along with a pen. And George wrote: "Saw window with bugs and typewriters. Is writing some kind of insect or parasite or disease or virus? A symbolic load dropped into the psyche of the reader from the bubbling guts of the writer? Is writing the surface layer onto which all the intricacies of what has happened or formed or been structured beneath (in the writer's bowels) paint their linear sequence forward, somehow articulating who or what's there, in a mysterious and hopefully infectious type of way? The surface, like standing on a clear sheet of ice, allows the reader (and writer) to gaze into the depths and see the creatures and ecosystems developing/lurking below." He looked over what he'd written, handed the pen back to the old man, and carefully folded the piece of paper and put it in his pocket.

The old man said he wanted to develop an army, an empire, a kingdom, but first, they had to become warriors.

"Warriors?" said George. "Why in the hell do we need to become warriors?"

"To gain their respect," said the old man.

"Whose respect?" asked George.

"Theirs, them, our future subordinates and allies and ruffians."

Ah, he could see the logic now—formed in the archways of the old man's peculiar mind, a scheme to gain followers and win them a harem of beauties. He liked where the old man's head was at. They should hurry, but how would they become these leaders, these so-called "warriors?"

"To the sea," proposed the old man. "There, we will govern a vessel, a large attack ship, and we will set sail among the open waters and prove our bravery and power and worth."

"Fantastic," cried George. "Now, which way to the sea?"

When they got to the pier (after quite a lengthy ordeal and roundabout adventure), the duo went about questioning the various ship captains as to whether or not they had work for two strong and strapping sailors. All except one laughed in their faces: an old, brittle man and his inexperienced cohort—no one wanted or needed them, and only an elderly man (far older than even the old nameless man) and his fishing vessel agreed to welcome them aboard. But George's companion declined the offer ("Fishing's an arrogant and ignorant pastime for *pussies*," he said. And when George asked him why he thought that, he just swatted him away and walked back towards the road. Mumbling that he'd find a more modern way to manipulate the hearts and minds of the world, not lowering himself to this level of buggery; he pulled out his telephone and started tapping away at its screen.). George, conversely, accepted the fisherman's offer and said he'd give it a try, test his might against a big marlin or a giant squid; he'd do his best to help the elderly fisherman any way he could. The fisherman introduced himself and asked George to call him Joe; he beckoned him aboard, and George was eager to learn the ropes and get out to sea and do battle with some prehistoric aquatic brute.

They got themselves out on the water, far enough away that George couldn't spot any land in any direction. "Back to the comfort of a directionless zone of pure uncertainty," thought George, and he also thought that it looked a lot like a maze. But a maze that was an anti-maze, no walls, and pure space, with no hints or clues as to where anything should be or go, an abyss of openness. He thought back to a puzzle he'd made back at the asylum; it was supposed to be of an idyllic scene lifted straight from a fairy tale or fable or a postcard reminiscent of an old New England countryside. The box showed a cabin in the woods by a creek on a sunny day with a waterwheel turning and deer grazing in the distance. When he opened the box, all the pieces were blank. An error in its manufacturing, no doubt, but he tried to assemble it anyway. With no pictorial guide, he looked to the edges and the shapes of the pieces to provide hints for their assembly; he put the puzzle together in little sections or clumps and sometimes had to restart these little mini-constituents; it took him almost a month to complete, and when he looked at the finished product—a white canvas stitched together from hundreds of pieces—he couldn't help but feel disappointed. He tried to stifle this feeling by showing it to one of the nurses, but her response reiterated his own. Nothingness or blankness (a void devoid) rarely incited awe.

Down in the ship's cabin, with the door closed, Captain Joe was watching some show on his portable TV set. George knocked and asked what he should be doing (readying the rods?), and Joe cried out in an angered voice to get going and scrub the deck and prepare the lines and start reeling in those *goddamn* fish, or at least that's what George thought he said; the tirade from the old man was rather incoherent and strung together almost like one long and multisyllabic word. Wow, what a grump, thought George. So he stood on deck, and not having fished since his youthful days, he found what he hoped was the bait and started hooking them to the ends of two fishing lines, and then he sat back and enjoyed himself, peering out at the canvas of pure blue, dangling the rod over the water, pretending he knew what the hell he was doing.

When he woke up (he'd fallen asleep at some point), the sky was black, and he jumped up, startled and frazzled, and went knocking down on Joe's door. He heard a commotion; Joe whipped the door open—and the strong smell of whiskey stung George's nostrils as Joe, blotchy and red and hoarse, breathed heavily and close.

"Holy fuck! We've missed the goddamn day."

His eyes rolled mechanically from left to right and back again. He'd obviously drunk a rather sizeable amount of booze, and he no longer seemed to make any sense. He talked about the moon and navigating according to the stars and Neptune and Poseidon, and he started the engine, and George was told to hang on as he accelerated the boat to full speed, which wasn't all that fast; and they kept this up, this straight shot into the night, for over an hour before some sign of land appeared in the distance, and Joe shouted, "Hurray!" and George was happy to see terra firma, but uncertain exactly what type of land or place they were heading towards.

They dropped the anchor and left their boat close to the beach, and George and Joe hopped out and swam the little distance to shore. Joe shared his bottle of booze, but it wasn't long before he passed out, and George was left to his own devices; he left his shipmate drunk on the beach and went into the bush behind him to pee and explore the cluster of trees and marshy grounds.

Upon entering the woods, George swore he saw fire. He followed its glow, and, lo and behold, a group of eight women, stark naked, dancing and chanting with painted faces and great heaps of pubic hair adorning their crotches, beautiful and vivacious bodies gyrating about. George, a little drunk, walked right up to them, ready to introduce himself, and someone screamed, and George tried to show that he was a friend, but before he could, something smacked him on the back of the head, and the whole world went black, and George went limp, and blood started leaking from his wound, and he lay still, spread out near the glow of the fire.

Chapter 27

When he woke up, George saw, or rather heard, the screech of monkeys, and he opened his eyes, heavy and ornery lids, and saw stacks of cages filled with primates and lizards, four-foot by four-foot sturdy metallic things. He tried to lift his head, but the pain was excruciating. A lady approached him; it was still dark. Morning? He asked her where he was, and she told him to lie still and be quiet. She rubbed salve on his head, and her bare breasts hung inches away from his nose. He repeated his question, and she told him that he'd surprised them, out there in the dark, hence the crack on the head, but that they'd found Joe, who told them who he was. *Was Joe a friend of the nudists?* He mumbled the words "Joe" and "friend," and she said, yes, Joe was a friend—he brings supplies and alcohol, and sometimes he even dances with them when the whim takes hold. George tried to mumble some more questions, continue the conversation, but his headache was killing him; it reminded him of when he was a young man with a penchant for booze, but not so young that drink—in this case, spirits—

did not have dire or costly effects on his health and on his next day's well-being and performance. After such nights, he'd wake up, usually with a raging hard-on, and have sex with the woman lying next to him, and if no woman were present, he'd masturbate, still drunk, and believe himself none the worse for wear. But soon the reality of his predicament would surface, and he'd run to the toilet and puke with such force that he'd blow a bunch of blood vessels in his face, giving him a horrible complexion for days, and he'd spend the rest of the morning and afternoon (and sometimes the evening) hunched over, rocking, praying desperately for the passage of time so he could recoup and have some semblance of his former health and life back. These were the only times he ever asked God for anything: please, God, grant me my health back, perish this sickness, yada yada yada.

When he woke up for the second time, he felt much better, still achy and dizzy, but the salve or time or the bandage around his head was helping. He sat on a log and saw Joe talking to one of the women. Where were all the men? thought George. Joe came over and patted him softly on the back and asked how he was.

"Not bad, took a good crack on the head, though."

"Yes, I heard. Best not to disturb the coven when they're in their groove."

Coven?

"So, where are we?" asked George.

"Oh, just some island not too far off the mainland. These ladies live here, have been for quite some time. I met them, not unlike how I met you. They approached me back at the pier, and we struck up a deal. I'm their unofficial delivery man." He chuckled at this. Old dirty Joe with all his side hustles and schemes; never one to shy away from some unorthodox venture, particularly if good money were to be gained and if the workload were minimal.

That night, George partook in one of their lū'aus or séances or soirées of sorcery, dancing around the fire, painted up, his dong flinging about as bouncing tits and hairy groins and Old Joe's saggy balls mimicked and mimed seizures and chaotic krumping styles; they summoned the respiratory and bronchial flu of ages past and asserted this witchery with their prancing vocal cords, lowering their voices by several octaves; they summoned the binding will of all ancient and highbrow magic, gathering it up in their tippy-toes while paying homage to the forest's cockeyed spirits; they sang and moved and grew together in song—a developing chorus.

George was not particularly into their quirky musicianship or their baritone cries, but he felt the need to partake anyway, and although naked and without pockets, he found an old Walkman near one of the tents that he was able to carry along in his hand. He put on the headphones and was overjoyed to find a Lou Reed cassette inside; he blared "Walk on the Wild Side" and "Satellite of Love," catchy riffs sounding off against his eardrums. He moved maniacally with the rest of them; he gripped the Walkman firmly in his left hand; his right arm jabbed out at the billions of stars unseen above; he carelessly partook in their festival of worship and danced alongside the nudists to an altogether different tune; he energized the scene, provided an outsider's allure with a glamorous touch, and he found himself content at having been stripped of all his inhibitions, just another stark raving lunatic stumbling along next to the fire.

He sat on a log and rested a bit, and Joe came over and took a seat next to him. George asked him what he was doing before, back on the boat, below decks. What was he watching on his little TV set? A movie about Mozart, replied Joe, and some other composer. George mentioned that the other composer was a man named Salieri; he, too, had seen the film and enjoyed it very much.

"Yes, yes, it's a fine movie."

Old Joe mused on the works of Mozart, never highlighting any particular piece and keeping all his praise vague and wishy-washy. George guessed he wasn't too versed in classical music or Mozart but probably had a strong emotional connection to the film, one that wasn't necessarily tied to any historical facts or music per se, but maybe to ideas and genius and madness and mediocrity. Joe told George that he thought Salieri's (he kept saying Salo-harry) main defect wasn't mediocrity (even though he was, for all intents and purposes, a true-blue nonentity) but blindness; how could he not be content as a rich and influential man at that time in that epoch in Vienna? He had the exact post he wanted—so what if a little snot-nosed kid was better? What did that have to do with anything? Eat, drink, fuck, and die: why did he need anything more—why complicate this mess? Why did he need or long for immortality or, less romantically put, longevity (as everything dies including the greatest works of art) when he could just enjoy the immediate luxuries all around him? Why so much vainglory? Embrace the hedonist within, said Joe.

George didn't know how to answer; he supposed some men were blind, just as Joe said, to the gifts and luck they possessed, and then he readjusted his previous claim and said that all men were blind—even Mozart and himself and Joe and probably the witches, too. Joe laughed at this and stood up and apologized for yelling at him before on the boat. He told him he'd been drinking most of the morning and was tightly wound because of the booze and the movie and the fresh air and the stranger (George) he had on board, and when he got overwhelmed, he got angry, like a stupid bull in a plaza (did he mean bullring?), or a child who'd been out playing in the sun for far too long with far too little to eat.

Late into the night, as the festivities were dying down, George decided to lie down next to a log and try and get some shut-eye. One of the women, all painted up and naked and dark and beautiful, came up and extended her hand. He took it, and she led him to one of the tents. He expected it to be empty, but two other women were there snoring, and she led him to an empty corner, and she grabbed his penis, and George motioned with a worried look towards the sleeping pair, silently posing the question as to whether or not the women might wake up. The woman—one hand still stroking his junk—shook her head and smiled and pulled him to a corner of the tent, and she kept a firm grip on him even as they got down on the ground; and she led him inside of her, and George and the woman made love, and the snores of the others never ceased, and he pulled out and came on the side of the tent, and then the woman held him close like a child, and he fell asleep nestled against her bosom.

In the morning, he helped the women organize the camp. He realized they never talked much, a silent lot, and in the sunlight, they became something else. Far more ordinary, the theatrics of the night before forgotten, a distant dream, their tasks now focused on the mundane and no longer cloaked in the mystery of the firelight. Joe told him it was time for them to go. Back to the mainland, he said. Joe talked with one of the women who slipped him a piece of paper. George bid the women farewell and kissed the one he'd slept with awkwardly on the cheek; he blushed as he did so. He and Joe boarded the boat, and the journey back took them roughly four hours, neither one spoke much. Joe drank from his bottle of booze and offered some to his shipmate, but George politely refused. Once they arrived back at the pier, George thanked Joe for the adventure and said he was going into town for a while. Joe extended an invitation and said that if he ever needed work, or just wanted to go out to sea or visit the dames, to let him know.

"Farewell, Joe."

"Farewell, George."

George walked in the direction of the nearest town by the side of the road. An old pickup truck stopped, and a man and his dog gave him a lift and dropped him off near Main Street. It had been a long time since George had set foot here, at least ten years, he supposed. He looked at the new storefronts and the people busying themselves about their day, and he saw the church he'd known as a boy, and he thought of his old friend Father Tom. He walked around for an hour as dusk slowly overtook the day, and he sat on a bench in the park and threw away his bandage and closed his eyes, wondering how strange it was to feel simultaneously trapped and free.

Chapter 28

George decided to go visit his mom. Was she still at their old house? Probably, and he headed in that direction, catching the time on the big clock in the main square: 8:30 p.m. The clock hung at the center of a large stone building with four pillars stationed along its front entranceway. It had once been the town's courthouse but now served as an information center as well as the town hall—jazzed up with enough emanations from the old-timey days to warrant its central position as the structural mascot and the town's most iconic marker. Folks and families used its picnic tables daily, and small fairs positioned themselves on the front lawn. Many happy memories from George's early days—i.e., his four- to eight-year-old period—were housed and played out along that cluster of well-groomed grass.

He walked towards his old home.

He knocked on the door, and a lady answered. She was not his mother. He asked if she knew a "Mrs. Dilgunk" or the previous owner or residents of the household. She said that she did not know anyone by that name and that the previous owners were Mr. and Mrs. Cockdoe. George was confused— certainly, this was the house; it was so familiar, just as he'd left it, but all the actors had been replaced. How strange. A change of cast in the original setting; he was sent down a spiraling visual preamble towards distant memories, "the past," or a weird trek trying to justify the here and the now with what was and could never be again. He apologized and stumbled back towards the road. Had time eroded everything?

He walked aimlessly; he needed to repurpose himself; he needed to have a destination, an easily accomplishable goal with little to no room for complications. He needed a place to stay, a place to sleep. He went to the cliffs.

They remained largely the same; at this hour, a destitute spot, the grass brown, or at least the patches he could see, illuminated by a distant flickering streetlight. He went to its edge, dangled his feet over the precipice, and lay down facing the sky. He listened to the wind, and he fell asleep without trying to.

When he woke up, the day was breaking. He hadn't changed his position; his first visuals were those of a grey sky. He got up, wet from the dew. He opened his wallet and fished out two twenty-dollar bills. He grabbed a coffee and a donut and went back to Main Street. He didn't know which day it was, but the bank was open, and he went inside. The teller was a kind young woman; he told her his name and gave her a piece of ID, and she pulled up his information on the computer. She handed him his statement and gave him a new debit card. Within ten minutes and his goal accomplished, he was off to the hunting and camping store; he purchased a tent and some camping supplies, and then he went and rented a campsite and paid for a week's stay. He set up his tent and got groceries and made a fire and sat around smoking a cigarette he'd bummed off a neighboring camper, a woman named Nancy who was vacationing with her boyfriend, Todd.

George had forgotten all about money. Years had passed, and, little by little, royalties had accrued from his books. Monthly or quarterly payments deposited into an account that he'd barely touched. He grabbed a stick from the outlying bush and carved it to a point and stuck a wiener on the end. He'd forgotten buns and was forced to eat his hotdog as is. How many books had he written? Three, five, ten, twenty? The charred hotdog was incredibly appetizing, and George ate four more and made instant coffee, and he sat alone gazing into the flames. This wasn't a bad existence, he thought, not tonight anyway; and then a wolf or coyote or a drunken buffoon howled in the night, and he heard his neighbor Nancy quiz her boyfriend as to its source, and he said that it was a giant beast, slender and tall, that stalked the woods at night and ate its occupants. There was giggling and then a pleading tone and then silence, and George put another hotdog on his stick and shoved it into the fire.

That night he dreamt that he and Nancy and Todd were sitting around his campfire in the bush, roasting meat on sticks. George was carving it from his very own thigh, taking out long, thin chunks with a knife that they then folded and impaled with their wooden skewers. Nancy said it was delicious and asked for more. He carved her another strip, and Todd asked how he created such flavorful meats. George said the key was to not try *too* hard but to also try just hard enough—to find the perfect balance of hardness. And then he asked Todd if he wanted more, and Todd nodded his smiling head. After each chunk cut, George would grab a paintbrush and dip it into a bucket of silver paint and coat his wound with thick brushstrokes—marinating it with metallic opulence.

When he got up, George unrolled himself from his sleeping bag and went to work building a fire and making some coffee. He saw that Nancy was up, and he invited her over. She accepted and came by wrapped in a blanket, her hair held back in a ponytail. She told George they were from out of town, traveling along on a camping trip. She spoke of Todd, the outdoorsman (he'd planned the itinerary), and she told George that she didn't really care much for this style of holiday, but that she liked spending time with him, and since he (Todd) did most of the work, she had fun. George sat quietly, listening. He made the odd comment; he smoked another of her cigarettes, and then she left when she heard stirrings coming from her tent. "Off to wake the beast," she said.

That day, George walked around the woods; for some reason, he felt like avoiding town today. He ambled through the tall pines and firs and spruces and was on the lookout for animals and intriguing sights. He mused on death and the passage of time and on beautiful neighbors and morning coffee. He felt like getting a book and inquired at the campground's front office if there was anything to read. A young girl, probably in her late teens, offered to lend him one of hers. It was a novel for teenagers about love and jealousy, and she said there was a murder plot woven throughout with an okay twist near the end. He thanked her and took the book. He tried to read it while sitting at one of the picnic tables stationed randomly around the outskirts of the campground. After a chapter or two, he grew bored and gave up, and then he heard whistling and two men approached: one with short hair (the whistler) and the other carrying a rifle.

They introduced themselves as Floyd (whistler) and Buddy (gun), two wayward thugs (they humorously said this as if the term meant the opposite of what it implied) hunting bounties in this here vast land. George invited them to sit with him, and they got along famously. They reminded him of Butch Cassidy and the Sundance Kid, or maybe more of Paul Newman and Robert Redford, or maybe just of likable criminals. They had a banter and style akin to the joker and the thief; they seemed to feign hostility towards each other, but George could intuit a genuine affection shared between the pair. George asked them what kind of bounty they were looking for, and Floyd said, "Booty?" and Buddy laughed, and he said they were on the hunt for the great American booty.

"She was said to move briskly around these here parts," he joked. "Tight denim shorts snug against a bleached asshole." George laughed, and they asked him about the book he was reading, and he told them a storyline that had nothing to do with the actual plot of the book. He made up a story about hunters and a town and a beautiful girl and an evil boyfriend and a mysterious stranger and a wild beast: he gave it an apocalyptic end. Buddy seemed intrigued, but Floyd's mind was elsewhere. They asked him where he was staying, and he said at the nearest campground. They told him they'd pay him another visit if time permitted, and he said he'd be there for another five days or so; he gave them his campsite number (B56) and bid them farewell.

That night, alone at the fire, George opened the book again and gave it another go. This time, he fell in love with the novel. It was about a girl named Jordeena. She was sixteen, a typical kid from the sounds of it, and she had a crush on a boy named Luke, and Luke seemed to like her (or so it was hinted at because they'd barely spoken at this point in the book; the whole thing was inferred in looks and glances and descriptions and such), but then some masked killer started going around at night and cutting the throats and chopping the heads off citizens and residents of this small, quaint American town (mostly teenagers and mostly women), and Jordeena started to receive threatening phone calls, and Luke, whose girlfriend was one of the first victims of this evil psychopath, started talking to Jordeena and wanted to help because she was supposedly next on the killer's kill list, and Jordeena and Luke strike up a friendship and devise a plan to catch the killer, and while they're waiting to apprehend and ensnare the killer, the two of them kiss and reveal their feelings for one another and fondle each other and then have sex in a closet, and the killer sneaks by and kills Jordeena's neighbor, an innocent old lady who just happened to be at the wrong place at the wrong time (checking in on a suspicious noise she heard coming from the Gershwins' or Jordeena's house), and because Jordeena and Luke were in the throes of love and passion and were having sex and not paying the slightest bit of attention, they feel guilty when they find the neighbor's headless corpse, and Jordeena pushes Luke away, and Luke goes after her, and in her emotional breakdown, she runs into the woods, and then she sees the killer—he's followed her, or she's accidentally run after him—and he's dressed from head to toe in black with a ski mask or balaclava covering his face, and he's carrying a hatchet, and Jordeena makes a sound, and the killer sees her and walks deliberately in her direction, scraping his axe against the bark of the trees as he approaches...

Chapter 29

The next morning started a lot like the previous morning: coffee and a friendly chitchat with Nancy. The day was going to be beautiful; somehow, it was written in the air. It was a special day, carried out to a sacrificial hymn, but one that'd already been paid for, waiting in constant anticipation for the prize that had taken so long to arrive. A pristine day, one to codify the loop and vanquish the final foe—*oops*... never mind, wrong story.

When he woke up, it was raining; a hole in his tent bled debris water onto his pillow and face. He squeezed his striped pillow and tried to fix the hole but only made it worse. He put on his hat and boots and stood outside in the rain.

A man, mid-forties, tighty-whities—he sees her smokes lying alone on the table, dry beneath the tarp. He sneaks into his neighbor's campsite and steals three of Nancy's cigarettes; George retreats quickly and quietly zips himself inside his tent and blows smoke through the hole in the roof, his makeshift chimney. He smokes all three in a row. It's too wet to make a fire; he gets into his sopping clothes and walks towards town. His shoes are soaked and squish with each step. He sees a diner and enters; the hostess invites him in, calling him darling—she even fetches him a towel from the back, and he dries himself off, steps out of his shoes as he sits at the booth, and orders three eggs, hash browns, sausages, bacon, toast, a side of fruit, orange juice, and coffee. He smothers his meal with hot sauce and syrup and eats it like a man on a mission and is warmed and cheered on by the fuel of this greasy and scrumptious spread.

He pays and leaves, and the sun is starting to peek out. The rain has stopped, and the other citizens seem to have woken up, and they walk out and organize themselves along the walkways and paths of the city. George sits on a bench near the town hall and notices a woman in her early thirties (or late twenties) that looks strikingly familiar. He goes up to her and apologizes for disturbing her and asks if she knows the Dilgunks, and she smiles and says that the name is familiar—wasn't one of them a writer?

"Something like that," says George.

George introduces himself, and the woman says that she's read one of his books but can't remember the title. George says he can barely tell his novels apart on his best days, and she laughs, but George wasn't joking. She introduces herself as Suzy Jenkins, and George remembers... the girl that Father Tom was fond of—smart and cunning and preternaturally psychotic. George remembers her as the little girl in the front pew he'd sometimes see at church services or by chance around town. He asks her how she is and what she's doing now. She says she runs the local movie theater over on Park Avenue. George shows adulation and tells her about the time he'd gone and seen an Italian horror movie there with bright and exuberant colors, turquoise with pinks and reds and mauves with lots and lots of blood, and he tells her about one scene where a man's intestines were torn out, "—like sausage links coming out by the bucketload." Suzie says it was probably *Midnight Madness* by Antonio Del Giorgio or *Red Hatchet* by Gregory Bava. George isn't sure, and he asks her what's playing today, and she tells him that it's an underground movie from the 1970s (very violent, she says, with one scene where a pipe is pushed through a guy's skull, and the camera just lingers on his face which is twitching and oozing blood and brains and goo, and it seems excessive, but it just holds there for an eternity or millennia, and somehow, back then, they thought it was art, and because of the way it's shot and sculpted in time, it kind of is).

"It starts at 3 p.m. if you'd like to come," she says, and George agrees, and Suzy says to meet her at the theater entrance around 2:45 p.m., and she'll escort him in free of charge—even give him a tour if he'd like. George and Suzy shake hands, and George goes to the corner store and buys a pack of cigarettes and a turquoise lighter.

***

The movie was about a detective and his partner as they chased a notorious killer around the city whose M.O. was running over select pedestrians in a black and orange souped-up muscle car. He'd stalk them in his vehicle, with most of these scenes filmed as if the car were an animal or predator or monster; each kill was decorated and photographed in a flashy and slo-mo style, presented and framed in an oblique or angular way. In all honesty, George didn't care for the movie much and found the subplot with the detective and the gas station attendant much more interesting. There were scenes between the pair that were filled with pathos; the attendant and the detective mostly talking about mundane things—cars and women and weather and life and manliness—in mostly short and pithy declarative sentences or brief and curt aphorisms; and they were a pleasure to watch, like two weary bulls or travelers or soldiers who understood, just by looking at each other, that the other had suffered or seen some shit or tiptoed onto the alabaster floor of craziness. These parts he liked, but the greater whole was a disappointment, and the killer was an embarrassment, and his motives were boring, and the overall rhythms (including the visuals) were repetitive—not to mention the one-dimensional and slovenly constructed arc that governed the narrative, the so-called engine, the one that supposedly drove the show. He didn't say any of this to Suzy, though. She said she'd enjoyed it, but that it wasn't one of her favorites of the genre. And when George asked her which genre that was, she said it was the killer car genre, which is a subgenre of a subgenre within the horror genre.

"So long, Suzy, and thanks for everything."

As George was about to leave, Suzy yelled out after him and told him to wait. She almost forgot that she'd promised him a tour. Was he still interested? George accepted, and she said, "Good," and she grabbed his arm and escorted him up the steps from the main lobby towards a wooden door that led to the upstairs balconies ("Only open for special screenings and VIP events," she said.).

She showed him the projection room, and he met the projectionist, a cheerful fellow named Phil, and when George shook his hand, he was lost in its immensity. Phil smiled and flashed George his big white teeth, telling him to come back anytime. George paused and asked him what his favorite movies were; Phil said, "*Jaws*. That was a good one, and maybe... *The Wizard of Oz.*"

***

Suzy shows George behind the screen, and George remembers a junior high play he was cast in decades ago. The behind-the-scenes setup reflects that of his play and gives the space a nostalgic overtone even though he's never been in this specific place before. She tells George that she likes coming back here while the movie is playing and watching its inverse image. She tells him that she sits in a chair and chain-smokes cigarettes and looks at the gargantuan image only ten or twelve feet away. She finds it relaxing and has spent some of her happiest moments sitting alone right here on this empty stage.

"Isn't that sad?" she says.

George says no and tells her that it sounds fantastic.

"I think I better get going, but thanks for everything," says George. "Can I come visit you again?"

"Please do."

And she walks him out, and George returns to the street and buys some hamburgers and eats them as he walks back to his campsite.

That night, he sat alone by his campfire. Nancy and Todd were confined to their tent, and George only heard faint whispers coming from their direction. His mind was focused elsewhere, on Suzy and the influx of memories and thoughts of his childhood attacking him all at once. He smoked and looked carelessly up at the sky. He heard the howl of some creature, but it didn't register dread or fear; it had become part of the backdrop to his nightly scene, something expected, even if that thing were foreboding and ominous and hinting at death. Then he heard footsteps, or the cracking of branches and twigs beneath footsteps, and he turned into the darkness and saw two figures emerge from the nothingness: Buddy and Floyd.

"What are you fellas doing at this hour?"

"Hunting," said Buddy. "Hear that godawful howling? We're searching for that little fucker, gonna put it out of its misery. Just one rifle shot and... Bam! Down she goes."

"What is it?" asked George.

"Hell if we know," said Floyd. "But we figure it's worth pursuing. Anything that makes that type of racket this late deserves to be hunted, drawn, and quartered. And well... we like being out in *these* woods at night."

"—so long as we have our rifle," added Buddy. "These here woods got some strange things lurking within 'em. Believe you me."

They sat for a while with George, and they offered him some of their booze. George, in return, offered them his cigarettes. Their talk centered on the woods and then moved off to women once Buddy and Floyd got a peek at Nancy exiting her tent.

"Got yourself quite a neighbor there," said Buddy.

"Yes, sir. Quite a neighbor indeed," said Floyd.

Floyd told a story about a girl he'd once tried to pick up at a campsite. The tale was long and had an abundance of plot holes, but in the end—contrary to what George was expecting—Floyd didn't get the girl, and he ended up falling down a bank and into a river where he accidentally shit himself due to being struck in the guts in just the right way by a rock or a root so that he evacuated his bowels right then and there; and as if on cue, they all laughed, and George couldn't stop; he howled. And it must have sounded like a crazed animal having a terrible fit to those who could not see the three men doubled over in the firelight, dying in a frenzy of laughter.

Chapter 30

In the morning, George sat at his picnic table smoking and eating crackers. He saw a dice embedded in the dirt near the leg of the table and dug it out. He told himself that if he rolled a three or less, then he'd go for a walk by the cliffs; if he rolled a four or more, he'd venture into town and see Suzy. He shook the die and rolled a two. So it goes, and he went to the bathroom and showered in his flip-flops and got dressed and brushed his teeth. He saw Todd rummaging about the campsite, and he offered a nod, and then he was off—off to the cliffs, carrying with him his stick, fashioned with a sharp point, the roaster of wieners, and he plunged it into the earth like a great staff or a good walking aid.

The day was grey, and when he got to the cliffs, he spotted two pairs of couples: one old and one young (and attractive). He walked by the old couple and nodded to them, they smiled, but when he got a few paces away, he heard them call him a vagrant and a busybody. He imagined turning around and piercing them each in the heart with his stick; but instead, he let out a fart and hoped it'd catch a ride along the proper air current and sting those stodgy old folks' nostrils. Both denouements seemed farfetched, and he retaliated against reality by kicking a stone over the edge of the crag. He watched it fall and tumble along the rocky terrain; he heard it hit the water.

He dangled his feet over the edge and pulled out a notepad and a pen. He heard a shuffling behind him, and he turned to watch the old couple depart; he could hear them moaning about something—probably him—and then he heard the old woman yell, "And why don't you just jump? Go ahead, you dang fool!"

"Shut up, you old bag," whispered George, but somehow he was certain she had heard him.

After that, things quieted down, the young couple lay still, and George looked out at the horizon. Then a sudden gust of wind tore the notepad from his hand, and he saw it somersault and land in a nook near the cliff's winding path. George steadied himself and began his descent, taking it slow along the steep downward trail. He crept forward, carefully, one hand on the rock face; he got to the notepad and pocketed it; he was midway down and decided to continue on. "Might as well." He remembered the caves and entered the first of the pair and examined the graffiti he'd expected to find there. He entered deeper into the lair and was surprised to find that it kept going, far more profound than he'd remembered. He heard water dripping and was forced to rely on his phone for light, and then he saw it. A head? It looked like that of an elk or deer but bizarrely configured with its mouth jutting out— like the poor creature had some terrible underbite—and George got close to it and inspected it and noticed that its teeth were actually keys, marked with letters. A writing apparatus?

"Exterminate all..." What was that thought?

But it was gone, and he was left alone with an empty brain and a horned and uniquely serviceable writing machine (or so he assumed based on its make and model and presumable function), and he got on his knees and wrote "hello" on the keys, and the type hammers swung the corresponding letters up to a point near the horns' upper protuberances, and, lo and behold, George had found his new instrument. He grabbed the machine and carefully scaled the rock; he tucked it beneath his arm. When he got to the top of the cliff, he noticed the old woman far off in the distance; she gave him a thumbs-up, but the old man was nowhere to be found.

Chapter 31

When he got back to the campsite, he set his new typewriter on the picnic table. "Look at this beaut." He pulled out a cigarette and admired the craftsmanship of the device. The girl stationed at the campground's main base of operations gave him ten pieces of paper free of charge, and George slotted one in the mouth of the machine. Dusk had already set in, and Nancy and Todd came by to see what he'd unearthed, but George was in the zone, too busy tap-tapping away to the melody in his head—a cosmic midwife birthing an unknown saga.

"What are you writing?" asked Todd.

"Oh... uh... writing"—yes, yes... I am writing, thought George—"a novel. A-a novel—"

About what? Or better yet, for whom?

"—for demons... and, uh... darlings," he mumbled.

"Well, it looks like you'll need some more paper, then. Huh, hotshot?" observed Todd, and George concurred (only half-listening to the man's muttering). More fodder was needed for the fire; this ancient and foul beast demanded it.

Nancy and Todd stood beside him, keeping an eye on his progress. Transfixed by his methodology and the glint in his eye, insinuating the mania within. He needed fuel, and he saw a lone packet of ketchup on the far corner of the table—left over from some unknown lunch—and he lunged and grabbed it and squeezed it into his mouth. There was no time to stop; there was no time for anything. Continue this *wretched* dance forward, he thought; continue it right on through to oblivion. But then he got a cramp ("Goddamnit!"), and the machine jammed ("Fucking bastard!"), and his cravings inundated him all at once. Break time. And the greedy animal lit two cigarettes and undid his fly and spread himself out in his lawn chair, completely unaware of the gawking eyes of his forgotten guests. He noticed a ketchup stain on his shirt and said: "Fuck it."

That night as he rolled around in his sleeping bag—duct tape lining his shoddy tent—he heard noises outside, someone or something rummaging about before moving on, and then the familiar howl, this time, not too far off. He turned over in his tent and faced his new writing machine; it was an odd device, to be sure, but it seemed to function gracefully under the guidance of his tactful motions. The horned machine with its loud and unmistakable carriage return and bulky design, perfect for his forays into the experimental interzones he was picking up, hovering in the air, floating like radio waves—dispersed in the ether, and then concentrated and re-envisioned and remixed in modules and subsets, and then in words and letters. What a triumph of the world and all its folly, thought George.

He got out of his tent, and it appeared to be the blackest

part of the night; he could see next to nothing and hadn't slept much. He saw the tip of a glowing ember and whispered a "hey" into the night. The illuminated spot (and by spot, we mean speck) maneuvered in his direction, and Nancy appeared, or her voice gave her away, as she was still cloaked in blackness or caked in midnight.

"What are you doing up?" she asked.

"Can't sleep."

"Me neither."

George pulled a cigarette from his pocket, and his eyes got used to the darkness, and an outline started to form, the contours of Nancy, a slightly distinguishable silhouette. She came over and leaned against the picnic table.

"What were you writing about today?" she asked.

"Not sure yet. A story of sorts, I guess."

George took a long drag of his cigarette and noticed that Nancy wasn't wearing any pants. Even in all the darkness, her beauty was apparent, or insinuated, which made it exponentially more alluring. Supple and youthful skin, a hanging T-shirt, hard nipples. Was he imagining this? Or was it a creation of two separate spheres? Reality and unreality converging, the darkness acting as a melting pot brewing a concoction of wishful thinking and romanticism and erotica (with a spooky forest setting). He could feel the beginnings of an erection but paid it no mind; it would be difficult to spot in the darkness, and if she did, well... whatever.

He asked her about her life. She was in her twenties, studying to become a nurse. Todd was an engineer. They were planning on getting married, but she didn't know when. She wanted kids but couldn't provide any definite timeline. George asked her if she was in love, and she said that she was. She was madly in love. She and Todd had met at a bar, and she thought he was cute, and when they first made love, he would constantly stop midway to pepper her with little kisses, and then he would continue, hard and rough, and then he would slow it down and restart and perform this ritual over and over again. She found this to be strange, and she wondered if it was his technique or style or way of cultivating endurance. But then she got to know him and realized it was just the way he was. An extremist of sorts working at the ends of the spectrum: volatile then kind, aggressive then sweet, bold then tepid. She found this, at first, to be revolting—even goading on a gagging fit once—and because of it, she'd planned to distance herself from him, break up or push him away, become a ghost in his life, but then she started (slowly at first) to think about him at unusual hours, or when she was doing small menial tasks, like cooking or studying or going to the bathroom. And then, little by little, he took over her world. It was odd—she'd always thought of herself as a rational person—but her infatuation with Todd, beginning with revulsion and ending (or reevaluated) at this moment (or, more precisely, a month or so before their camping trip) as love, gave her second thoughts and cause to doubt and question her assurance and hardheadedness and its manners and its potions—and she thought of her manicured and organized and color-coded map (her way of seeing the world), with all its symbols and demarcations and lines, and were they, in fact, all wrong. Was her map hogwash or useless or just too darn small? Was it inaccurate and naïve to the discrepancies of the world? And George waited in silence until she had finished, and then he said, "Love is an ethereal thing—beautiful and enigmatic, but I sometimes think it's got another face, a secret face, a devil face, staring right back atcha, too. It's like a poison or a virus or a mood or a

storm that overtakes everything and, all of a sudden, upends
the world, and then, as swiftly as it arrives, it's gone. Clear
skies, perhaps a tattered shed or a blown-off roof, maybe a
car or two flipped over and destroyed, and that's all the proof
we have. The only proof of it ever existing, a landscape in
ruin—or maybe just in slight disorder, depending on how it
was built up and organized and how much luck the person
had in the first place."

When he'd finished, he took another drag of his cigarette
and felt Nancy's hand press against his side; she leaned
over and kissed him; she placed her hand against his
crotch. He put his hand on her back and slid it down and
squeezed her backside. He wondered if anyone was
watching, but then she slid her tongue into his mouth, and
all thoughts were eradicated.

In the morning, George got dressed and ventured into town
at the crack of dawn. He needed supplies, and he headed to
the grocery store, and whom did he see? Captain Joe, out of
the woodwork to fetch supplies for the ladies of the isle.

"Those *goddamn* women have me runnin' around like a
rooster with its giblets cut out. 'Goddamn, get me this, and
goddamn, get me that, Joe.' For Christ's sake, make me a
list, and don't just be yelling at me every goddamn chance
you get!"

George could see that the old captain was tired. Poor
bugger was at his wits' end. George assured him that
everything would be fine. "Just do your best, Captain; all
will be well in the end."

Old Joe nodded and left, and George came across another
blast from the past: Tim's mom. She was dressed in a colorful
sweater, pushing a cart chock-full of goods. George went up

to her and introduced himself. At first, she was apprehensive, but then she recognized her son's old friend, and a smile crept across her face.

"George!" she exclaimed. "How wonderful to see you. How are you? How's everything going? How you've changed!"

***

After getting his provisions, George heads back to the campsite; he stops by the main office and pays for another week. He's enjoying his stay. As he's walking back along the winding road, smiling at the families and fellow campers, Nancy and Todd drive by. They stop and unroll the window and tell him they're off, that it was nice getting to know him. They wish him luck, and he does the same. He looks at Nancy, and their eyes linger, and she says goodbye, and she winks at him, or twitches, and then the window starts to go up.

"Goodbye, George."

They drive off.

"So long, neighbors."

That night, George attacks the page. It's strange not having anyone next to him, no movement in his peripheral view, but his focus is on the task at hand. An empty campsite means nothing to him. He clacks away at the keys. Words appear on the page, and a story is taking shape. What is a story? A transgression against reality, or the norm, or against the modern map; a battle raging on, injecting mystery and magic at the price of sowing chaos—or, if not chaos, uncertainty and absurdity. In other words, replacing reality with another reality, but a reality that's molded and birthed in a cave or deep in a stinking lair, in the primeval goo of the human psyche. Them's where the real stories are, thinks George, cave stories, and George tries to remember them. For all creation is nothing other than an act of remembering. One has only to remember the original nightmare, and then everything falls perfectly into place.

He can't sleep. He sits alone after having discharged a good five pages. He hears the howl in the darkness, and right on cue, he howls back. He laughs, and he thinks he hears laughter out in the darkness, too. He goes over and sits at Nancy and Todd's picnic table. He puts his nose close and smells it. It smells of wood and paint, not the faintest smell of its former guests. He returns to his tent and sees a piece of paper folded up in the corner.

"Keep writing, you miserable fool. Miss you already. Much love, Bugbear."

Chapter 32

I wonder about the levity of all things—about how some things are prone to having considerably more weight than others. Why is this? Who decides on the mass of everything? Who decides on the gravity? An underlying system at play? A system of values transposed over a play of codes? An underlying governing body with an everlasting exposé of rules? Superfluous human design and inference—we give it names and dress it up with consonance. We try to bend it. We attempt to control it. We the lame. We the submissive. We can do beautiful and terrible things when we let it in—let it govern. A coin with two faces: the devil and the darling. The All... The Powerful... The Infinite... The Holy... The Grim... The Paradoxical... The Bugbear.

Now, what the fuck did that mean? George woke up from one hell of a weird dream with some hideous character morphing into being, corrupting and personifying a cute nickname thrown out on a whim a few nights before, landing smack on the ass of the gorgeous, horny twenty-five-year-old

Nancy. No subtext was meant, no pretext for its induction, just a pet name thrown around to jokingly jilt a lover, all the while—its actual goal—attempting to lure her in, win her grace and favor. A teasing remark to get her to suck his dick. Why did his subconscious do this shit? Why did it make a mockery of everything and erode the foundation of his terms? Of his memories? Of his terminology?

That day he decided to visit Suzy at the theater. After performing his usual morning duties and getting himself in respectable order, he left for town. It was still early, so he went to the diner and read the paper and filled up on coffee and bacon and eggs. He watched out the window as a group of youngsters decorated a truck. They hung tinsel around the back window and spray-painted designs on its sides. A girl wrote, "Hail, Chiefs!" and George asked the waitress who the Chiefs were, and she said they were the town's famed hockey team. They were playing tonight in the semifinals against the Sexsmith Blue Devils. "Are you going to go?" inquired the waitress. He hadn't thought about it, perhaps. A cold beer and a rough-and-tough game of hockey sounded like a fine evening. He paid his tab and left.

He thought of Nancy as he strolled about. She was one hell of a beautiful woman. He wondered why she had sacrificed her flesh and candor to a slightly fat and grizzled older man. The mysteries of the feminine mind, thought George. He walked along the sidewalks and lit a cigarette as he stood in front of Father Tom's old church. He thought about the old preacher and decided to go visit his grave.

The cemetery was well kept; the carctakers were out mowing the lawns and trimming the hedges. It took him a while to spot the grave, and when he did, he couldn't think of anything to say. He nodded politely to the plot of grass. The epitaph on Father Tom's gravestone read, "When it all comes to a point." George asked one of the workers if there was a bathroom close by, and the man asked if he needed it for number one or number two; George said he just needed to pee, and the man directed him behind a row of trees to an overgrown and tattered section. "Piss wherever you please," said the caretaker, and he left, and George unzipped near a bush and let 'er buck. When he finished, he pushed some branches aside and saw a headstone hidden underneath. He'd accidentally peed all over it. All that was engraved on the headstone was the word "Brutus." He checked his phone; it was half past noon. He tipped his hat to the workers and went to the theater. More cars bearing the words "Hail, Chiefs!" and "Go, Chiefs!" passed him by.

When he got to the theater, it was locked. The marquee showed that a movie called *I Bringeth the Wind, He Bringeth the Change* started at 3:30 p.m. George turned the corner and headed down the back alley. A crackhead emerged from behind a doorway and startled him.

"By God, friend. You gave me a scare."

The crackhead looked nonplussed and offered George his pipe, snickering slightly, eyes averted, a shifty son of a gun with a grimy grin.

"I better not," said George.

The crackhead kept on, and George fell victim to his persistent peer pressure. He lit the pipe and inhaled and sat down in a euphoric haze among the dustbins and dumpsters and rats. The sky was clear and blue.

"Thank you, friend," he mumbled in some incoherent verse, and the crackhead scurried off, or away—or disappeared entirely (*poof!*)—and George closed his eyes, and he saw the horned machine staring right back at him, great Wagnerian orchestrations accompanying its image. He stared at it, his eyes wide shut. This lasted for God knows how long, but when he opened them again, the sky was the color of television.

What the *hell* had he just smoked? Surely that wasn't just crack. Emanations of some unknown land now permeated his surroundings. He rounded the corner, and a giant centipede bid him hello. He looked left, and all constructions oozed red, organic and pulsating, a jungle of reptiles in heat (or were they bugs?). A vehicle painted shades of green croaked along the main drag and backfired around the bend, an unknown assailant camped out in an adjacent window fired an Uzi and eviscerated the car; a fireball illuminated the scene. The driver's head fell at George's feet, and the centipede turned around and scurried back on its many legs and ripped open the skull and devoured the cerebellum—the sweetbreads of the brain. It peered up at George, dripping red, and said, "*Howdy!*"

"Fuck me," was George's response. "What the Christ is this place?" Had he seen this shit before—a comparable tone or atmosphere? Hell was opening up on his doorstep, or the town's anyway, and here he was at its mercy—at least until the narcotics wore off. He wandered around catching hold of many memorable sights: the pterodactyls swooping in every chance they got. "Goddamn vipers!" He was holding an umbrella and fending them off as best he could. A man wearing a bear suit came up and asked him for a light; George poked him in the eye. "Stay back, you beast!"

Somehow George had ended up being drawn into a great torrent of people, joining their ranks. They arrived, and George took his seat. The drugs were waning. Banners—now legible—bore encouraging words and slogans.

George watches as a man skates across the ice, past the defensemen, and dekes out the goalie to add one to the scoreboard with ease and elegance. George claps and cheers and yells, "Take that, you fools!" He realizes it's the Blue Devils—the town's nemesis—who've just taken the lead. A worm with the head of a man crawls along the rafters, and George excuses himself and goes to the bathroom. He splashes water on his face and notes his grotesque and bulging appearance. The deformities he has tried to hide for so long now reappear. Talk about bad timing, thinks George. He puts his hood up and exits the arena as stealthy as possible; he now has the cover of darkness to accompany him home, and when he gets to his campsite, he zips himself inside his tent, finally able to relax. He grabs his typewriter and writes: No more drugs. He pauses, then continues and adds one more word: today.

When he wakes up, yesterday's events are a blur, but George is able to distance himself, provide some perspective, perhaps even some clarity. What a ride, he thinks. He grabs his phone and takes a picture of himself. How does he look? Awful and normal. No longer an outward monster, thank God. He grabs his typewriter and crumples up the piece of paper left in it from the night before and tosses it into the firepit. He realizes that that was his last piece and makes a mental note to get more ASAP. He gets dressed and wonders about the pterodactyls.

After making some purchases and replenishing his supplies, he returns to his campsite to get to work. Fuck everything: the town, the people, his strolls—all of it. He readies the typewriter and slots in a piece of paper between its horns, and just as he's about to begin, he hears Floyd.

"Howdy, partner."

Goddamnit!

George and Floyd and Buddy sit and smoke and drink most of the afternoon. George can feel the mounting anxiety caused by not being able to write or work. But polite social conduct trumps this sentiment (for now, anyway), and he sits with the duo shooting the shit. Booze seems to help, and in no time at all, he's having a great time with the lads. Day becomes night, and George tells them about his sexual escapades with Nancy, and the boys laugh, and they tell him that they *too* have been down that road. They met her in the woods one night, and she approached Floyd, and one thing led to another, and she unzipped him and started jerking him off; they each had a go with her—twice with Buddy, in fact. George is somehow hurt by this reveal, and his mood is darkened. (Perhaps they're lying, but George doesn't think so.) He wants the two lads to go, and he excuses himself and says he needs to get to bed. Buddy and Floyd linger, and he hears them drunk and loud late into the night. When he wakes up, Floyd is passed out on the picnic table, and Buddy is curled up on the ground using his coat as a pillow; the rifle still slung over his shoulder. George grabs his typewriter and ventures for a walk. At the cliffs, he loads a piece of paper in. He starts writing. He feels better almost immediately.

When he gets back to his campsite, Floyd and Buddy are gone. He puts the typewriter in his tent along with the pages he's written and heads into town. He sees Suzy, and she waves him over.

"Hey, George. How are you? How you been?"

George is reticent and doesn't feel like conversing much. His replies are brief but polite. Suzy goads him on, and her friendliness brings him out of his gloom. She invites him to the theater the next day; she tells him she'll treat him to a movie. He accepts, and by the time their conversation is over, George is feeling good, content, back to his pre-crack, carefree ways. Suzy, the once-youthful psychopath, walks away and rounds the corner. A kid tosses a firecracker, and an air conditioner falls from a windowsill making a great commotion; a bird swoops down and nearly hits a businessman in the face. George looks left, and a little old lady says, "Hey!"

Chapter 33

George woke up to his phone ringing. *Who is this*? His sister, Trisha, calling from the big city. "How are you?"

"I'm okay... listen... I went out to Mom's grave last night and someone—some *fuck*—has spray-painted all over the goddamn thing. What the fuck..."

She continued on in this vein, and George told her to calm down. He, too, was trying to stay calm. He'd somehow forgotten all about it. How had he forgotten? When had this happened? Then he remembered, eight or so years back, a car crash visiting Trisha, just outside the city center, smashing into a garbage truck. Tears welled up in his eyes as he tried to pacify his sibling.

He needed coffee and six successive cigarettes. Afterwards, he could think about the day to come, plan it out. He'd promised Suzy a movie, that much he remembered. Was there something else? What else was he forgetting? Was it all his fault? How had such an oversight occurred? How had he buried such a monumental event? Things were not adding up. But were they ever supposed to?

He was beginning to understand that his mind wasn't exactly a reliable source of information. Perhaps this worked to his advantage occasionally (creatively), but today—upon hearing (or relearning) about his mom—he cursed its very nature. Unable to find a soothing narrative to grapple with the pain of his reality, had his mind tricked him, crafted an error of omission? Or was he simply born with a broken brain, one that skipped over things at random, the large and the small? Were whole years and months wiped out, replaced, or simply left as gaping holes?

It would be difficult to tell. No point in getting too upset. Whatever he knew, he knew—and anything else that wanted to float up to his conscious level was welcome to do so; the errors and omissions he would just have to live with. He was a man who preferred to remember things his own way—or he supposed he would have to adapt to that maxim. To hell with reality! Let the accountants and historians fritter away in its meager shadow. I will live in a hell of my own making, thought George. And then he heard the monster's howl coming from the woods—but it was only noon; what could this mean? It was a topsy-turvy time in the forest today. Things were all over the place. They were not what they seemed.

He met Floyd and Buddy on the path into town, winding their way through the woods. They stopped and chitchatted briefly. They too had heard the beast and were hot on its trail. George told them that it was strange—this midday howling. They concurred; both men seemed unnerved, and George hastened his exit, and the hunters went on their way.

It was almost 2:30 p.m. when George got to the theater. He asked at the ticket booth whether Suzy was in or not, and the lady picked up the phone, made a call, and within a minute,

George saw Suzy descend the staircase and wave him in. She asked him how he was, and he told her about his mom and her death and his forgetfulness.

Suzy went quiet, confused, paused, then she put her hand on his shoulder and offered her condolences. "I'm so sorry, George."

She led him towards a bench in the main foyer, and the two of them sat. She patted him on the back and asked thoughtful and poignant questions, and he changed the topic and asked her about the movie.

"Oh, it's a gem from the 1980s, a real strange concoction. Have you ever heard of *Captain Sven and the Enigma of the Four Herdsmen*?"

George laughed. No, he had not.

She said, "Here," and she gave him a large popcorn and beverage and ushered him into the theater. She said he'd missed the first ten minutes but not to worry; the plot was secondary in the movie, or nonexistent, really, with the real fruit being reaped from its style and cinematography and over-the-top acting, not to mention the big action-packed payoff at the end. George smiled, and Suzy patted him on the back one last time before leaving him at the mercy of the thirty-foot projection, standing tall, in living color.

***

"*Mother of God*! That was one hell of a movie." George walks out a new man. What has this film told him? What has it whispered into his occipital lobe? He feels refreshed, topped up, overflowing with fuel. Suzy is outside, giving him a big smile.

"What the fuck!?" says George. "What was that?"

"Did you like it?"

"Best goddamn show this side of the Timbuktu."

His excitement has made him mildly incoherent, and judging by his merry state and the looks he garners whilst donning it, he seems to be a disturbing presence all around; his happiness is a revolting sideshow, brought on by his overindulgent manner and the way he walks/jogs along the sidewalks. "Never misjudge the meteoric impact of a good drug or disease or virus on one's soul and psyche," he mutters. He feels rejuvenated and joyous. Time for him to hit the keys, stroke the consonants, pluck the vowels. When he gets back to the campsite, he immediately puts himself to work, smoking like a chimney in his tent, sitting cross-legged, and trying to keep pace with his mind. "Slow down, you bastard!" But it will not; he will have to speed up. "Come on, hands! Get your goddamn shit together." He writes on well into the night, sweating like a mule, depositing a plethora of verbs and adjectives on paper and sending out contradictory vibes into the marshes and forest; he smiles like a dang fool during this ungodly hour, this evil hour, this hour of the wolf.

Chapter 34

George was tired as hell in the morning. He was unable to sleep, and any chance of recouping some form of rest in this unholy predawn was ridiculous. He showered and put on some clean clothes and walked around town as the sun came up; he passed his old house and other nostalgic haunts. He walked by his school and thought of Nikki, his first love. He walked by the creek and remembered the summers long past. He bought a slice of pizza and some potato wedges from a relic of a convenience store and thought of Ricky Allen, his first friend. This town was an echo chamber of past lives and memories, and George found himself in a strange mood as he sat down on a bench to finish off the wedges.

That day, he packed up the campsite and moved into a motel in town. He paid for the month and sat down, first and foremost, to watch some TV; something he hadn't done in a long while. He sat on the edge of the bed; images beat at him in a barrage or whirlwind of climactic gimmickry—a fucking onslaught. He turned the thing off, steadied himself, drank four beers, and lit two cigarettes. Was he ready to face such a beast? He flipped it back on, and the first show he watched was a reality show about love—love in the modern age. A dramatic tantrum, it rekindled his misanthropy. He could not take much more of this. He ordered a movie and abandoned himself to its formulaic rhythms. He took a bath and jerked off.

"What's your book about?" asked Suzy.

"It's still figuring itself out," said George.

He was finishing off the tail end of a middling chapter. Suzy waited in the doorway, supper at the diner awaited them both.

"Hurry up, slowpoke."

It was already dark as they walked across the roadway and through the lit streets. Suzy told him she had taken the liberty of inviting a friend. George made an incomprehensible noise, neither showing dismay nor excitement at this reveal. They took a booth near the window, and Suzy's friend Gary showed up a few minutes later. He and George shook hands.

The conversation was lively, and George took to Gary right away. A friendly fella, animated and jovial, and the trio talked of films and books and the history of the town. They even mentioned Father Tom, and Suzy expressed a deep love for the old preacher. They ordered beers and nachos and hot wings and kept chatting well into the night. Gary excused himself, mentioned that he had an early morning coming up, and Suzy departed not long after. George insisted on paying the bill, and then he wandered around and stumbled into a bar just off Main Street.

The clientele eyed him in a queer way as he came in through the door, and he returned their peculiar looks with one of his own. He took a seat at the bar and ordered a whiskey. A dog walked by, and the man seated next to him asked if hell was real. George said that of course it was—that it could barge in at any moment. That heaven and hell were one and the same, markers read off an internal barometer measuring the agony and longing and fear one felt at any given time. Hell was nothing but that all-consuming pain and need dialed up to the breaking point. He looked over, and the man stared into his eyes, a foggy stare, an intense stare, with no room left over for any kind of listening, one that was all-in with the eyes, visually hyperaware, tuning out the sounds to mine the secrets of this world through the shape of an iris or the dimming of a bulb or the geometry of a billiards game. George returned his attention to the barkeep and asked for another whiskey. "The Cat Came Back" sounded off from the speaker system, and George closed his eyes and listened.

The next day he decided to stay in and write. Just write, no distractions. He pulled the curtains shut, unplugged the TV, turned on the lamp, took a shit, and sat in front of his typewriter, ready to get to work.

An abridged version of the story George was working on:

He would not enter it—He could not. It had gone too far. Its growth had exceeded anything He could have dared imagine. But what had He imagined? His goal had been the antithesis of imagination, but perhaps the counter was, in fact, its purest form. He adopted a "flight forward" philosophy to see what would become of it. He'd made a room; He'd decorated it; He'd made a machine—His crowning jewel. A machine to do away with all the decisions and misdemeanors associated with creation. A machine capable of creating sentient bodies and immobile structures—all from the written word: books, scripts, musical notation, biblical verse, advertising, anything at all. Feed it the nomenclature, and it creates the beast. A thoughtless form of creation, quarantined in a room, with Him—*God*—sitting above, watching the experiment, pointing a large pistol at it, ready to destroy it if need be. But then everything goes haywire; somehow, He'd lost supremacy. The machine had created a new God, and that God had phased Him out. He'd lost control, and the new God was opening the door, allowing the creatures out, to run amok, the experiment no longer under His command or supervision, but rabid and crazed and hungry and experiencing rapid and seismic growth. In a way, He had achieved His aim; He'd fashioned a world that didn't need Him. A world that could go on without Him. It could sow its own destiny, one that seemed more and more inclined towards destruction, but perhaps that would change. Perhaps the machine would create a new entity, one to shift the balance or smooth everything out. God sat down, no longer of any use to anyone; He sat in His vacuous non-space and created another machine, a machine with one drive, that of hunger. Its sole purpose to eat and God set it loose in His world, in His non-world, and it ate up everything, all the negative space or non-space, and then it ate God Himself; and when it was done, it found its way into the other world, the world of space and time, and it started eating everything in sight. Feasting on the people and animals and buildings, and when it had eaten everyone and everything, it ate the creating machine and sucked up the air and all the compounds and chemicals and dark matter until nothing was left in the entire universe, and finally, the machine decided to eat itself, and then it exploded, and everything it'd eaten was regurgitated or vomited out, but in a backwards and strange order, all willy-nilly-like; and God was a tramp, and one machine was a meat grinder, and the other one was a typewriter. And God smiled, impressed how everything had worked out. All's well that ends well, said the beggar.

Having had a successful day of typing, George goes for a walk around 8:30 p.m. He heads back to the woods. He feels out of place, like a guest; before, for some reason, he felt like it was his home, his birthright, so to speak. He understands that that was a silly feeling. He has no claim over any of this, but in his blood, in his loins, there is a connection. And then he hears the beast's howl... and it's close. He turns, and he can see the unmistakable outline of two long and scrawny arms dangling on the forest floor, razor-sharp claws at their base. It isn't moving, and it's camouflaged well in the woods and in the darkness; he has to try hard to keep it in focus. He can hear its rugged and coarse breathing, its sickly panting. He hears another noise, and he turns—just a young couple out for a walk. He shifts his focus back to the monster but can't find it. Is it still there hiding in plain sight? George hears a hooting owl and thinks that he should return to the motel. As he walks, he confuses tree limbs with monster legs. He becomes increasingly unnerved and paranoid (is it stalking him?) until he exits the forest's path and sees the town's lights. He hears the howl one more time, and then a woman screams, but he decides not to go back and investigate. Perhaps tomorrow under the light of a new day, he thinks. He is shaken and cannot sleep; he watches TV until the early hours of the morning. It's the same show again—the one about love. He can't take his eyes off the screen.

The day is bright, and George wakes up refreshed around 11 a.m. ready to seize the day. He goes to the motel's front office and grabs the paper. He wishes the receptionist a good day, and she disregards him with a mumble.

He showers and flicks on the TV and watches the local news. A grisly crime has occurred. A woman and a man were torn to shreds in the woods last night. Their corpses appear to have been ravaged, and the TV anchors seem more than a little disturbed—a wave of ease envelops them as the next story appears on their teleprompter, guiding them out of this hellish narrative towards a story filled with happiness and puppy dogs, involving a local girl and her fundraising efforts for a charity supporting blind canines. "Ah, isn't that sweet," thinks George. He dresses and goes to the diner; he orders steak and eggs, and the waitress asks if he wants it burnt or bloody, and he responds without having to think, as if there was ever a choice.

He spots Phil on a bench, the projectionist from the theater, and gives him a big wave. The day feels like any other until he sees Floyd and Buddy a couple of minutes later. They seem panicked, and he asks them what's going on. The two men are drenched in sweat even though it's actually a cool day with a brisk breeze. They are unable to concentrate and neither is able to articulate much. Why such distress? Why the alarm? Does this have something to do with the murders last night?

"Of course," says Floyd. "That fucking beast..." But then he trails off.

Buddy taps him—Buddy who looks so odd and naked without his gun on his shoulder—and they leave without saying goodbye, without really acknowledging him at all. They disappear around the corner, and George lingers on the curb. He watches the sewer across the way and wonders if crocodiles really do live down there, and if not, where did that myth come from? Crocodiles in the sewers, monsters lurking beneath the crust—George feels good, and he moseys on with his day, a stomach full of meat and a productive recent run of writing. What more could he ask for? He passes by a group of children, maybe four or five years old; they stand near a dumpster squashing bugs—cockroaches from the looks of it—laughing and playing, doing their part to keep the facade up.

Chapter 35

That night, George returned to the bar. Many of the same faces greeted him. This time the peculiarity of the visages didn't seem so stark or off-putting. He sat in the same seat; the inquisitive theologian was nowhere to be found; there, instead, a younger man in a hooded garb graced the chair. He kept his eyes forward and his ball cap tilted downward. George found his neighbor less hospitable than the one from the other night, but no matter, beggars can't be choosers.

It began with a memory, one involving his mother. He remembered it in flash edits: the way she'd make him breakfast when he was a kid—porridge or French toast—and serve him tea in the mornings. She'd even sing him a funny little tune each time she woke him up for school. The drink, along with the memories, caused him to stir in his seat, and he stepped outside to regain his composure and smoke a cigarette.

Upon returning, he tried to chat with the hooded man seated next to him to no avail. The man simply grunted in response to any query, and George let it go. He finished his whiskey, paid his bill, and left. While walking back to the motel, a man yelled, "Hey, faggot." George, intoxicated and cockeyed, ignored him. But the man persisted, and George saw that he wasn't alone. They came closer, spewing more insults and vulgarities. Laughing? Were they jokesters? Bona fide thugs? Last night's murders flashed before George's drunken mind. He heard the sound of an organ, and he reached into his coat and realized he had a hammer in there. "Where the hell did this come from?"

The two men neared, and George tightened his grip.

He didn't even wait for them to begin. Shit-faced George advanced; he swung the hammer, catching one on the jaw. He went down instantly. The other man tried to run, but George chased after him and caught him on the shoulder with a heavy blow; the man lost his balance and fell. George got on top of him and smashed his left hand to smithereens; the man screamed. George stood up, wobbling, and looked at the man's gnarled and broken fingers, one or two of which were severed. And as he passed the other miscreant, he looked down, and he saw the man trying to speak—his jaw dislocated, blood pooling and swelling mounting. George's vision was kaleidoscopic. The man on the ground made nonsense sounds. The world increasingly blurred. George staggered back to the motel, and he fought back the urge to hurl, and he smoked another cigarette, and then he turned out the lights and went to bed.

He didn't hear anything about the incident the next day.

Where had the hammer come from? Did he always carry it with him?

He got food at the diner and wrote until late in the afternoon. He was compiling a book; he saw it now. Interwoven stories and he figured he was about halfway through. God was central to the tale, and the devil had no small role either, peppered with humanoids and secondary characters and mischief-makers and monsters and old gods and cleverly concocted ones. He looked at the hammer sitting next to the horned typewriter; there was still blood on it that he'd never bothered to clean off. He put it away in one of the drawers.

"*Oowoooooo!*"

It came from outside. "That fucking howling again," and he opened the door. A great storm had snuck up unannounced, dark and ominous clouds, gale winds, garbage and debris blew across the roadway; a mother shielded her son as they tried to hurry home. George walked out and saw it clearly for the first time—standing forty feet tall, slender and terrifying; it emerged from the other side; it had no eyes, just four mouths signaling to the east and west and north and south; it feigned a stare, and all four mouths howled in unison from across the street. It walked towards him. George stood still; he could feel the monster's appraising eyeless gaze, contemplating his tiny stature.

"What do you want?" asked George.

"*Oowwwooooooooo!*"

It let out another guttural wail, this one louder than the last; and then he blinked, and he was back in his motel room hunched over, drool seeping down his cheek. He lifted his head and saw a woman in a bikini on the tube. He turned off the TV.

When had he fallen asleep?

Later that night, he paid for a hooker.

Chapter 36

The prostitute was a girl in her mid-twenties. George had never seen her before and had to take a taxi down Main Street (near its dodgier end) to find her. She wore a crop top and had beautiful and lush skin. They negotiated $200 for two hours, and George seemed to think this a fair price. Her name was Jewel. George hailed a taxi, and it took them back to the motel. He asked her where she was from, and she said, "Just another girl from another place," and he asked her if that was a line from a movie, and she said she didn't know.

At the motel, he undressed, and she put him into her mouth, and then she undressed, and he put his fingers inside of her. He came, and she swallowed, and then he kissed her (just the once), and they spent the rest of the time talking. He drew on her skin and traced little shapes with his hand, making his way across her back and down to her buttocks, along her hips and up to her ribs, then down her thigh. She would shiver from time to time or let out a slight sigh or a girly giggle as she answered his questions. Who was she? What was her favorite

TV program? What did she want to do with her life? Did she believe in God? Did she have any kids?

She was apprehensive to answer his questions at first, but then she opened up and even went ten minutes over the allocated time to finish a story. She was telling him about a particular curiosity from her youth.

Jewel's story:

In the small town where Jewel grew up, the kids knew an eccentric old woman known as the Butterfly Eater. She lived in her sister's barn near a large wheat field. The nickname started one day when one of the kids from Jewel's school approached the old woman; she was sitting alone outside her barn on a lawn chair. The kid was selling cookies for a local fundraiser. He asked the woman if she'd like to buy a box: he had chocolate or maple. She said, "Why do I need cookies when nature supplies me with such rich and delicious treats? Huh, kid?" And at that, she caged a butterfly resting on the arm of her chair; using her stained fingers to trap the insect, she tossed the poor beast into her mouth. Shocked, the kid ran away, and he heard shrill, hyena-like laughter as he booked it back across the fields towards home. The story traveled like wildfire, and all the kids thought she must be crazy, living off snakes and cockroaches and butterflies; and when Jewel told her father about it, he laughed and said that Betty (the Butterfly Eater) had always had a flair for the theatrical. He told her that Betty used to be the most beautiful girl in school, with everyone vying for her hand. And for some reason, knowing that her father had gone to school with the Butterfly Eater unnerved her, but her father was very cavalier about the whole thing and seemed to reminisce fondly about the woman even after Jewel had revealed to him her newfound dietary habits. Jewel asked him what had happened to her to turn her into the woman she was today—the woman who eats butterflies—and he said, "Life and time, sweetheart."

When she left, George could feel the pangs of love and affection attempt to strike a match in his insides, but the match tip broke, and he was left with a soft feeling of calm and peace briefly offering him repose before everything returned to the way it was. It was past midnight, but he knew the diner would still be open. He wanted a piece of pie, and he got dressed and set out to get his fix.

When he got to the diner, the waitress, a hefty woman known as Dolores—a woman he'd often seen, gotten used to, a familiar and friendly face—told him to be careful, that Buddy was out looking for him. Floyd was in the hospital, but Buddy was out. His arm was in a cast (and two of his fingers were missing), and she said all he could talk about was evening the score, and he kept mentioning George—George *mother-fucking* Dilgunk. His eyes fierce and foul.

That night, George dreamt of Jewel and Buddy and Floyd. He dreamt that they were back in the woods near his campsite, and he heard a noise coming from outside his tent (the Great Howl), and he went out to investigate. He had a flashlight and followed the noise and crept through the darkness and the bush, and then he saw them. Buddy was on top of her—his pants around his ankles. Floyd held her arms back, and her mouth was gagged and stuffed with a bandana or handkerchief or sock. There was blood running down her forehead. She looked at George with pleading eyes; he went running to her aid; he gripped the hammer in his hand—the hunters watched him approach, but indifferently, not sensing danger, not addressing the threat. As he was readying to crack Buddy on the head and rescue Jewel, a giant hand swept down and picked him up and caged him in its long and spindly fingers. He could feel himself being raised into the air, and then he saw its mouth and teeth, and the thing threw him inside and munched away and chewed him up. And George was able to get glimpses of Jewel and the hunters and the rape taking place below as he was being eaten, and he heard Jewel's voice: "Life and time, sweetheart." And when he woke up, he was drenched in sweat. But then he realized he was still dreaming, and the giant bug, the musical monstrosity from his early days, was over in the corner of his motel room, next to the bathroom, playing that *godawful* organ. It said, "Don't you recognize me?" And George said, "Of course. You're that fucking bug from the cabin." And it said, "No, that wasn't me. I am Jewel," it said, "the prostitute." She had come back to deliver a warning, urging him to leave. Things were not what they seemed. "Leave in the morning," she said, and then she began playing the organ, and she serenaded him as he lay in bed. He asked her if she was all right, and she said, "Fit as a fiddle. But hush now and listen." And she continued to play a beautiful requiem, and then he fell asleep, and that's all he could remember.

In the morning, he wondered what he should do. Certainly, an apology was in order, but things had presumably gone too far between him and the hunters. He would have to leave for a while. Get out of Dodge, so to speak.

He packed up his clothes and sleeping bag and stuffed them into a backpack he'd bought at an army surplus store not far from the motel. He threw the rest of his camping gear in the dumpster and grabbed a pack of peanuts from the vending machine and set off with his typewriter to find new accommodations.

He took the road out of town, heading to the pier to see how Old Joe was doing.

When he got there, it was just after lunch, and the pier was quiet. He caught sight of Joe's ship and boarded and knocked on the cabin door.

"What the *fuck* do you want!?" cried Joe.

"It's me, George." The door swung open. Joe emerged, shirtless and tattered. His curled grey chest hair on end and his sun-soaked visage grinning back at him. He noticed that Joe was missing some teeth.

"Where the *hell* you been, my boy? I could have used you. I was out gettin' the shit kicked outta me. Fightin' those fucking scavengers over some cargo. Got into quite a squabble, believe you me."

George smiled, and the old pirate sat down with him and poured them each a glass from his mysterious booze-filled bottle.

"What can I do for you, George?"

"I was wondering about the ladies over on the island. Could you take me there?"

"Why do you want to go there? I'm not sure they'd appreciate a visit right now, son. They're in the middle of something. I'm not sure what, but I'm not even allowed there myself. I just drop off the goods near the shore and then skedaddle. They're kind souls, but get on their bad side, and well... you remember what happened when you caught them by surprise."

George touched his head, remembering the blow he took that night when they'd first arrived on the beach. "Yeah, I suppose you're right," he said. "I'm looking for a place to lie low for a bit. Thought the island might be a good spot."

"You can stay here if you like, free of charge," said the kindly captain.

George thanked Old Joe for the offer but politely declined. He drank up and told him that he'd be back soon for another visit. They shook hands, and Joe wished him luck, and he left the same way he came—and as he walked down the pier, he heard the old sailor singing some tune, crooning away with horrible pitch. "Fuck your fish and fry your itch, and every day's a *paaaaaaarrty!*"

He followed the road, knowing full well that he was returning to his beginnings or, put more accurately, his most recent (apart from his stopover in town) domicile. The asylum emerged once he ducked down a hidden road, an alternate path to a side enclosure where he figured he might be able to jimmy a door and find a vacant room, accessed from some obscure annexed wing. He wondered what had become of his former place of lodging, this palace in the woods. Was it now in ruins? Vines and vegetation climbing its steeples? Nature reclaiming it as its own? But it mostly just looked the same apart from some broken windows, lackadaisical graffiti, and overgrown lawns. He decided to walk around to its front, not sensing any movement or activity, and when he got to its main entrance, all that stood in the way of him getting inside were a couple of boards that he was able to pry loose with his hammer. He sat on the steps and smoked a cigarette and looked out on the vacant parking lot as the sun set just above the tree line.

Chapter 37

His first task was securing some food. He had a general idea of where the kitchen was in this Brutalist labyrinth, and with the help of a map located on a wall near the main entrance, he found it—one floor down—without much trouble. He searched the cupboards and scoured the pantries and found a sizeable collection of canned goods. These rations alone would undoubtedly last him a month, if not more. He piled them into three garbage bags and slung them over his shoulder, and he kept on with his downward theme; he found a small common area (with kitchenette) one floor down, and he decided to set up shop there for the night. He unrolled his sleeping bag and heated a can of beans on the stovetop. He slept soundly that night, just him and the rats lounging in the catacombs.

It surprised him that the asylum still had electricity. Not all the light switches worked, but many did, and he had ample luminosity to guide his efforts forward; he'd even found a flashlight lying on the table in a staff common area. He upgraded his chamber the second night and found a spacious gymnasium-like suite, similar to the activity center where he'd spent most of his time while engaged here as a patient. The TV area was set up in a similar fashion at the center of the space, and a ping-pong table was placed over in its westward nook. Couches haphazardly tossed near one end would serve as his bed. He concocted a fort, laboriously pulling the couches over to the center of the enormous space near the TV area; and he ran laps around the enclosure afterwards to stifle some of the joyous energy he felt accruing at the sight of his splendid and bountiful housing arrangement. The television had a DVD player and a small assortment of movies located in a binder on top of it. He grabbed a disk called *The Damsels of Devonshire* and popped it in and snuggled up with a can of creamed corn on his couch/bed.

In the morning, he decided to explore more of the asylum and see what else he could scavenge around its cavities and corridors. Many of the rooms were similar in nature and decor—stark and housed in raw, unadorned concrete—the rooms and suites seemingly continuing without end. He avoided the elevators and kept to the stairwells. He went four floors deeper and found a tramway with a set of small attached cars—an industrial roller coaster; and with the flip of a switch, he was able to put the beast in motion. He took the serpentine vessel and found it to be an enjoyable means of touring the lower floors of the architectural substratum. He ate another can of beans (his chin glistening with its juice) as the tram circled back and returned him to his base of operations.

He had neglected his most important task, at least that's what his mind was telling him. During moments of lag when he sat unbothered from his exploratory efforts, he sensed that he was forgetting something. But what? The writing! Holy Hannah, the holy palindrome! He was in the perfect place to solidify his efforts into a cohesive and structural whole, and here he was, pissing it away, exploring some concrete animal without ever getting down to the meat and potatoes of it. Sloppy due diligence, he proclaimed in his head. Come on, George!

That night, he sat at the far end of the room, gazing at the space in front of him. His own private abyss. A sanctuary of madness with a beautiful vaulted ceiling. He thought of it as a church without exit, incubating the birthing process for the one who was trapped within. Sealed off from outside perspectives and influence. Insanity *à la max*, or the flowering from within.

George kept typing. The goods were coming at an alarming pace—he and the horned typewriter, at it again. It came out like a flatulent shitstorm. It was disgusting to witness, but why stop? The ecstasies of creativity harbor no grudges against the crude and the despicable, or the vile and the bold. Urban myths by troglodytes—she bestows her gifts to the most promising and worthy, the most obscene and defiled, the horniest and most sadistic, the most depraved and previously innocent.

What story is he concocting now? What tales of wonder and woe sign and sacrifice their loins to the printed page? He is finishing his book of stories—about God and His abhorrent creation, a new draft with alterations—the one he'd begun before, under the grey-blue sky and the wooded awnings. He's nearing its climax, although he is oblivious to what that is. No concrete phenomena pierce into his head; they possess his fingertips and leave his brain to rot unbothered. It's guts and hands all the way! Ganglions and gallbladder! As he writes these words (or words similar to these words, words looping and undulating around these words), he acknowledges that he doesn't rightly know what he's doing. He is defiled by a dream that has rerouted his senses and placed him at the throne, kneeling to the king, ass to the crowd; he reworks the image, and the king is kneeling to him (charity and graciousness demeaning to all involved, supplementary souls included), and he cracks the monarch on the head. *Boof!* The sound escapes the king, as does his last breath; and he's spread out and dead, surrounded by his royal court. George sits on the throne, his revolutionary act a success; the new head transposed upon the snake. But alas, he's sucked in. The throne pulls him through. A trapdoor? What gives? And he hears a rustling and wakes up, lifting his head from the table and the typewriter; he spots two men entering his abode. "Hark! Who goes there?"

At first he thinks it's Floyd and Buddy. Come to seek revenge (the talented tracker and triggerman). But it's not them. Strangers or runaways like him. They tell him they're his neighbors; they live on the upper floors with a small clique of others. They offer supplies, gifts (more canned eats and another binder of films). He waves them in; they sit on the couches and swap stories, describe how they've come to take up residence in this here asylum. The one fella is named Jim, Jim O'Sullivan, and he's been living here for a few weeks, and he speaks of the place as if it were a castle, and George can understand his enthusiasm. They offer George some of their concoction, swill crafted in the laboratories of the edifice. Under the guidance of the other man, Dexter Hartright, a part-time toxicologist and full-time vagrant, they've distilled a liquid hallucinogen capable of illuminating the dimmest parts of even the most calcified brain. They each take a sip from the flask. George imagines it has an azure tint. It burns his throat. They continue their chat, and a few minutes later, they bid him adieu and tell him that if he needs anything, anything at all, to come and see them on the seventh floor of the L-wing. He nods and waves and smiles at the swill merchants as they exit his den.

***

"Ideals" bend to truth, or
"Truth" bends to ideals.

He saw the bastards in the corner, rutting and circling, hyenas all jazzed up by some locomotive impulse seizing them, all eyes on George; they ready themselves to charge—horns first.

For six hours, he's imagined himself reinvented as a matador, chased and hunted and gallivanting by and past made-up beasts in a perpetual state of terrifying transition, moving from one nightmarish state to the next. Beasts with two, three, five, or eight heads—in keeping with the Fibonacci numbers—jutting out at horrifying angles and surprising recesses, tracking him with their many eyes; he runs around with a blanket like a crazed banshee. "Where did you cocksuckers come from?" But alas, he gets the horns (or he thinks he does), and the stampede starts and all the bulls or beasts or what-have-yous charge, and George is down for the count.

Morning finds him passed out on the hardwood floor. He didn't even make it to the couch, just passed out at some hour right then and there. What a fun night, he thinks. He must request more of that blessed swill from those devils upstairs. He sees movement over in the corner. More guests! A familiar gait and a recognizable countenance—his mother, by God! And she's not alone. A nearly headless chap in a cassock walks beside her, arm in arm. Perhaps he took too much of that delightful drug last night, and the dead now walk among the living—times are strange. He says hello to the pair. His mother scolds him, asks him if that's any way to greet his long-lost materfamilias. He rushes over and embraces her in a dutiful hug and kisses her cheek. She asks him how he's been, what he's been doing, why is he here in this rank subbasement squatting in a gymnasium. He keeps his answers brief, and the headless chap next to her, or Father Tom, nods his chin, and George has great difficulty not staring into the inside of his head. Snippets of meat are strangely overlaid in there and flap about like thin tongues trying to communicate some claptrap vernacular. The pair tells him that they're a romantic item now (in actuality, Father Tom just nods, making loud forced-breathing sounds, a chronic sufferer of apnea). In the afterlife, they've bonded and found solace in each other's company. George gives them a thumbs-up, and he asks his mother if she'd like a tour, and he and she and Father Tom do a lap around his newfound kingdom and then off on an exploratory excursion; he takes them around through the concrete beast and down to its tramway; he shows them all the wonderful areas he's discovered: a canteen with a still-functioning refrigerator full of Orange Crush, a padded room for psychopaths and the genuinely disturbed, a sea of passageways and bunkers and hideaways. And all his—he mentions this with great pride (a slight fib) and mutters a quiet aside, "There's also some friends who rent the upper floors, tenants who mostly keep to themselves." Mrs. Dilgunk is agog and gleeful, and Father Tom remains difficult to gauge, inscrutable without a head, but he pats George on the back, and this can only be read as a sign of approval and good faith.

Everyone returns to his bunker, and George sets up some couches for them in the corner—naptime, and about time, George's hangover was beginning to get the better of him. All the swill was used up, and he was running on reserves. When he wakes from his afternoon slumber, Father Tom and his mother are gone. Apparitions? Hallucinations? Or antsy guests?

While he's got the time, he decides to write and continue one of his tales—his tale of Jonathan and his journey as God's most hated abomination: Jonathan the Great, Jonathan the Wise, Jonathan the Heel.

Chapter 38

Jonathan had incurred the wrath of God. He was a pianist. He was a born winner in every conceivable sense: handsome, loved, strong, generous, intelligent, and self-aware—but God, in His infinite wisdom, just didn't like him. He'd created him (He'd created everything), but something about Jonathan irked Him a great deal. Perhaps it had something to do with what Jonathan represented, a microcosm of the overall problem, all that was easy and surface. For all of Jonathan's challenges ended in victory, minor defeats scattered here and there (sprinkled for interest's sake)—the odd tough year—but all in all, a consistent scheme of victory running throughout an unimpeachable surface existence. Contrary to this lifestyle of ease and facility, God thought it important (nay, downright necessary) that all His creatures bear witness to the insurmountable, that the true weight of unworthiness be felt, its burden conveyed, if not carried. And God wanted him to know that there's a thin line between a detective and a pervert.

When he met her, he thought she was a real big fat thing with meat shaking all over her bones. He didn't think much of her. A homely girl, her youth dissipating from her every pore at an alarming rate; her most "beautiful" days already behind her at the ripe age of twenty-three. But she caught his eye up at the bar an hour later, the way she leaned and tilted her head and shimmied her hips with a certain *je ne sais quoi*. Something about her was pulling at his focus. He'd look away, survey the scene, and then be brought back to gaze at this strangely captivating creature. She was one of his best friend's girlfriend's friends, and they'd all come out together for a night of dancing. Jonathan, being a good pal, dutiful to the bonds of friendship, accepted Jack's offer to accompany him and Daisy and her friend (the plain and burly Jane) out for the night. Jack explained that Jane was a sweet girl, and from what Jonathan could tell, she was—a kind and polite gal, smiling and inquisitive but not in an overindulgent sort of way; and Jack asked Jonathan to keep her company and enjoy the frivolous and fun nature of the night. But as he spoke to her, more and more at the bar, he began to notice her face; it was morphing somewhat—what he once described as plain was becoming virginal, even angelic. Was it the booze, the drugs, the club's lighting? A coalescing of all three flattering the fat girl's face and remodeling it as a baroque vision of beauty? At the end of the night, Jonathan walked Jane to her door and firmly planted a kiss on her lips. The next day, he called her and continued this telephoning trend for each of the subsequent days of the following two weeks. Why had she suddenly captivated him so? He'd been with many women far more beautiful and far more interesting than Jane—he couldn't figure out the reason behind the draw, but he certainly felt it.

***

Jonathan becomes increasingly desperate as he continues to make a fool of himself over and over again, quickly losing interest in all other pursuits, goals, and hobbies—even losing his ability to see other women as potential mates. His eyes are only for Jane, and every time he sees her, she somehow (inexplicably) becomes more beautiful; time is working to her advantage: she is slimming down; her boobs are getting bigger; her ass's getting tighter. She is a virtuoso on the violin, drums, and even the piano (more so than Jonathan even); her talents and interests know no limits. She rebukes him time and time again and refuses his advances; and one night when he's over at Jack's (all four characters are hunkered down there for the night due to an unexpected snowstorm coming from the east, trapping them with road closures in Jack's accommodating household), he sees Jane take Jack's hand in the middle of the night (while Daisy's sleeping), and she sneaks him off into another room (the guest room) and fucks him loudly, but Daisy—the sound sleeper—doesn't hear, but Jonathan does (with his mock love seat/bed near the action). He's heartbroken, aroused, ashamed, and maddened. He feigns sleep as they tiptoe past him, and the episode only increases his appetite for the girl. He continues to pursue her in the passing months to no avail, calling her and leaving messages, as every other aspect of his life falls apart: he stops going to work; his appearance is a mess; people avoid him, and every time he mentions Jane to someone, (without fail) they compliment her style and charm and beauty and praise her virtue. In an attempt to end his suffering, he decides to end her. Kill her, shoot her, stab her—and rid himself of the longing and pain coming from that atrocious hope of a potential embrace that'll never come. And as he hides behind a corner, gun in hand, ready to pounce and attack the beautiful Jane, God comes down, assumes the appearance of a beggar. "Hey, Jonathan," He says. "Whatcha doin'?"

God convinces Jonathan to leave Jane alone, and He makes him a deal. "Kill yourself right now, and I'll let you come up to heaven, and I'll show you a love so great your heart will burst with joy." Jonathan accepts and promptly puts a bullet in his brain, and God chuckles as Jonathan makes his bed and now must lie in it. "Fuck you, half-wit," says God, and He laughs heartily at the folly of the fool as He ascends to heaven, and Jonathan descends to hell.

For the Universal Creator was an asshole, a mirror of His creation.

He liked making his characters (including that of God) morally fluid, bastards of moral relativism, and he found each of them to be divine apparatuses (the bigger the prick, the holier the tramp!), and he felt that every victory was somehow Pyrrhic in nature.

Some hours had gone by for George since he'd begun typing away. He barely paid attention to time anymore, and not having seen the sun in days, his habits adapted to his newfound underground lifestyle (a dark, nocturnal life), and activities (including those of sleep) were undertaken only when the mood or necessity dictated. He went down the hall to the bathroom and noticed his disheveled appearance in the mirror. He hadn't brushed his teeth or showered or kept up an even modest level of hygiene since reentering the asylum. He fetched his bag and got his supplies and cleaned his teeth and wandered the hallways until he found a washroom with a fully functioning shower (he knew he'd come across some in his exploratory efforts), and he came out a sparkling new man. He washed his clothes in the sink and hung them over a random wire dangling in the hallway. He whistled a tune as he performed these menial tasks necessary to the daily upkeep of each American citizen—or modern human being, for that matter.

He went over the pages he'd written, tallying up the final score of his stories, reading them all from the beginning to the end. He'd begun it in the woods and now completed it in his bunker (his tapestry of tales), and he felt that the two hundred-odd pages were quite an accomplishment, especially since he hadn't completed a book in over a decade. But what now, and perhaps it was the asylum murmuring to him his next plan of action, whispering to him and prodding him on. He felt the electricity bubbling up in him, which was always the case when a new idea was forming, its ominous precursor. Still without shape or form, he felt it emerge, first as a hazy structure—a grim outline—then, in more concrete parameters, as a character or two, and then as an arc, and then as a general map or course to chart. He needed a cigarette, but he didn't have any—and where had his mother and Father Tom gone?

It takes him a while to find the swill merchants, Dexter and Jim, and he spots them on the third floor. There are six of them in total, and he asks if anyone has any cigarettes he can buy or trade. They sell him two packs, all for the low price of two cans of creamed corn and three DVDs, which George, unfortunately, has to return to his lair to retrieve, but he smokes while touring the dark corridors, and the trek is rather enjoyable. Upon his return, the swill merchants ask if he'd like another taste of their new and improved merchandise. He takes a swig and hustles back to his basement lodgings before its effects become overwhelming. He makes it and cuddles up on the couch and tosses in a movie called *The Dice People* before succumbing to the poison and entering its warped world of deranged visions and apocryphal imaginings.

When he wakes up from his delusions, he decides to write a play, a one-man show that he'll perform right here for his neighbors. Its opening line of dialogue went: "The world was divided into two factions: Pussies and Fascists. And you were *forced* to pick a team."

He performed it three days later in the asylum's theater where he'd attempted his audacious breakout performance not too long before. Someone asked him how he came up with the title, the structure, and the plot of the warring parties. And he said, "I let each side pick the other's name and waited to see who could dig themselves out, and then the wheels began to turn, and the story emerged like a ripe old turd."

He called the play *Martha's Fountainhead*, and he had immersed himself so far into it—into the writing and acting— that he'd completely blotted out who he was, actually rewiring certain aspects of his circuitry through this strange inward journey. And for some reason, he thought back to when he'd given Mr. Mickelson one of his early short stories, and the comments he made regarding its incoherent flow, juvenile stylings, chaotic perspectives, and suboptimal structure, and George said, "All your rules are mere suggestions, and your critique mirrors your ignorance." (Or he imagined he'd said that.)

The truth of the matter was that there were two parties: Creators and non-Creators.

But are those who destroy Creators, too?

He sat around smoking cigarettes and wondering what to do with himself. He figured it might be time to go out and get some fresh air. See what was happening in the outside world, or at least on its periphery. So George packed a light bag for a day's journey; his intentions to come back in a few hours after surveying the woods, or heading into town, or visiting Joe, whichever whim took hold while he was up and out there. He ascended the staircases and exited the main doors. The day was dreary and rainy, and the overgrown grass was a lush green, and George sat on the steps and lit another cigarette, contemplating his move. He heard a rustling among the trees. Could it be the growling beast? And sure enough, he heard its howl—warm and welcoming (at least to George's ears), and he walked off into the woods with no directional marker beyond the bellows of the beast, turning over questions in his mind as he went along: was he a Pussy or a Fascist?

Chapter 39

He told himself a story as he walked about a man who was talking with a woman, and he asked her why she didn't like a certain creator, and she said because of what he represented, his ideology; and he asked her if she felt anything when she experienced his creation, and he said maybe, and she said because of what he represented, and he said, *huh*?

And for the first time, when he asked himself what he believed in, he knew the answer: the sanctity of the maze.

In the beginning was the Word(s).

You can only ever play as good as you ever were. (The peak, or its preeminent potential, twisted and coded in the makeup—disguised in the blood or the book.)

He saw conversations as mental masturbations plus guests, and wisdom erroneously prescribed as painkillers.

He watched the branches sway, and through the obscuring mist, the shape of the four-mouthed beast emerged, its head nearing the top of the forest's height. A dark blur in a grey fog. It roared and swooped down, swiping at George who stood still; perhaps if he didn't move or make a peep, the beast would leave him be. The beast took in long breaths, exhaling all over George. Its head rotated, and each mouth took its time (and turn) discharging its foul breath on the poor fear-stricken man. George was carefully going through his bag in search of his hammer; he gripped its wooden base and swung it, catching the bastard square on one of its jagged teeth. The beast jumped back and howled in hysterics and performed a circular dance of pain, lifting its hands to its broken tooth, knocking trees back and over as George snuck behind a large Douglas fir, watching the scene play out between its prickly branches. The monster tumbled to the ground, and George figured the beast was a bit of a baby: "Not much of a fighter, is he?" he thought. And at that, with the beast sprawled out and George's courage resurfacing, he went over to the downed monster and said a meek hello. The beast's head rose from the ground, and a strange recording emerged, "What **do you** want?"

George was utterly surprised by the monster's sudden gesticulations and vocal eccentricities (not to mention the English), each word accompanied by a new voice; it sat up and began conversing with George, who apologized for the tap on the tooth, citing fear as the reason for the smack, and the beast accepted, saying that it too had violence on the brain and was thinking of tearing him apart (limb from limb)—but due to an error in recognition, because it thought that he was a bear or a buck, certainly not a human being. The beast explained that humans tasted like cheese (an apparently abhorrent flavor to the beast), and suffice to say, they weren't its preferred choice of chow—in a pinch, perhaps, but generally avoided. They continued to chat, and George loosened up and decided to help the beast, warn it about the hunters, its devout pursuers (because, after all, they were now his pursuers too), and he told it about the target looming over its head, or on its back, about those that meant it harm, out to kill it, take it in—downed and cut up, then mounted and displayed, a four-mouthed trophy for some thickly carpeted rec room. The beast said that it knew all about that (old news) and that it did its best to either avoid or eliminate these (cheese-tasting) types, generally hillbillies but not always—the urbanites could be as kill-crazy as the rest. And the beast asked George what he was doing out in the woods: it asked, "*What* **are** you <u>doing</u> here?" And George explained that he was living in the asylum out back, writing and hiding out while some minor hiccup blew over, and the beast asked him what this minor hiccup might be, and he said that he'd beat the hell out of some fellas with his hammer, and the beast said, "Go **figure**."

He asked the beast how it navigated—if it could see or hear or touch its way to its goal, and the beast said that it used its immaculate sense of taste to navigate the treachery of the woods and the vileness and unwholesomeness of the land. It showed George its dog-like tongues, pink and also lizard-like, and it said that it tasted everything, a constant consumer of flavors. And George said, "Wow," and the beast thanked him for his praise, and they continued their leisurely stroll through the dark forest.

"It **was** <u>all</u> **ABOUT** possibility... the possibility *of an* **island**, *far off*, **OUT** of **sight**, <u>*but*</u> still there. So *real/***you** could TASTE it."

We shall call the next bit of our story *Pandemonium!*

"First, you shit it <u>*out*</u>, **then** you **beat** it *into* **SUBMISSION** with <u>a</u> **hammer**. *Does **that*** sound **about** right?" (In reference to George's summation about the act of creation.)

They continued their walk, and all of a sudden, George realized where he was, in that strange desert, monolith intact, way off yonder, and he noticed his fashion accessories (a costume change!), a sweet bandolier and an accompanying pistol. Back in the cowpoke garb, he thought. *Yippee-ki-yay!*

He shot a cactus, then a small scurrying lizard, showing off his skill for his new pal, the beast, who looked at him with a bored grin and then a toothsome one, and then it rotated yet again to its other mouth with its tongue hanging out, licking its lips, tasting the scenery.

George asked how they'd got here, arrived at this mysterious locale. The beast said that it didn't know; it was following him—not the other way around. Shit, thought George, how the hell had he ended up here yet again?

The monolith's door was open, and he saw a stream of crustaceans and gruesome-looking dudes and disoriented corpse-like damsels dashing out, a colony on the move, populated by the undead, or dead-like things, a diabolical crustacean-cum-*H.-sapiens* horde or an ant army bred with Cro-Magnons and thrown into a meat grinder or a pixelated murder machine with a desert arena functioning as the showdown's rustic milieu: two players against everybody else. They had stumbled unknowingly into a battle, and George reloaded his pistol and hoped the beast was prepared for the rushing onslaught coming their way.

"**Bring** it <u>on</u>, *bitch*!" (Growled the heads.)

The monster horde from the monolith was waging war, coming towards them at an alarming pace. Fuck it, thought George. Bring it on, thought the beast. The first of the enemy to arrive lunged at George's quadruple-headed pal, and the monolith-based bugs took it down, crawling all over his fallen comrade who snapped its many mouths in a defensive strategy that was both sorely disappointing and dimwittedly ineffective: it was being eaten alive because of this lackluster stratagem and its misguided notion of strength and lack of preparation. It was succumbing to the bugs and bad luck—and, ultimately, to the demands of fate: it would soon forfeit its life. George was shooting as fast as his trigger finger would allow. Killing those cocksuckers left and right. Retreating, reloading, halting, then back to killing. Rinse and repeat. He did his best to aid his downed friend, but it was already overrun and all in vain; its blood and guts and entrails were thrown up like mixed-meat confetti from a bursting balloon. George stepped backwards firing nonstop. He knew he was done for unless a miracle happened (just too goddamn many)—and, lo and behold, he tripped over something: was God listening? A big motherfucking machine gun, an assault rifle, cocked and loaded with a full clip and spare ammo hitherto unnoticed, right next to his foot, lying in the sand. Lying in wait? No time to think! *Shoot*, goddamnit! A time for revenge, a time for payback, a time for fun—and he mowed those motherfuckers down. Singlehandedly decimating an entire populace, a genocidal desert scene painted by Picasso or Dali or van Gogh on the eve of his suicide, an array of bug parts and human brains and limbless corpses baking in the sun. He knew he should hurry; soon the smell in the wasteland would be overpowering. He reloaded his pistol and put another clip in his assault rifle and shot the last of the withering bugs who still had a bit of fight left in their broken carapaces.

The pistolero known as George made it to the monolith and peered inside. Not much going on in there. A couple of screeching baby bugs and their mothers, George fired his pistol at a few, blowing off a couple of heads for kicks, and then he resumed his desert wanderings. It was beginning to get dark, and the horizon disappeared as the sun did, and no moon rose to replace it. He walked on tasting the air, blind but moving, and thinking of his monstrous pal spilled out on the sand. He might not have been much of a fighter, but he did what he could, thought George, and he spit on the ground as a show of respect for his dead friend.

At some point unbeknownst to George, he'd collapsed, presumably from fatigue, but memory eluded him, and when he woke up, he looked to his left and to his right; he was on the forest floor, on a hill, near the beginning of the town. He had mud on his face, and he snuck into the first backyard with an unlocked gate and used the garden hose to clean himself off. It must be early, he thought. He saw a convenience store on the corner of the residential street and headed inside. Smokes and coffee, maybe even something from the delicatessen counter like a good, greasy hotdog to put him right. He sauntered in with the jingle of the door announcing his arrival. The clerk said good morning, and he returned the greeting. He purchased his goods and sat on a bench and smoked and watched the sun come up and the early risers wander off to jobs and assignments pertaining to the daily hubbub of their lives. He felt like writing a story but had neglected to bring his typewriter for obvious reasons pertaining to its bulk and grandeur. Anyway, it was something to look forward to when he got back. He smoked three successive cigarettes, and a young boy, no more than ten, came and sat next to him.

"You shouldn't smoke, you know," said the boy.

"I've heard that before."

"So, how come you keep doing it?"

"For kicks, to spit in the face of life, to corrupt my organs and pummel them into submission via the cancerous smoke of an inhaled dart."

"I guess those are good reasons," said the boy. "I'm John. I'm waiting for the bus; then I'm off to school. What are you doing here?"

"Killing time. You want a cigarette?"

"No thanks."

There was a lull, and the two just sat there.

"You know, my teacher smokes. Her name's Ms. Randall. She doesn't like me much. She says I fidget and interrupt the class too often with stupid questions."

"Oh yeah?" said George.

"Yeah, and she called me a retard once, too. I told my mom, but she didn't believe me."

"Tough breaks, kid. You tell Ms. Randall to go suck a cow's teat the next time she calls you that. Okay?"

The kid giggled. "I can't say that."

"Suit yourself," said George.

The school bus rounded the corner, and the boy got up.

"I gotta go, mister."

"You take care, kid."

George sat awhile longer; the kid waved to him from the bus, and he waved back. It was good to stretch his legs, and he was glad he'd found his way back to town. For all his misanthropy, he enjoyed the lighter side of daily life, the menial chitchat and musings on the weather, particularly in these early morning hours. He smiled as the sun shined down on him, and he drank his coffee.

Chapter 40

"Which came first," said Bill, "the intestine or the tapeworm?" Bill: the smartest person George had ever met; he worked at the post office. They nodded to one another, passing furtive and knowing glances back and forth, a slight telepathic exchange accompanied by a grim grin; they cut through the alley in opposite directions, and one passed the other.

He wondered if Suzy was around; it was early, but perhaps due to a malfunctioning projector or a sticky, pop-soaked aisle and a shortage of custodians, the young woman would be up and at 'em, hard at work, already seizing the day; so George hobbled over in the cinema's direction, hoping to have a chat with his friend.

As expected, the cinema was locked. He peered in to see if anyone was moving about, and he saw flickers of movement, and he knocked on the glass, and Suzy came over and unlocked the door.

"Howdy, stranger. Come on in."

She asked how he was, and she said he needed a shower and a shave and a new wardrobe—he was a real disheveled mess; and then they sat quietly on a bench, and George lit a cigarette and offered Suzy one. She lit up and told him about the movie playing that night (a flicker of light dancing on a screen, hobnobbing shapes, adorning 'n' disguising the dream), and she said that he just *haaaadd* to see it (a personal fave according to the cinema's steward).

"Playing tonight," she said. "It's a gem from the '70s taking place in Nazi-occupied France. A real violent and fucked-up thing about a bloody rebellion—mixed with sadomasochistic undertones and dubious theories about censorship and love, with a strange brew of authoritarian overtones and duality and deceit (some Nazis helping the French and some French helping the Nazis); a clusterfuck of bedlam featuring plenty of depravity, and a climactic battle at a zoo with tigers eating the Germans and piranhas eating the French."

George said it sounded like a swell movie, and he bid Suzy adieu, knowing the young woman had plenty to do, and he agreed to come back that night for a cinematic soirée if time and chance permitted.

He felt ambivalent about most of the town's attractions that day, and he wandered through it in an expressionless haze. Moments of joy were quickly eroded by boredom, and nostalgia was replaced by monotony, and George wondered why he always came back to this place, this home, this community of his. He allowed his feet to be his governing guide (relegating his head to the back seat), and he walked to the cliffs, following their lead. There wasn't anyone there, and George stared out into the murky waves and let out a bellowing howl. He sat down and began to cry; he didn't know why.

He stayed there for an hour and smoked and turned over thoughts in his brain. He felt like he'd had a minor emotional purge and needed a cup of coffee to refuel. He ventured back and detoured along the path through the campground and wound up at another convenience store hidden off a gravel road near the edge of town. He walked in and poured himself a coffee and asked the clerk how he was doing. Voices rose up from behind him—familiar voices, talking behind a row of sweets and candy bars—voices belonging to his former hunting pals, and now, presumably (or more accurately), to two men carrying firearms with intentions to kill or maim or punish him in some horrendous and vengeful way. George ducked out as quickly as he could, his bag slung over his shoulder, and he spilled half his coffee on the road in his haste.

He hid out in the bush until he saw Floyd and Buddy (Floyd with his jaw wired shut and Buddy with his left arm in a cast) drive off to God-knows-where. Hopefully far off and away from George, who still felt that he owed them an apology, but certainly not a face-to-face one, not yet anyway, perhaps a nice postcard with a pretty picture and a brief but sincere apology written on the back. He followed the road into town and saw that it was already four o'clock.

Having subsisted mostly on canned goods as of late, George was eager to get some tasty fare into his guts and had the notion of visiting Aunt Carole's BBQ Shack on Abson Ave. near Main Street: one only had to follow the scent—slow-roasted pork and smoked beef layered with sauce, and George salivated at the thought. He quickened his pace and held out hope that they still had some of their buttery biscuits for sale.

When he got to the eatery, it was closed. *Son of a bitch!* He turned in a full circle, eyeing his options, and saw another convenience store. He was ping-ponging between them today. They seemed to function as wayward markers.

As he opened the door and offered the clerk his habitual salutation, he noticed that he looked strikingly similar to the other clerks from the other stores and wondered if there wasn't a typical type that gravitated towards these humble haunts or menial jobs (brothers or cousins or strangers with similar anatomical modeling and professional bents). This clerk, however, appeared more weathered and less enthused or neighborly (depending on how one looked at it) than the last few; and George browsed the gourmet section of rotating hotdogs and potato wedges to satisfy his growing hunger.

The door swung open, and George paid it no mind until he heard the voice, devoid of emotion, flat and unfeeling. "Give me your money, now." George turned and saw a man in a hoodie with a gas mask and a bulletproof vest on. He sported yellow kitchen gloves, and George could see no exposed skin; he wielded a pump-action shotgun. "You, get down." He motioned to George who got on his stomach. "Put the money in the bag." "Yes, sir," said the clerk, and he did as he was told, and he was nervous and fidgety, and George dipped his hand into his bag, reaching for his trusty hammer. "Hurry up," said the gas-mask man. A kid entered, about seven or eight, he stopped dead, his smile faded, and the gas-mask man smacked him across the skull with his shotgun, and the kid spilled out on the floor, knocking over a stand of comic books. "Hurry up," demanded the gas-mask man. George could see blood coming out of the kid's head; he wasn't moving. George gripped his hammer. He waited—the gas-mask man went for the money. George got up and swung the hammer. The man screamed, and the shotgun went off, and the clerk's brains sprayed all over George. He stared down at the gas-mask man (quivering) with the hammer rooted in his skull and then at the headless clerk whose blood painted the tobacco display and, finally, at the kid, spread-eagle, dead or unconscious, splayed out on the floor. He wiggled the hammer out of the man's skull, prying loose some part of it, and he exited the store. Many people were staring at him in the street. He looked at his hammer; a portion of meat clung to its claw.

Once again, he followed his feet; his mind was locked up, unable to properly deal with what actions should or could be taken next. He was back at the cliffs (a day of repeats), and he ventured down along the path. He entered the first of the caves and figured he had an hour (maybe two) before the coppers searched them. He heard movement, and he went further inside and saw the flickering of firelight along the roof and walls of the grotto. A woman was huddled around the fire, cooking something on top of the flames. It smelled delicious, and George, too hungry to abide civility, asked if he could join her and taste some of her victuals. She said he was more than welcome; he was, after all, an old friend, a savior of sorts. And when George looked closer, he saw that it was Suzy—Suzy O'Connor, from the hut (57 Cherry Lane) and the cliffs, with the screams and the fits. "Wow, what are you doing here? You sure seem to pop up at the oddest of times."

"Tell me about it," said Suzy.

She fed him, and they ate in silence; she asked him why he had blood all over himself, and he told her what'd happened— about the dead crook and the dead clerk and the possibly dead kid.

"Quite a day," said Suzy.

"Yup," confirmed George.

Although preoccupied with his own troubles, George still had plenty of questions for Suzy, about her past and her disappearance and her reappearance at 57 Cherry Lane; and knowing he had to skedaddle soon, he asked her who that creature was in the basement. Was it her abductor? The one who'd kidnapped her and Nikki and all those kids way back when? Was it the town's true devil terrorizing the land? The evil that George had suspected of poisoning his hometown, which he'd thought of as faceless—and metaphorically, he pictured as a towering spider or a giant squid floating above their municipality and connecting and infecting their mojos. She smiled at him and told him to eat up; the devils weren't going anywhere. Then he heard the sirens, and he jumped up, and he took one last look at Suzy, and she winked at him, and she said, "Give 'em hell, tiger."

He followed the path down to the rocks and the water and crept along the shoreline until he could climb back up a mile or so down. He was near the campground and decided to orient himself back towards the asylum. At least it was a place to lie low for a bit. He moved through the woods as the sun was setting, and he caught an unusually vibrant sky peeking through the trees, fading azure giving way to calm mauve and then violent red and blazing vermillion, then darkness, and George stumbled on hoping some internal compass was righting his directional lumbering. Hours passed, and then, out over the treetops, maybe a mile out, he saw the high-pitched roof of the asylum: his castle. And he breathed a sigh of relief, and then he thought of Suzy, the other Suzy, cinema Suzy, and he wondered what sort of movie he'd missed that night, and he allowed his imagination to succumb to the spell, speculating on the illusion he'd skipped by formulating a brand new one inside his head.

Chapter 41

The Nazis came out of nowhere. Jean-Michel ducked down and crept low alongside the broken concrete border, crouched in the vicinity of the enemy, rebar exposed. He liked to destroy the body while praising the soul; it was just the kind of soldier he was. And the inebriated warrior took some potshots at some Nazis, and he hit two with strangely concise headshots, then kept onward, forward skulking, parting his way through the ruins of a town bordering on the Seine, his spirit strong—a rusty rifle over his shoulder. He carried a bottle of rum beneath his arm. He thought back to an hour before when he'd had a truly beautiful thought, but he forgot what it was. He never wrote anything down; he believed in the Darwinism of ideas. If an idea were sublime enough, a truly remarkable firmament of celestial polyphony, condensed and broken and recreated in the aggregate of words, then it would surely return at some later point, ready to be plucked from his consciousness— whether it came about in the exact same configuration or not— the tone true; the parasite composed and ready to be harvested, as it always was when it resurfaced, fully formed and waiting, its strength corresponding to its permanent residency (the returning clientele or the strongest of the strange). The method itself somewhat of a self-fulfilling prophecy though. (Were the forgotten ideas really the weakest of the bunch? And could an idea's ascent be based on arbitrary factors entirely outside the scope of its strength—at least strength in the traditional sense?) He heard some German words and readied his rifle.

She loved to read. She'd sit at the café in Montparnasse and thumb through Céline (the genius traitor) and Kafka (the enigmatic Jew) and enter lives and mazes and heptahedron fantasies to keep her mind and soul rich while she and her city were held captive and burning: prisoners of the Third Reich— the reigning establishment whose philosophy was to destroy and discard all that was degenerate: art, people, anything that did not adhere to its strict and rudimentary principles. An aesthetic philosophy even going so far as to construct its temples with decay in the game plan, embedded in the mortar, prophesizing or preparing for the ruins of the future—a strange ode to entropy—readying for its demise even during its ascent. ("A forceful philosophy is always due to self-destruct."—Albert Speer) She looked out the window, a commotion was underway: two young men were running; they halted in front of her window. They kissed, and then one backed up and took out a gun and fired it into the face of the other; afterwards, he placed the gun against his temple—and the exiting bullet broke through the café and shattered the window along with the restaurant's composure. Up trotted an SS officer followed closely by his Nazi pups, and the clientele watched as the Nazis stood over the bodies and stared at the two dead men; the SS officer unsheathed his pistol and fired at the corpses. He rubbed his eyes and walked away, astutely and rigidly. One of the pups yelled, "*Schwuchteln!*" and spit.

Luc was living out in the woods. He was a communist. He was Black. He was friends with Jews who lived in his building. The night he left, he heard the Gestapo coming to fetch his neighbors. He saw an old man being thrown from his fourth-story window, and he heard the ruckus as the families were carted out and loaded in the backs of trucks. He hid and packed a small bag of supplies and left in a hurry the moment the coast was clear. He'd been living in the woods for over a month now. He'd seen no one and heard no news. He sometimes ate bugs, and he was adept at making a fire; a stream close by supplied his water, and he constructed a roof between three closely separated trees. At night he'd sometimes forget about things and stare up at the sky and fall into a lull. A young boy wandered into his camp one day, and Luc caught him eyeing his abode as he segued out of his daydreams. The boy was not afraid and asked many questions. Luc was thankful for the company, and they sat conversing, and the kid asked Luc why he was living out in the woods, and Luc said because he had to. The boy promised to come back and bring food. Two days later, a group of German soldiers came by and shot Luc while he slept.

She met him exiting the movie theater after seeing *Pandora's Box*. He was a Nazi; she was a French girl who liked the read. He said, "*N'était-ce pas un film merveilleux?*" She said, "*Oui.*" He kept walking with her, and the more he talked, the more his French seemed to break down. She didn't say much; she was nervous and wanted him to leave her alone. She smiled politely, and he asked her about other movies she liked and then about the books she read—but he never mentioned the war. He asked if he could see her again, and she said yes, and two days later, he turned up with flowers at her apartment where she lived with her mother. They went out on three dates over two weeks; and on their fourth date, he took her to his room in the 10th arrondissement on the fifth floor of an occupied building with a beautiful view. He kissed her, and he undressed her, and she didn't refuse. The next day, he came by her house and talked with her and her mother and whispered things in broken French for only her to hear. A week later, he told her he had to leave; they made love again, and this time, she was more involved; she didn't know if this was because she was getting rid of him or because she'd probably never see him again. Two months later, she realized she was pregnant. When she told her mother, she started to cry.

***

Jean-Michel wanders the road drunk and knows that his supplies are dwindling. He will need to restock soon at the nearest town. It's in shambles, and he waits until dark to move in. The first house is abandoned and hides nothing of note. He hears voices outside and sees light coming from a house down the way. He sneaks through the alleys and climbs an adjacent building and gets on the roof. He sneaks from the rooftop into an open window and finds an MP40 just lying there. He takes the gun and opens the door a crack and peeps through and slowly steps out onto the stairs and sees a card game in full swing. Six Nazis sit, drinking and having a laugh and smoking and playing poker. He aims the gun, knowing he'll have to be quick once the shooting's over and take what he can. This will make a lot of noise.

As a means of escape, he takes one of the Nazis' uniforms along with as much booze and ammunition as he can carry. He sleeps on a roof that night and is making his way back to Paris. He is a one-man killing machine and is surprised at this dormant talent that the war has propelled to the forefront, without which he'd have never known anything about. He dreams of a beautiful woman who works at a zoo and has a calming effect on tigers. He wakes up full of love for an imaginary angel.

Jacky stands out in the cold. She's told to line up at the camp with the other prisoners. The officers stand in front of them, walking. They have been out in the cold for hours, and anyone who falls or falters is shot. Twelve women down, a corpse to her left, four away from her, an elderly woman (her face bloodied, unrecognizable). Snow falls, and night creeps in. Still, they stand, barefoot, outside, and shaking. She notices a dog limping through the camp. She hears another shot, and she tries to think about her gardenias and her lilies; she tastes iron in her spit, she falters, and she hears footsteps coming towards her.

The liberation of France: the Allies have arrived, and Paris is celebrating. She goes out; her belly has grown for eight months. She kisses her mama and runs into the streets to celebrate. A weight is lifted; she lets out a sigh of relief. People sing and dance and run and frolic, and the day is beautiful, and a celebration ensues. She sees the American soldiers, and she waves. One blows her a kiss. Then she's grabbed, dragged, and someone punches her. She begins to cry—what's going on? Other women are crying too, and someone is cutting off their hair. She is on her knees. Chunks of her hair are being cut; blood runs down her face in trickles and mixes with her tears. What is happening?

They curse her in French and call her a Nazi, a slut, and a collaborator; someone kicks her in the stomach. She screams.

He's drunk again, along the road, nearly made it to Paris—he thinks. He is dressed as a Nazi, a disguise, and he sees their retreat, and he figures it's time for him to bag a couple more Germans for his illustrious kill count as they scatter back. He sees a bell tower and figures that's the spot. He spends the morning waiting for the regiment to pass him by and pops out, firing at the backs of their heads. They don't wait to engage, but continue on, altering their course so he doesn't have a shot. He sips whiskey, and near the end of the afternoon, having marked each kill on the stone of the church tower, he notes that he's successfully killed twenty-four men. He sees the approaching Allied forces behind him and continues shooting at the last of the straggling Nazis and wounded German soldiers. When the Allies arrive, he waves. He sees them scatter, and he remembers he's dressed in the wrong attire (team swastika); he laughs as an American kneels and aims a bazooka his way. He takes a stiff drink and thinks that all a man can do sometimes is sit back and watch it burn. God save the Queen!

Chapter 42

When he got back to the asylum, he went right to his usual campout locale—after heading to the bathroom first, of course. George had needed to take a large bowel movement for quite some time. The relief was palpable when he was finally able to drop off this cumbersome load.

Apart from his gastrointestinal urge, he was also overcome with an equally pressing compulsion to write: come hell or high water, he needed to get this shit out of his system. He sat down at his horned typewriter, and the machine asked if he was ready, and he nodded, smiled, and rubbed its horns the way a doting father might do to its good-natured offspring or pet. He wasn't sure how much time he had until the paddy wagon arrived to cart him off, but it didn't seem to matter, or at least the thought faded away as soon as the words came running out. George sat hunched over with his jaw jutting out as the words disentangled themselves from the knot in his gut and spewed forth—ink hurled at the page.

He'd written a monologue, a one-man show. He had no idea how long it had taken him; he'd fallen back into his timeless subterranean state. Was it day or night? Monday or autumn? Writing under duress had the urgency of a blackout state. He hung a white sheet between two freestanding coat racks and wrote, "Music + Math + Myths + Sisyphus (or Syphilis) = Labyrinth," in black marker in a bold, barely legible typeface. The sheet was to be his backdrop, and as he readied himself, wearing a custom cap concocted by taping odds and ends together and mirroring the battle helmet of some ancient, barbaric tribe; musing on the ferocity of falcons and other raptors, he created an homage to the talons and beak by taping knives from the kitchen to his hands and helmet. He dimmed the lights and waited for the audience to take their seats before starting the show.

"I met God on the corner of Pumice Ave. and Main Street. He said He needed a dime, and I said go to hell. I met the devil a mile down, and he said God asked him for a dime, and I said, "What'd you do?" and he said, "Told Him to go back to you." I met God on the corner of Pumice Ave. and Main Street..."

We are always blind to the present, spoke the serpent to the thief.

And he said I have an ambivalent nature solely to match my grief.

At 1 I was a fascist,
At 2 I was a saint,
At 3 I was a nihilist,
At 4 I ate some grapes,
At 5 I was a communist,
At 6 I had no faith,

At 7 I was a god,
At 8 I passed away,
At 9 I was reborn,
At 10 I was dismayed,
At 11 I was alone,
At 12 they never came,
At 1 I heard the music,
At 2 it was the same,
At 3 is when I surrendered,
At 4 I walked away,
At 5 I disappeared,
At 6 I saw him play,
At 7 I fell asleep,
At 8 I dreamt the day,
At 9 it all repeated,
At 10 I felt ashamed,
At 11 I asked a question,
At 12 the answer came.

He looked out at the audience. He saw Ricky from his youth. He saw his mother, Jill, and his father, Walt. Trisha was in the corner, Gordon too. Some old asylum pals—the Laura sisters and Willy—were seated near the aisle. Captain Joe and Tim were there. And Suzy O'Connor and Suzy Jenkins (both in their youthful and more mature forms, a doppelgänger of a doppelgänger) were taking up four seats scattered throughout the crowd. Nikki was there and Floyd and Buddy, too. Nancy even made an appearance, and the beast with the four mouths was lounging in the back, eyeing the play from the far wall. Some creatures from the monolith were there, and he noticed that the bug with the organ was supplying his soundtrack, stationed stage right. Father Tom was seated in the front row, and he gave George an encouraging and subtle nod. He noticed other faces too, past and present, real and unreal, coexisting as the perfect audience for his debuting play and its sole performance.

He raised the knife high above his head and knelt on the stage. "I am the freest bird in the biggest prison," he yelled (a palpably cheesy line), and he plunged the blade into his guts as the audience watched wide-eyed and captivated. A disemboweled performer going for broke, and as he lay still, blood and intestines pouring forth (actions overtaking words), a chorus of angels came down and harmonized the maxim, "No man shall be considered fortunate until he is dead." George smiled at the resounding cries and the gush of applause from the packed auditorium. He whispered a "thank you" before closing his eyes, content with his ending but hoping his body would hurry up and die since the pain of his wound was excruciating, and the shock and bliss of the moment were wearing off.

The lights burst on. The audience disappears. George sees his upstairs flatmates come running. "There's a fucking knife in him!" yells the first to arrive. "Call an ambulance."

Fuck, thinks George. Fuck, Fuck, Fuck, Fuck, Fuck.

He has a Bob Dylan dream. He dreams of the folk-rock-pop icon, and they share an intimate chat about being on the road, and he says to George, "Hey, bucko, we've been out here a long while now. I think it's about time we head home, bring it all back. This trip's gone on long enough, hey? Let some other schmuck take its victory lap. Let the *new* Bob get all garbled up in front of this hitman's parade. Hell, it's time for a new mask, man. A new face. A new visage, you know?" A head pops in from an empty doorway. "Five minutes, Bob." "Five minutes, eh? All right, all right. When there's no one to lead the show, but the show must go on, what's a fawn to do but play on?" He puts on a Venetian mask and tips his hat to George. "So long, old boy."

George is strapped to a gurney and is being pushed through the halls as hallucinations come rushing forth and as demons and doctors and friends and foes come out of the woodwork to bid George farewell. He feels the cool air as he exits the asylum, and far off, above the treetops, he sees a funnel cloud touching down. The paramedics halt, and violent periwinkle skies turn demented amaranthine. They are frozen in the midst of a medical crisis by the beauty of destruction. George breathes a sigh of relief; the world has not forgotten him.

Chapter 43

He was sentenced to eight years in prison. His past misdoings including his assault on Floyd and Buddy were brought up, along with his fleeing the scene of a triple homicide and him planting a hammer in the face of one of the deceased; they also saw fit to bring up his past as a lunatic, along with his most recent suicide attempt. George found the judge to be a bit harsh, and he scratched at the route of stitches crossing his midsection, a map accurately depicting the trajectory of the knife's journey. He thought of the miracle of the medical workers and all their technological savvy, as they must have had their work cut out for them as they taped and spliced his bod back together. The judge even commented on his novels at one point, an abrupt aside, stating that she didn't like them, not one bit. George piped up at this point (his only outburst during the entire trial), and he let out a loud, thunderous fart.

Jail was an odd bit of business. At first, George was terrified. He was fresh meat, entering the factory where the war of attrition was written into the concrete and embedded into the sweaty and disgruntled glands of the inmates. On his first day, his cellmate, Diggs, told him that his cracker ass would be fucked and prolapsed six ways to Sunday if he didn't show some meanness—some tooth and vileness right outta the gate—to throw up some smoke and disorient the other inmates so they'd rape and beat some other fresh-faced, mushy-assed White boy.

George asked him if he should pick a fight, and Diggs said yes.

The next day at mealtime, he beat the hell out of a prisoner named Joshua. He'd seen Joshua squash a butterfly out in the yard and thus were his reasons. George beat him so bad his eye socket caved in, and his brain was (mildly) damaged. When George returned to his cell—after having spent a few weeks in solitary, which turned out to be quite lovely, contrary to what George had expected; a time when his hallucinations kept him company, and George was able to replenish and build upon his strength—Diggs told him to watch out, be careful, because that fella he'd beat was part of a crew, and they were aimin' to kill him.

He was coming back from the laundry when they attacked him; he went down, and all he could see were big leathery boots coming hard his way. Once they'd finished, they got him on his knees—his face was bleeding, and two men held him upright under his arms. The leader grabbed his chin and made him face him as he spoke. "Now, why'd you go and attack our boy? Huh? Why'd you do somethin' stupid like that, son?" George had never met this prisoner, but Diggs had spoken of him before. Big Henry was his name. A tattooed hyena of a sinewy man, his sneer was legendary (something fierce), as was his penchant for knifing inmates and sometimes performing his own sloppy castrations on them. George figured he was done for, and Big Henry asked him another question, "Who's your enemy, son? Tell me that."

George spoke without thinking; fear loosened his tongue. "Film critics and cyclists."

"Huh?" said Big Henry. "What the hell you talking about, boy?"

George didn't know, but he kept on. "In my opinion, no job does more damage and adds less to the world than the film critic; their job requires no risk, no creation. They are even woefully inept at destruction (or castration or damnation). It is a ridiculous job and attracts the most morally reprehensible sort. The pseudo-intellectuals flock like moths to a flame. They have no respect for the movies; they are weasels working and exploiting the scene, dipping their grubby fingers and contaminating this powerful illusory art—and more and more often, the movies themselves are relegated to the back seat, a tool to prop them up, in the service of their callous personal crusades, an attempt to gain a cult-like following that bows down to their interpretation, their worldview. Standing on the shoulders of giants (movies), they yell tommyrot. The modern state of film criticism is an embarrassment and should be eradicated at all costs."

"Huh," said Big Henry. "What the hell are you on about?"

"I hate cyclists too. Cars and pedestrians hate them; everybody hates them; even other cyclists hate them. They adhere to no rules and run lights and zoom past at close range and criticize as if they were the kings and queens of the roads and sidewalks. They are outlaws in the worst sense of the word. They lack style and are crude and dress in spandex with NASCAR-like logos strewn every which way with silly, uncouth helmets; every time I see a cyclist fall or wipe out or get doored, I rejoice. Twice those cocksuckers have hit me while crossing the road."

Big Henry laughed. "Amen, brother." He lowered his knife. "Fuck it. You're a strange one, kid. You know that?"

They stood George up and patted him off and told him that he'd work off his debt, suffer through servitude. He was now one of them (like it or not): a Brother Beelzebub.

At first, his tasks with the gang were mostly focused on helping sneak in supplies and drugs and joining in during a few choice beatings. He watched as Big Henry cut the nose off of one inmate; his butchery awarded him two months in solitary. George adjusted to prison life, and he and Diggs got along just fine. He didn't care much for being part of a gang though, but life was full of such inconveniences, as was prison. When Big Henry got out of the hole, he caught up with George in the yard. He'd read one of his books (*Territorial Pissings*) while he was down there. He said he was a big reader, "... ever since I'd come to prison," and was proud to have an artist among the ranks of the Beelzebubs. George smiled, and from then on, his status within the gang rose significantly, and all he had to do was meet up with Big Henry a few times a week to discuss art and books and narratives and structure and icons and parasites and violence and sex and architecture and joy and climaxes and denouements and red herrings and love and puzzles and beauty and death and inversions and starts and stops and anything and everything that literature could (and would) be said to contain (given it were handled by a keen practitioner).

One day, years later, Big Henry cut out George's eyes. He did it in his cell with a switchblade while Diggs was out. George screamed as two lackeys held his eyelids open, and the blade cut across. Big Henry had read another of George's books (*Hand Covers Bruise*) and was appalled by it or hated it or was severely disgusted and disturbed by it (whichever way you look at it, he'd been rattled by it). Such stupidity and hokum and trash coming from another Brother Beelzebub were beyond what he could tolerate—and Big Henry passed sentence and took his eyes.

George was moved to a hospital while he recovered and spent a long while there before being transferred to another care facility. He served the remainder of his sentence quietly in a comfy room and was released six days before his fifty-fourth birthday.

George, now blind and free, used his remaining funds to purchase a small house on the east side of his hometown. He sat quietly on the couch most days, his journey ever inward. He smiled often, and many memories from his childhood flashed before his darkened gaze. He sipped coffee and smoked and listened to music. Many moons went by this way, happy and quiet. Sometimes he would have visitors, strangers and friends, curious of his state and of him in general. He welcomed them so long as their visits weren't too frequent. One day, he heard a crash, and he went outside to investigate. He bumped into something on his front lawn. He slid his hands over it; he felt the smooth wooden texture and then the ivory keys. Someone told him that there'd been an automobile accident: a station wagon had T-boned a car. One of the drivers had paid a kid for his shirt and then run off. The other driver was dead. George took the instrument inside. Everyone was paying attention to the crash; no one was looking at him. He played the keys and heard nothing; then he felt around and found a latch and turned it and some accordion-like apparatus dropped down. The machine had breath and bore its first words.

Sitting in the dark, his soul was roused once more. He and the machine formed a partnership and strange songs rose up into the world.

Song titles: (Song #87) Someone Who Deepens the Art, or Deepens the Game, Is Inherently on the Side of Good; (Song #52) People Sometimes Fight for Their Ideals (Even to Death) in Order to Not Look at the Truth; (Song #124) Take Violent Joy Any Day, or Exhilaration, or the Gladiator's Battle Cry; (Song #6) Under Their Auspices, He Was Their Augur; (Song #93) The Immaculate Gait; (Song #62) It Had Nothing to Do With Good or Evil, or All That Matters Is Who Sings the Sweetest, or Whose Songs Last the Longest; (Song #83) There He Goes, Walking the Cow

Once he started writing the songs, he noticed more and more people coming to his door for a variety of reasons: salesmen and door-to-door gospel preachers and kids selling chocolate bars for school fundraisers and old acquaintances and lovers and enemies. He tired of these constant interruptions and sought refuge in his basement. He took the instrument with him, and he played in the soothing corner of a dank nook. He felt himself changing, evolving as it were, and as he evolved, the instrument morphed with him. His tentacles expanded, he squeezed and bore down and attuned himself to the movements of the machine. Beautiful songs stayed hidden: the monster and the apparatus rejoiced, and they kept to the bowels of their church. Until one day, George heard footsteps and a young person's voice. She asked him about his music, and when George tried to speak—his voice muffled and cracked, his tongue now alien—he fell upon his instrument to translate: his vocal surrogate. At least once a month (with increasing frequency), kids would somehow find a way in and sit and listen, and then up and disappear. And George kept on, changing and playing and performing—the accursed

Pied Piper—until one day, someone entered and bared their fangs and swung a hammer, and that was that for George.

***

He woke up sitting at a desk; the man across from him was speaking about preparation. He handed him a sheet of paper with the number 76 circled. And then he saw the sun... and the Great Lakes shimmered, and he emerged from the shadow of a tree, and he gleamed with golden chitin, and he walked on through the rubble and the detritus, marching along the forest's undergrowth, ever onward; he cut his path through the unknown, and he kept on like some forgotten king of old.

Notes

www.ingramcontent.com/pod-product-compliance
Lightning Source LLC
Chambersburg PA
CBHW050230110726
47898CB00007B/2088